THE MASTER'S QUILT

THE MASTER'S QUILT

Michael Webb

CROSSWAY BOOKS • WHEATON, ILLINOIS
A DIVISION OF GOOD NEWS PUBLISHERS

The Master's Quilt.

Copyright © 1991 by Michael Webb.

Published by Crossway Books, a division of
Good News Publishers, 1300 Crescent St., Wheaton, Illinois 60187.

Cover illustration: Chuck Gillies

First printing, 1991

Printed in the United States of America

Library of Congress Cataloging-in-Publication Data
Webb, Michael, 1944-
    The master's quilt / Michael Webb
        p.   cm.
    1. Jesus Christ—Fiction. 2. Bible. N.T.—History of Biblical
events—Fiction. I. Title.
PS3573.E1982M3 1991   813'.54—dc20   91-11625
ISBN 0-89107-619-0

99		98		97		96		95		94		93		92		91
15	14	13	12	11	10	9	8	7	6	5	4	3	2	1		

*Although the desire to write has been
simmering inside me now for over twenty years,
it was only six and a half short years ago
that the flame flickering deep within my soul
suddenly ignited into a crackling fire.
Nevertheless, I take little credit for the writing
of this novel and even less for the idea.
All the glory belongs to Jehovah Elohim, the
Lord God Almighty, Creator of
Heaven and Earth.
Even before I was conceived, I was betrothed
to the Lord, dedicated to His service from the womb,
like Samuel. However, it took thirty years for me
to finally acknowledge that I, like so many others, was
"born into the kingdom for such a time as this."
My heart and my passion now belong to
Him who sits on Heaven's throne.*

*Thank You, Father, for loving me first
that I might love You. Thank You, Jesus, for
turning a "heart of stone" into a "heart of flesh."
And thank You, Holy Spirit, for never leaving
me or forsaking me.
May this work glorify You, Triune God,
and You alone.*

ACKNOWLEDGMENTS

Many people have influenced the outcome of this work, both directly and indirectly, but a faithful few stand out in my mind. First and foremost I give thanks to my parents, Jack and Margaret. Without their steadfast love and support I would never have written this, or any other, novel. To my mentor and friend Lurlene McDaniel: What can I say that will do justice to your hands-on involvement? I trust that you know my heart and that mere words are woefully inadequate to express the gratitude hidden there. To all the prayer warriors: Mark and Susie Miller, Rick and Kathy Rosiere, Bill and Susan Gattle, Gregg and Margaret Eaves, Bob and Sue Stowe, Todd and Barbara Ratliff, David Zambrano, Richard Pitoni (and Richard Junior), Ron Stowe, Gina Campen, and all those I don't even know about, my sincere thanks. To Tim Timmerman, hacker extraordinaire: thanks for all your help, especially for turning me into a quasi-literate "user."

Last, but far from least, to the person above all others who believed in me, prayed for me, exhorted me, and never gave up on me, even when I gave up on myself — Elizabeth Gail Zambrano: you deserve more credit than I could possibly pen in the short space the vagaries of publishing allow. Your unwavering friendship and faith, not to mention your many helpful ideas, are all woven into the fabric of this novel. Thanks, "Lucy," for your laughter and your unfailing encouragement.

Both were like the balm of Gilead, applied expertly and with a great deal of love to the aches and pains of the birthing process of this novel.

Michael Webb
Palm Bay, Florida
October 1990

PROLOGUE

The night sky was unusually dark, even though a full moon was rising, as if the stars of Heaven had forgotten their stage positions for the drama about to unfold. But that was not the case, because it was the kind of darkness born in the hearts of men, not in the heavens above the earth. And that was why there was a night yet to come that would be darker than had ever been.

It was a cool, unpredictable April night. A spring night pregnant with uncertainty for three of four men traversing the mount on the outskirts of the Holy City. The three followed one they called Rabbi on the well-worn path pressed out of the fabric of creation, one of many crisscrossing the dusty landscape that was now only a parody of former splendor.

By day, the starkness of the locale impresses itself into the spirit of a man. At night, there is only the moon or the occasional flare of a campfire to break the monotony of the darkness.

Three of the four shared a common, unspoken sense of foreboding. Gone were the feelings of good cheer and camaraderie experienced earlier at dusk. The mealtime celebration had ended on an ominous note. Their Master had announced during the feast that betrayal and denial were imminent. Cries of outrage and concern had followed. The Master had calmed the twelve with soft words of understanding and wisdom, as He'd done on several occasions during the previous three years, and a final hymn was sung.

The meal was finished, and now three accompanied Him to the garden.

Deep within the slumbering city that lay spread out below the mount, an old man, his once-abundant and jet-black hair and beard now thinning and grey, began the task of preparing for the ensuing eight days of celebration and worship. Just after midnight he left his humble home and walked quietly through the dark, deserted streets. His whole body tingled with expectancy as he inhaled the familiar musk odor of the city. He did not have to walk far, and upon reaching his destination he reached forth with a stubby, callused hand and unlatched the gate.

The men reached the garden.

The moon, only hours shy of being full, rose big and round above the crest of the mount. The bright yellow light, reflecting off the deep amber-colored wood of the finely grained, squat olive trees, outlined in caricature the somber faces of the four companions. They stood silent, unmoving. And yet their shadows rippled in the moonlight. The wraithlike silhouettes bounced off the two gigantic cedars standing atop the mount and etched themselves upon the canvas of darkness.

A fine mist, with the almost imperceptible taste of salt and smell of fish, hovered above the arid soil.

Time slowed . . .

The old man, his senses attuned to the various rhythms in the sea of night surrounding him, moved among the animals with the practiced ease of one long accustomed to ritual. The collection of male lambs crowded in the pen — none younger than eight days nor older than one year — represented the finest sheep of twenty different flocks. The initial selection had been accomplished in broad daylight, and each had been chosen carefully to insure that none had blemishes or imperfections.

The old man, however, did not rely upon sight to tell him of imperfection. Instead, he depended upon his acute sense of smell during the final test. For he was blind.

He smiled and sniffed the air. The odor was faint, but it was there. He'd been asked many times during his seventy years to describe the scent, and his reply had always been the same: "I'm not sure exactly. But I *am* sure of three things. I always smell the peculiar scent after only a short time among the lambs, I never smell it on more than one animal, and I know that the gift is from God."

Without further delay, he reached down swiftly and grabbed hold of a pure white lamb baying softly to his right. *This is the one*, he thought as he carried the animal inside the building adjacent to the pen, handing it over gently into the outstretched arms of the waiting priest.

None of the four had said a word during the brief trek. Finally the man who'd been in the lead spoke. His voice was soft, troubled. "My friends, My soul cries out in grief and My heart is heavy with thoughts of death." He stared off into the darkness, scanning the surroundings with sagacious eyes. "I've come to this place on many occasions, when My heart was burdened and My feet weary, seeking rest . . . here in the land of My Father."

His face became somber, His voice subdued, matching the

lighting on the hilltop. "Tonight is different. Will you wait with me and keep vigil while I pray?"

The three nodded their assent, not trusting speech, and watched the Rabbi walk towards the center of the garden.

"The night is short," He called over His shoulder, sighing it rather than saying it, "and darkness is heavy upon the earth."

The three waited, reclining against the old, stone wine-press — used to press olives into the lifeblood of the region's commerce — from which the garden took its name. A gentle gust of wind nudged the mist that enveloped them like a cocoon, rearranging the night. The quiet moments froze together — into sleep — and the three companions breathed in tense rhythm, as if silently rebelling against their own ambivalence.

Two times their Master returned from solitary separation. Two times the three were awakened and admonished to remain faithful in their vigil lest they be caught unawares. Two times they lapsed into fitful slumber, oblivious to the silent battle their Master waged.

Upon His return the third time the three were awakened abruptly by crisp, commanding words. "Rise, we must be on our way. Behold, the one who shall betray Me is near."

Before they'd gone far, there was a flurry of activity. A group of angry men appeared out of the darkness and surrounded them. Judas stepped forward and said, "Hail, Master" as he grabbed Jesus about the shoulders and kissed Him upon the cheek.

The night gave way to morning and the morning to afternoon. The old man had returned home, slept, and was now back at the Temple. It was time.

Although it was early afternoon, the room was dark except for the light provided by several tall candles. The color of the wax was almost as pure white as the coat of wool covering the lamb held in the arms of the priest.

The Levite, one of several present, carried the lamb to the altar, carefully stretched it out upon the deeply stained, grooved wood, and secured its four legs firmly with leather straps. Only then did he withdraw the razor-sharp sacrificial iron knife from his robe.

First the Levite, then the other priests closed their eyes and began to sing in unison, filling the Temple with the sonorous sound of the Great Hallel. The old man added his own deep-throated voice to that of the others, singing with vigor. Outside, in the immediate vicinity of the Temple, the sounds of the city were swallowed up by the ritual chanting.

Gradually the singing stopped. The Levite opened his eyes and grasped the head of the lamb. He stretched the animal's neck backward, exposing the soft, vulnerable flesh to the light and the knife. His right hand was poised above his head.

Swiftly, with a precisely articulated motion, he brought his arm down, turning the blade ever so slightly as the knife dropped downward through its arc. In one deft stroke he drew the shining blade across the animal's neck, severing the jugular vein.

Several of the priests blew a threefold blast from their silver trumpets as bright red blood spurted from the wound. Special silver and gold ceremonial bowls caught the warm, sticky fluid, which was then splashed in one single stream at the base of the altar.

A small amount of blood escaped the confines of the altar and fell to the foot-packed ground. The desiccated, yellow-brown earth and the burgundy-red, liquid life blended together in a copper-colored mud.

The Levite grasped the dead animal by its hind legs, took

a length of rope, and secured the sacrifice from two hooks mounted in staves nailed together in the shape of a cross. It was flayed, and the entrails were taken out and cleansed. Afterwards, the inside fat was separated, put in a dish and salted, then placed in the fire of the altar of burnt offering.

The ritual was repeated continually for several hours. The old man was one of many who were waiting for their paschal sacrifice.

Once again twilight settled upon the city. The old man stood in the doorway of his small hovel and stared at the sky with sightless eyes. A penetrating shiver danced up and down his spine. For some strange reason he could almost feel the darkness seeping into his bones through the pores of his skin, and somehow he knew that even though there were no clouds in the ebony sky, there were also no stars.

Hastily he dipped the hyssop he held in his trembling right hand into the wooden bowl he cupped in his left and sprinkled the blood of the lamb upon his doorway, wondering why he felt so strange on this very special night.

The priest lit the incense. The room was smoky, the air thick with *ketoret*, the special blend of spices he'd prepared earlier. He took several deep breaths as he went about his tasks, smiling contentedly. His nose twitched as he savored the unique, aromatic smell: frankincense, galbanum, stactate, onchya, and myrrh.

Finally, as the thick night began to seep into the cracks and crevices of the Temple, he trimmed the lamps in preparation for the evening prayer.

Hear the word of the Lord, you children of Israel,
for the Lord brings a charge against the inhabitants of the land: There is no truth, or mercy, or
knowledge of God in the land.
By swearing and lying, killing and stealing and
committing adultery, they break all restraint,
with bloodshed upon bloodshed.
Therefore the land will mourn; and everyone who
dwells there will waste away with the beasts of the
field and the birds of the air; even the fish of the
sea will be taken away.
Now let no man contend, or rebuke another;
for your people are like those who contend
with the priest.
Therefore you shall stumble in the day; the
prophet shall also stumble with you in the night;
and I will destroy your mother.
My people are destroyed for a lack of knowledge.
Because you have rejected knowledge, I also will
reject you from being priest for me; because you
have forgotten the law of your God, I also will forget your children.

(Hosea 4:1-6)

I

Deucalion Cincinnatus Quinctus tasted fear. The flavor was cold, like iron, and it lay on his tongue with the sharpness of a battle sword.

Around him stretched a stark and shadowy landscape. He gripped a spear in his sweaty right hand, tight enough to soak the wooden handle. Cautiously he walked towards a mound littered with skulls. The mound, adjacent to the deep, narrow glen called Hinnom by the Jews, held three wooden crosses.

In the distance a wild dog howled. He turned in the direction of the unnerving sound and saw the city of Rome — or was it Babylon? Sweat burned in his eyes, and when he blinked the scene dissolved.

Around him the shadows shifted, seemingly alive with things that made his skin crawl. Even though it was almost summer and he was in the middle of the desert, he suddenly felt chilled to the bone. He walked on, shivering uncontrollably. Finally he stopped before the center cross and looked up.

Above him a man hung with his head slumped forward, so that his chin touched his chest. He wasn't breathing. There were three bloodied holes in his body; one each in the palms of his hands and one through both feet, where the two-pound nails that secured him to the crossbars had punctured his olive-colored skin. He reminded Deucalion of a flayed animal pelt, stretched taut to dry.

Deucalion winced, knowing that somehow he was responsible for the man's hanging there. That thought caused bile to rise in his throat, and he retched. He noticed something else. Although all else was in shadow, the site where he stood was bathed in light. A strange, ethereal light that seemed to glow with a pulsing force. Fear began to overwhelm him. He'd fought in a hundred battles, but had never known the darkness, the hopelessness, the soul-wrenching agony of such terror. His heart pounded furiously, as if it might burst through the walls of his chest at any moment. Instinctively he raised the spear and thrust it upward at the man — at the light. The razor-sharp metal tip pierced the man's side. Blood and water spewed forth, splattering Deucalion's tunic and face. Startled, he stepped backward, frantically trying to wipe the stains away.

Abruptly the scene shifted.

He stood before a tomb hewn out of solid rock, just before the column of dawn. Suddenly he was engulfed by an intense, blinding white light. He tried to run, but his feet were rooted to the ground. He had to get away! It was too bright . . . too bright . . . .

He screamed . . .

"Commander! Are you all right?"

Deucalion awoke with a start and turned toward the door and the source of the voice. He blinked several times, trying to wash away the stinging salt of a cold sweat. The room was dark, and he felt disoriented because the light in his dream had been so bright. "What in the name of the gods is going on?" he muttered.

"Commander . . . it's Malkus. I have an urgent message from Rome."

Deucalion shuddered with sudden realization. The scream

had been real! He sat up and shook his head back and forth, trying to clear it. "What time is it?" he asked in a scratchy, dry voice.

"Just after the column of dawn," came the muffled reply.

The tall, dark-haired Praetorian heaved himself off his cot, feeling as if he'd not slept at all, and splashed several handfuls of tepid water on his lean, angular face from a nearby plain porcelain washbasin. The water helped cleanse the stinging from his eyes, but did nothing for the nasty headache that was working its way to the top of his head from the base of his skull.

"I'll be there in a moment," he croaked, rubbing the back of his neck, trying to massage away the throbbing pain. "Prepare my armor."

"As you wish, Commander," came the reply from his second-in-command. Deucalion pictured Malkus' sharp, wolfish features and sighed. The younger man was ambitious, and Deucalion knew he'd have to watch his backside around him. Malkus had heard him scream, and he wouldn't forget it. An ironic, bitter smile crossed Deucalion's face. He'd have to remember to drink more heavily before he retired each night. The wine would drug him, and he'd sleep less fitfully. Maybe then the dreams would stop, and his capable junior officer would have less opportunity to circle him like a lone, hungry wolf.

Joseph ben Caiaphas, High Priest of the Most High God, felt the sunrise upon his face long before he saw it with his eyes — and feeling it, he began to dream.

He stood in the marble hall, before the Sanhedrin. Seventy old men stared down at him with hollow, vacant eyes. He felt fear — gut-wrenching, heart-stopping panic.

The balance of power, painstakingly developed through years of study and worship, was disintegrating. Joshua had returned. And he'd commanded the sun and moon to stand still once again. Forever. Never again was the earth to know darkness. Never again was man to be allowed the luxury of exercising his debaucheries under the cover of night. Light now reigned supreme. The sin of Adam could no longer be denied.

Suddenly the walls of the hall became transparent. Outside, thousands of fellow Jews had gathered. Roman soldiers penned them in on all sides, like slaves about to be auctioned. They had come, not to hear the High Priest speak, but to hear the message of the Christos — the Anointed One.

In frustration the Sanhedrin kept demanding that the High Priest give them an answer. "What are we to do, Joseph?"

"Crucify Him!" he shouted, and outside the mob took up the chant. But all he could hear was an echo: THE BLOOD OF THE LAMB — THE BLOOD OF — THE BLOOD . . .

Time and space dissolved, and he sensed that his order had been executed. However, the crucifixion of the heretical Jew, Jesus, did not cause the sun to move again in normal fashion. Instead, it glowed brighter. Caiaphas spun, facing angry faces on all sides. The walls started to close around him, but still the light consumed everything. The Council members began to shake angry fists at him. Several of them, including his own father-in-law, Annas, demanded that he order the sun to cease its rebellion and give darkness back its rightful place in the scheme of things . . .

Abruptly Caiaphas awoke, as he had on several mornings the past four weeks — mouth dry, tongue swollen, body drenched. His eyes were filled with tears, as if he'd been crying uncontrollably in his sleep. He groaned, then uttered a silent curse and hoped there was enough water on hand to quench the fiery thirst raging in his throat.

He glanced furtively at the heavens. His dream had been so vivid that he fully expected to see both sun and moon radiating in the crystal-blue sky. Instead, the morning looked normal and so perfectly ordinary that he wondered why he'd ever been afraid.

At about the same time Joseph Caiaphas was rubbing sleep from his eyes, a man of medium build, with a square-cut face and curly black hair pomaded with olive oil, paced the floor of his Jerusalem residence. The *Procurator Caesaris* had awakened hours before the sun began to rise hot and bright over the city. Sleep had become a luxury of the past for Pontius Pilate.

The man Rome had selected to govern Judea was wrestling again with his tortured conscience. The resulting headache caused him to cringe painfully. "It will be a hot, dry summer," he said aloud to the walls. He cursed the day he'd ever been sent to this land forsaken by the gods and filled with quarrelsome, rebellious Jews.

He poured himself a flagon of wine and greedily drank half of it in one gulp — knowing it would only dull, not eliminate, the pain — and watched daylight carpet the city that had become his nemesis. He could feel the desert heat working its way into his skin, and he grimaced as the prophetic words of Claudia, his wife, beckoned to him, as they had done daily for the past month.

"The Hebrew priests have beguiled you, Pontius," she'd said with defiance on the eve of the trial. "Beware, and touch not that man, for He is holy. Last night I saw Him in a vision: He was walking on the waters; He was flying on the wings of the winds. There was a mighty storm raging about Him. He spoke to the tempest and to the fish of the lakes, and all were obedient to Him. Behold, the forest in Mt. Kellum flows with blood, the statues of Caesar are filled with the filth of Gemoniae, the columns of the Intercium have given way, and the sun is mourning like a vestal in the tomb. O Pilate, evil awaits you if you will not listen to the prayer of your wife!"

He took another gulp of wine and pressed trembling hands into tired, reddened eyes. His headaches were getting worse. Why hadn't he listened? What evil, indeed, awaited him? *Gods, protect me*, he thought miserably, wishing desperately he'd never heard of Judea or Jesus of Nazareth.

Suddenly the throbbing behind his eyes became so intense that he cried out loudly enough to wake his servant, Antonius, who came running.

Not far away another man, a Jew in his mid-fifties, stood silently on one of the many balconies of the Hasmonean palace and admired the coral-colored dawn. His rectangular face was composed of deep-set eyes and a square chin that supported taut, thin lips.

Lost in thought, he barely heard the trumpet blasts that saluted the sunrise. He knew, however, that in each of the fourteen districts of the city the Praetorian Guard were synchronizing the water clocks, while throughout Jerusalem the elite of the Roman citizenry were waking, preparing to eat a breakfast of wine-soaked bread, pullet, and fresh eggs.

Herod Antipas, Tetrarch of Galilee, shared with the beleaguered Roman Procurator — though for different reasons and with different effect — a sense of frustration and impotence. He was a man of action, as had been his father, Herod the Great. But his failure to maintain the momentum of the powerful political apparatus the now-dead patriarch had forged disturbed him deeply. He sighed heavily, remembering a recent conversation he'd had with the one man he reviled most — the man who'd usurped his father's authority. And even though he would never admit it to anyone, the subject matter of that conversation had caused him many a sleepless night.

"You're a vain man, Herod," the Roman Procurator had said the day after the crucifixion of the heretical Nazarene as he offered his guest a goblet of wine. "And your vanity will be your downfall . . . just as it was your father's."

"Aren't you even going to thank me for helping you solve *your* problem?"

The short, balding man whom Herod knew hated Jews with a fanatical passion stared at him with cold, brown eyes, and the Tetrarch noted that the muscle along Pilate's jawline was twitching imperceptibly.

"What exactly do you mean by that?" growled the Procurator.

"Only that now you have no one to blame for your problems except yourself."

"You dare talk to me that way? It is *I* who occupy the palace your father built, not you. Too often you seem to forget that we Romans rule Palestine and not you Jews."

"There is not a day that goes by that I don't think about both those facts, Pontius." His reply had been as hard with contempt as it had been truthful.

"No doubt," grunted the Procurator. "However, if you're not careful, your appetite for power might very well choke you lifeless."

Now, weeks later, Antipas wiped the sweat from his brow with a white linen cloth he carried for just such a purpose. He thought about Pilate's unsettling words and the unusual events that had unfolded two days after they were spoken. What really *had* happened at the Nazarene's tomb? He chuckled without humor at his own mordant curiosity. Unfortunately, all he knew on this hot, dry May morning was that the lack of any breeze was a portent of a long, stifling summer.

"Master, a courier has arrived with a parchment from Rome."

He turned at the sound of his secretary's voice. "And?" he snarled, angry at being disturbed.

"The Praetorian says it's urgent."

What could be so important that Rome would send a message here to Jerusalem rather than waiting for him to return to Caesarea? And in the hands of a Praetorian, no less. Suddenly he had a premonition of impending doom. He shivered, then wrapped his robe snugly about him and reached for a brimming cup of *mulsum*, a wine and honey mixture he'd acquired a taste for as a result of his association with the Roman Procurator.

"Make the Praetorian comfortable," he said gruffly, "and tell him I'll be with him shortly."

Deucalion Cincinnatus Quinctus, Pontius Pilate's Commander of the Garrison, waited patiently for Herod Antipas' secretary to bring him refreshment and thought about how far he'd come in his career in such a short time. His father would be proud of him, were he alive.

When he'd arrived in Jerusalem eight weeks ago, he'd found the city, and the surrounding countryside, on the verge of violent rebellion. After organizing the garrison, he'd systematically dealt with the more dissident Jews — not by slaughtering them, but by giving them an opportunity to vent their frustrations. Utilizing a political instead of a military approach, he'd established three mini-tribunals to hear their grievances and persuaded Pilate to accede to some of the Jews' less offensive demands. Peace had been temporarily restored.

As a result, Pilate had taken an immediate interest in him.

"We share a common bond, you and I," said the Procurator the first night they'd gotten drunk together.

"What's that?" he'd asked, hoping he wasn't slurring his words, then realizing it probably wouldn't matter.

"Neither of us is willing to compromise our faith in the Republic and its future . . . even in the face of our growing doubt that Rome is as eternal as the Emperor leads us to believe."

During many subsequent hours, they'd solved numerous problems connected with ruling a stubborn and arrogant people thousands of miles from home, and within two weeks Pilate had asked Lucius Vitellius, Governor over Syria, to transfer Deucalion to Jerusalem permanently. Surprisingly, the request was approved. Deucalion found out why not long after. In addition to transfer orders, Vitellius had sent a special messenger with private orders.

> Deucalion Cincinnatus,
> Hail Caesar.
> As you are well aware by now, Jerusalem, though a hotbed of insurrection, is also the site of the Temple. Rome has certain pecuniary arrangements with the priests in charge of financial administration of Temple proceeds, monies received as tithes from the faithful. You are to make sure that Pilate does nothing to interfere with the flow of payments to the Empire.

There was one minor problem with the arrangement — he and Pilate had become friends. In fact, he suspected that Pilate saw him as the son he'd never had. And for reasons Deucalion never understood, he carried within himself a certain code of honor — one that might hamper a soldier's rise to ultimate power. One, he reminded himself grimly, Malkus did not share. Deucalion's sometimes allowing relationships to curb ambition was a definite weakness.

And now, there was yet another problem.

Something extraordinary had happened four weeks ago, three days after the Passover of the Jews, and he'd not had a full night's sleep since. Although he was still not sure exactly *what* had transpired, he was certain of one thing: the world he'd been born into twenty-seven years ago was not the same world in which he now lived. There was something different, something new and exciting afoot. It was as palatable to him as air and light. And he was determined to discover just what it was — no matter what the cost.

II

As Jerusalem roused itself from the night, Caiaphas groaned and sat up. Fighting dizziness, he focused his eyes on the black bark and soft green leaves of the *Shit'tah* tree rising twenty feet above him. He took several deep breaths, savoring the refreshing, sweet fragrance of the acacia's drooping yellow flowers.

Once again he'd fallen into a drunken sleep in the outer courtyard of the mansion, located a stone's throw from the Herodian Palace, in that part of Jerusalem called the Upper City, where he lived with his wife and father-in-law, Annas.

His late-night bantering with his old friend and confidant Simon ben Gamaliel was as fresh in his mind as the aftertaste of wine was sour in his mouth. Both the conversation and the wine had started out to be pleasurable; yet, in the short space of a few hours both had soured.

His former teacher had arrived unexpectedly just after finishing his evening prayers. Even more unexpected than his friend's unannounced arrival was the news he brought from the Sanhedrin.

"Joseph, the Council has asked me to convey their concern regarding the continuing unrest among the people," began the older man solemnly. He'd spoken with the same quiet forcefulness that had changed many a Pharisee's disagreement into agreement with and even at times enthusiastic support of the ideas of the predominately Sadducee Council. "Instead of quenching the fires of insurrection burning in the hearts of the rebels and zealots, your solution seems to have fanned the flames into epidemic proportions."

Caiaphas had been shocked at the harsh words. "That's nonsense, Simon. It's only been a month since the crucifixion, and we've heard nothing of the man's disciples. In fact, my sources tell me that they have all gone into hiding, fearing for their lives. They are completely disorganized."

"I fear not. Perhaps the disciples are in hiding, but the Romans have evidence that the rebel ranks are swelling, not diminishing."

"What of the *sicari* anyway?" he'd retorted, using the Latin term for the zealots to emphasize his distaste for those the Romans called dagger men or professional assassins. "Barabbas has not been seen nor heard from since his release." He paused, filled two goblets with the last of the spring wine and handed one of the brimming cups to Simon. When he continued, his voice was cold and hard. "Pilate should be most pleased with the results we achieved. One man dies, and the opposition to authority, both religious and secular, dies with him."

He gave Simon the forceful, intimidating look that all who knew the High Priest, save his long-time friend, found hard to withstand, and concluded, "Since when can Rome make the same claim?"

"All that is true. However, there are members of the Council, led by Doras, who feel that your handling of this matter was, shall we say, *incomplete*."

That was when he'd lost his temper, something he'd been doing frequently lately. "Doras is not even a member of the first chamber! He's merely an elder, an aristocrat who purchased his seat on the Council."

"Joseph, we have discussed this before," sighed his friend. "The Council has no proof, nor I might add, even allegations of any impropriety or wrongdoing on his part. And you know better than I that Doras is as cunning as he is immoral." There was just a hint of impatience in his voice. "Unless you're prepared to bring formal charges, the Council cannot sit in judgment."

"The man's a disgrace, Simon. His devotion is to his pocketbook and his daughter — in that order. And I doubt his daughter will help us ruin her father politically."

"Do not underestimate the power of Doras, Joseph," counseled the older man sternly. "His close relationship with Herod Antipas gives him access to the ears of the Syrian governor. Lucius Vitellius governs with an iron hand, and as a result he hasn't had the problems Pilate has encountered here in Judea. The Council, including Annas, believes that Vitellius is extremely displeased with Pilate's handling of the matter of Jesus of Nazareth. We can use that to our advantage."

"Syria is a long way from Jerusalem."

Simon scowled. "You're missing the point. We've worked hard for a very long time to achieve a measure of autonomy within the Roman hierarchy, and we cannot afford to have an incident such as this unleash the wrath of Vitellius *or* Tiberius."

"But, Simon —"

"Let me finish, Joseph. You always were much too impatient for your own good." The teacher was once again educating the student with practiced patience. "As you are well aware, Pilate has not exactly had an unblemished record since his arrival here seven years ago."

Simon was referring to the numerous confrontations between the Jews and the sixth Procurator of Judea. The five men who had preceded Pontius Pilate had all been diplomatic in their handling of the occupation of Jerusalem. Not so the current Procurator. Even his superiors considered him to be a reckless and tactless individual.

Pilate's predecessors had studiously avoided any unnecessary exhibition of flags or other emblems bearing images of the Emperor Tiberius, so as not to offend the sacred sentiments of the native population. Pilate, on the other hand, had been nominated by the late Sejanus, Tiberius' former minister and commander of the Praetorian Guard. He shared his benefactor's lack of sympathy for Jewish separatist manifestations and cared little for what he considered to be religious sentimentality.

Upon his arrival in Jerusalem he'd ordered his garrison of soldiers to raise aloft their standards and banners, emblazoned with the image of Tiberius, and had marched into the city by night with much pomp and circumstance. This brash demonstration of authority had provoked an immediate and massive protest on the part of the residents of the city.

The Council, led by Caiaphas, met with Pilate and begged him to remove the standards, fearing that the brazen disregard for Jewish religious custom — which did not allow the representation of graven images — would result in rebellion among the already tense populace. Pilate refused. The Council argued with him for five days to reconsider. Eventually Pilate became enraged and summoned the entire city to the racecourse, then surrounded the people with a detachment of his soldiers and informed them that unless they discontinued their harassment of his men, he intended to kill each and every one of them.

To his consummate dismay, all of them — men, women, and children — threw themselves to the ground, exposed their necks, and served Pilate notice that they, the children of Abraham, would rather die than willingly see the Holy City defiled. Pilate yielded; the standards and images were withdrawn. That event would forever blot the record of the career soldier from Spain.

"If Vitellius puts pressure on Pilate," continued Simon, "he will most certainly look for a way of escape — and you, my friend, would provide the perfect scapegoat. It was *you* who suggested that Jesus be sacrificed for the good of all." He paused, then added, "Make no mistake about it, Joseph, Pilate will not let the opportunity pass to serve your head on a platter to the Governor, especially to keep his own head *off* the platter."

"As always, Simon, your rhetoric is most persuasive. I do not intend to become an *Azazel* sacrifice."

Simon laughed, breaking the tension. "Never mind the patronizing, Joseph," he said without rancor, adjusting his robe. "Doras sees this as his opportunity to move up in stature in the Council. And he is steadily gathering support from some of the more conservative, disgruntled members."

"So?"

Simon shrugged. "He's already garnered support from among the scribes and certain members of the first chamber. If he sways enough minds, Annas may begin to have thoughts — if he hasn't already — about maneuvering his son Jonathan into a position of higher visibility among the Romans."

"To forestall any attempt by Doras to usurp his power," the High Priest muttered, thinking aloud.

The older man nodded. "We both know that where power and influence are concerned, your father-in-law is a master of manipulation. And your role in this Jesus incident is a prime example."

That comment had set Caiaphas to thinking. Was there more to the dreams that haunted him than he was willing to admit? Was it possible there was something of critical importance he'd missed? Was he somehow being manipulated?

"You are the first non-lineal descendant of Annas to hold the position of High Priest of the Great Sanhedrin," pressed Simon, "and you have ruled successfully now for fifteen years. Yet power is a fickle and persistent mistress . . . "

"What does all this have to do with the crucifixion of one blaspheming Jew? As High Priest of the Great Sanhedrin, I alone have responsibility for maintaining the sanctity of the Faith. While we might have tolerated some of the claims the man made, we most certainly could not tolerate His insistence that He was the Son of God and that upon His death His 'Father' would resurrect Him from the dead. Even the Pharisees were uncomfortable with those claims."

"Listen to me, Joseph . . . You haven't been yourself lately. There's been talk among a number of the Council members that you're not the same forceful man who boldly confronted Pilate seven years ago. We need a High Priest who is strong enough to keep the Romans in check."

"What do you recommend?"

"Reassert your strength. Let the Council see that you haven't forgotten what it means to be a Sadducee — and the High Priest. You must prove to them beyond a shadow of a doubt that there is no reason to be concerned about any loose ends in this affair."

Mounting morning heat brought Caiaphas back to the present. He belched involuntarily, then gagged. The sourness fermenting in his belly had risen from his stomach and scorched his throat with its foulness. He stood up on wobbly legs, and a wave of nausea threatened to shatter his precarious balancing act. He reached out and grabbed hold of the acacia, wishing desperately he had not gotten so drunk. The sun, a scorching irritant, added to his discomfort.

Glancing furtively at the sky one final time, he gathered his dirt-stained, wrinkled robes about him and, leaving the security of the acacia behind as a lame man leaves behind his staff, he headed for the house, remembering his last words to Simon.

"Tell the Council I shall make a formal report immediately. Tell them I intend to conduct a thorough investigation into the events surrounding the arrest, trial, and crucifixion of the Nazarene." He had paused, then added, "And, Simon, old friend, rest assured, I have no intention of allowing Doras, or anyone else for that matter — living or dead, to destroy forty-three years of hard work."

Annas, the seventy-first member of the Great Council at Jerusalem and the real power behind both the High Priest and the Sanhedrin for more than twenty-five years, gazed out the window of the inn at Caesarea Philippi and marveled at the beauty of Mt. Hermon, rising over nine thousand feet above the Mediterranean.

"Such beauty . . . yet such apostasy," he mumbled, thinking of his last conversation with Caiaphas. "What a contradiction Mt. Hermon represents," he had told his son-in law when he'd returned from his last visit to Syria.

"I don't understand, Annas."

"As you know, it was at one time the primeval religious center of Syria."

The High Priest nodded.

"What you might not know is that the ancient Canaanites sacrificed goats, bulls, dogs, and even men, offering still-warm blood from the dead carcasses to the demon god Baal." He knew by the look on his son-in-law's face that he had his attention. "And yet, in spite of the darkness it represents, there is light. The melting glaciers of the mountain provide the main source of water for the Jordan River. I have seen the cooling snows of its white-capped peaks from as far away as the Dead Sea, one hundred and twenty miles distant."

"There are those here in Jerusalem who swear that one can tell whether or not the crops will bring forth an abundant harvest by how far down the white cap sits on the head of the 'father of the dew,' Abu-Nedy, one of its peaks," the High Priest observed.

"There . . . you see what I mean," Annas had replied with consternation. "Man is easily deceived by his senses."

He sighed with the recollection and wondered how long it would be before he would have to intercede in his son-in-law's affairs. There were serious problems within the Sanhedrin.

Fortunately, however, his meeting with Vitellius had gone well. The Governor had agreed with him that Pilate was expendable and had informed him that he was receiving regular correspondence from Pilate's Praetorian. When he'd asked if Vitellius was referring to Deucalion Quinctus, the Governor had gotten extremely angry and questioned him at length about his source of information on the man he'd sent to spy on the Procurator of Judea.

Annas had been vague in his responses and was satisfied that he had not divulged anything of importance to the Governor. Nevertheless, he could not shake an ominous sense of foreboding. His instincts told him that the political climate of Palestine was about to change dramatically. Although he wasn't exactly sure what was in the winds, he could feel the change coming. He had no way of judging the magnitude of what he sensed, but he didn't intend to be caught unprepared when it materialized.

A cloud passed overhead, briefly obscuring the early-morning sun, and Annas experienced a moment of dread. If he believed in omens, it would be easy to believe that the dream he'd had just before the sunrise was a harbinger of disaster.

Like all Jews, he was a great believer in the power of dreams. Being but one of the many domains of his experience, they had intellectual, ethereal, and spiritual significance.

This particular dream had attached itself to his conscious,

waking thoughts as a parasite attaches itself to its host, and that made it unusual.

He stood in the middle of the desert, sweating profusely, and listened as Elijah rebuked him for his involvement with the Roman bureaucracy. The prophet, whose name meant "God is Jehovah," reminded him of his own problems with Jezebel and the consequences of disobeying God, then gave him a stern warning. "If you persist in your self-serving manipulations, Annas, no rain will fall upon Jerusalem and its environs for six years."

Before Annas could respond, the setting changed to the top of Abu-Nedy. He stood waist-deep in cold, grey-white snow, shivering uncontrollably. Frightened by his predicament, he tried to free himself, but could not. He cried out frantically in a hoarse voice, pleading for someone to rescue him, but no one heard him.

Suddenly, the stars in the purple-black sky melted together in an explosion of light, causing tears with the consistency of oil and the odor of frankincense to flow from his eyes like a river.

In front of him, swathed in the light of the sun, stood the Galilean — the Jew from Nazareth. Stunned, Annas raised his arm towards Jesus. He must touch the man . . .

He'd awakened at the first light of dawn, drenched in sweat, and even now, over an hour later, his throat felt raspy and dry, as if he'd been screaming in his sleep. He swallowed gingerly and took one last look at Abu-Nedy, then reluctantly pulled his eyes from the magnificent mountain as the sun crested its snow-covered peaks.

His servant was in the courtyard below, filling a bucket of water from the well. "Polonius, fetch my bags," he called out hoarsely. "It's time we were on our way."

III

Ten miles east of Jerusalem, eight miles south of Jericho, on the shore of the Great Salt Sea, which the Arabs call *Bahr Lût*, the Sea of Lot, the Watcher looked out over the greenish expanse of water and licked the crystalline coating of salt from his cracked, sun-parched lips. He was tall, over six feet, with silver-grey hair. His shoulders were broad and well-muscled; even though he was old, he seemed ageless.

As the sun passed its zenith, and as Annas headed for Jerusalem, he turned and walked briskly towards the cliffs behind him and to the cave where he knew Joseph ben Kohath waited for him. In a few moments he'd climbed almost to the top. It would have taken a man half his age in superb condition considerably longer.

Joseph heard Uriel enter the cave, but did not immediately look up from where he was tending the fire. The heaviness in his heart had not lifted during the past weeks, and he was grateful the old man had not pried into its cause.

They'd met on the day after Joseph fled the tomb of the Nazarene. He'd come to the great inland sea because he knew there he'd find what he desperately needed — solitude and time to think. He'd been walking along the beach, looking for shelter from the heat, when the old man had appeared, seemingly out of thin air.

"Come, I have prepared a place for you," Uriel had said,

staring at him with hazel-green eyes that blazed with a luminescence that was soft yet penetrating.

Although he'd been surprised by the old man's sudden appearance, oddly he felt drawn to the silver-haired stranger.

"Where?" he asked.

Uriel looked up. "There," he replied, pointing to the top of a sheer wall of rock.

"I don't see anything."

"The eyes of a man can be deceived, my young friend, and all is not what it appears to be. There is a cave . . . where you can rest."

That had been over a month ago. Unfortunately, there hadn't been much rest. Not because of anything Uriel had demanded, but because of the battle that waged inside Joseph. He'd attempted to rid himself of his inner torment by eating and drinking only the barest amount of food and water and by spending long hours in prayer late at night. During the day, he spent several hours walking along the beach, reviewing Scripture in his mind. The discipline had firmed up his soft flesh even as the sunlight had steadily converted the dull pallor of his skin into a handsome bronze coloring. Still, his dreams were often troubled.

When he looked up, Uriel was staring at him, and the old man's eyes seemed to radiate light. Suddenly Joseph made a decision. "How was your walk this morning?" he asked.

"The smell of great change is in the air," Uriel replied as he sat down across from Joseph.

Joseph wasn't sure what the old man was talking about, but he was accustomed to cryptic replies to his questions. His teachers had often spoken of spiritual matters in the same manner — always using words that held double meaning. However, the old man's words had an astounding effect upon him. An overwhelming surge of emotion welled up inside him, and abruptly he began to sob.

Uriel was startled, completely unprepared for the sudden outburst. Uncertain what to do, he waited patiently for Joseph to regain control, then handed him a ladle of water from a nearby bucket.

Joseph took several sips. "You probably think me foolish," he said as he wiped his face on his tunic.

Uriel remained silent.

"I was given the opportunity to share in the life of one who was bound by neither wealth nor poverty, knowledge nor the lack thereof," continued the younger man, "and I turned my back upon that freedom, unwilling to lose that which I perceived to be of greater value."

"And what was that?"

"Silver and gold."

"Aha . . . I see."

Joseph took a final sip of water, then handed the ladle back, taking care not to spill the precious liquid. "Now the one of whom I speak is dead," he added, looking at the old man with moist, red eyes.

"Oh?" Uriel poured the remaining liquid into the bucket without taking any for himself.

"We awaited His coming for a thousand years, and yet, in the end we denied Him. Now we cannot but swallow the bitter irony of our apostasy. Golgotha, the place of the skull, shall indelibly mark us even as Cain was marked for the murder of his brother Abel."

Both men were quiet, pensive, and each seemed disconnected from the present as they sat facing one another in the late-afternoon stillness, their eyes locked together. There was a loud *pop!* from within the fire, and an amber-colored slug of dried sap arced upward and outward, landing between the two statue-like men.

"It's not easy to battle wickedness, especially when one hasn't seen the enemy," Uriel said, breaking the silence. Then, as if reminding himself of something he must not forget, he added, "And the weapons of our warfare are not of the physical realm, but mighty through God, that we might pull down the strongholds of the destroyer and his minions."

Joseph had the impression that he and the old man shared a similar pain. Oddly, he felt that soon he would come full circle from his mistake in Bethel. "You speak of strange things," he whispered, frowning. "And your words remind me of my time of study with Rabbi ben Hillel . . . in preparation for my *bar mitzvah*. Yet with him I knew what was expected, what I was preparing for. But here, in this cave, separated from all I once held in high esteem, it seems that I am isolated from purpose as well."

"What you seek, Joseph, is Life and Light. Life that remains uncaged by the bars of time. Light so pure that its brilliance knows no limitation."

"I don't understand."

Uriel smiled. "Finish your story. If you still need an explanation afterward, I'll give you one."

He's doing it again, thought Joseph. *Speaking with words that hold double meaning.* Still confused but, strangely, no longer blindingly frustrated, he continued where he had left off.

"About the middle of March, my father sent me to Judea to purchase a new boat for our fleet. I'd concluded my business and was waiting for a boat to take me back to Cyprus when I chanced upon my cousin from Jerusalem, John Mark. As we'd not seen each other for quite some time, we sat down in the shade of a palm tree and caught one another up on what had been happening in our lives.

"I told him of the growth of my uncle's and father's fishing fleets and of my family's prosperity. 'I too have prospered,' he said smiling, 'but in a much different way.'

"When I questioned him about it, he asked me if I would

go with him to Bethel. 'There,' he added cryptically, 'you will find your answer.'

"By the time we arrived, a great multitude had gathered in a large semicircle. In front of them, reclining against a tree, was a man. The hot afternoon sun filtered through the tattered canopy of palm leaves, lighting His face as if it were glowing." Joseph sighed and poked the embers of the fire with a stick. "His gaze was penetrating, unwavering, and I had the impression that as He made eye contact with each of us He could read our character in an instant. I was overcome with an almost overpowering desire to *touch* Him."

"Why?"

"Because when He spoke, it was difficult *not to listen* to Him — His words were full of such power."

Uriel nodded with understanding. "Go on."

"I implored my cousin to get me close enough to the man called Jesus, so that I might address Him personally. He was on His knees, praying for a group of children. When He looked up at me, all I could think to ask Him was, 'Good Master, what good thing shall I do, that I may have eternal life?'

"He didn't answer me immediately, but again looked deep into my eyes. This time my whole body trembled as He stared at me.

"'Why do you call Me good?' He asked. 'There is none good but one, that is God: but if you would enter into life, keep the commandments.'

"'Which?' I asked.

"'You shall not murder, nor commit adultery. You shall not steal, nor shall you bear false witness. Honor your father and your mother, and love your neighbor as yourself.'

"'But all these things I *have* kept from my youth up,' I replied, bewildered. 'What do I lack?'

"'If you would be perfect, go and sell all that you have and give to the poor, and you shall have treasure in Heaven . . .

then come and follow Me.'" Joseph paused and sighed heavily, then added, "That was something I could not do."

Night fell as the two men talked, and the cave walls came alive with shimmering shadows of flickering firelight as Joseph placed another log on the dying fire.

"There comes a time," began Uriel as he watched the red-hot embers ignite the dry wood, "when an individual must make a choice between what his five physical senses tell him is real and what his inner man, what the Scripture refers to as *n^eshamah*, the breath of life, tells him to be aware of." His eyes sparkled with light coming from some other source than the now steadily burning fire.

"It is not an easy path to follow, but as you learn more about the enemy that has been the source of your torment, you will learn patience. Soon the thief will be exposed."

Joseph's whole body tingled. *This man seems to know more about me than I do about myself*, he thought, intrigued. *Strange . . . he speaks with the same authority as the Nazarene.*

"Continue your story, Joseph . . . we haven't much time."

"I went back to Joppa and spent two weeks of intense study in the Scripture at the Temple there. Although I had a vague sense that I would recognize what I was searching for once I found it, I wasn't sure I could ever explain it to anyone else. Even so, by the end of the second week I was beginning to despair.

"One afternoon, late in the day, I was walking on the outskirts of the city. I'd been studying Isaiah for several days, not quite sure why I lingered upon his words. I experienced mixed emotions as I read — alternating sadness and joy. The great prophet's words came alive in me as never before, almost as if he were reaching out with his visions and revelations, traversing through time to speak to me personally. But his message and its meaning eluded me.

"I found myself in the midst of a small clump of olive trees.

In the center of the stand was an unusually tall carob tree. Its branches swayed in the cool breeze, causing the sunlight to ripple across the leaves and coarse bark of the shorter trees. The effect was very unusual; the *whole stand* seemed to be swaying.

"It was cool in the shade, so I sat down against the carob and closed my eyes. I could feel the cool bark where it touched the back of my neck, and I imagined that I was standing on the deck of my uncle's boat, watching dolphins chase one another in the blue-green ocean. It was then that I heard the voice:

> "'And there shall come forth a rod out of the stem of Jesse, and a Branch shall grow out of his roots. And the Spirit of the Lord shall rest upon Him, the spirit of wisdom and understanding, the spirit of counsel and might, the spirit of knowledge and of the fear of the Lord: and He shall not judge after the sight of His eyes, neither reprove the hearing of His ears: But with righteousness shall He judge the poor, and reprove with equity the meek of the earth: and He shall smite the earth with the rod of His mouth, and with the breath of His lips shall He slay the wicked. And righteousness shall be the girdle of His loins, and faithfulness the girdle of His reins.'"

"What happened next?"

"I opened my eyes immediately. Much to my surprise, there was no one to be seen. Baffled, I stood up. Again the voice spoke. This time I realized that the words had come from *within* me:

> "'The people that walked in darkness have seen a great light: they that dwell in the land of the shadow of death, upon them has the light shined.'

"My heart began to pound. The haze of twilight blurred

before me as I cried out with understanding: 'Bethel, the place *of God*!'"

Uriel remained silent, unmoving. He studied Joseph through hooded eyes as he absorbed everything the young man said.

"The next morning I set out for Jerusalem. I'd been immersed in my studies, and it wasn't until I was on the outskirts of the city that I remembered the Passover would start that evening.

"It was just after the sixth hour, and I was about five miles away. In a matter of minutes the deep-blue, cloudless sky turned an angry purple-black. The wind began to blow with such force, it was all I could do to stand. I expected a torrent of rain at any moment, but no rain came. Instead, the wind began to howl, and great bolts of lightning crisscrossed the sky, like sparks created by the pounding of metal upon metal as the ironsmith pulls red-hot iron from the furnace and works it with his hammer.

"I imagined that all the forces of darkness had been loosed in the heavens above Jerusalem. I fell to the ground, trembling, and cried out to Almighty God."

Joseph's eyes grew wide, and his face became flushed as he relived the experience. The light danced off his glistening hazel-brown pupils, and his taut, finely muscled body was drenched with sweat. "Abruptly the wind stopped! The sudden quiet was deafening. Somehow I knew I was *hearing* death instead of seeing it." He shuddered with the memory. "An especially loud crack of thunder ripped through the silence. It reminded me of the singing sound the scourge makes before landing upon flesh.

"Then the rain came. Great torrents of it. The fat drops fell . . . and fell . . . and fell — like a flood of heavenly tears. I thought it would go on forever.

"I started to run, but hadn't gone far when, just as abruptly as it had started, the rain ceased. No drizzle. No light shower. The deluge just *stopped*!

"I arrived in the city just after dusk. The streets were deserted. Shortly thereafter I came upon a woodworker in the process of closing up his shop. 'Greetings, friend,' I said, my mind still contemplating the strange occurrence. 'I'm a stranger here, and I'm in need of lodging for the evening.'

" 'What business have you here in Jerusalem?' he asked me, moving forward from the shadows into the light of a lantern.' 'I seek a Rabbi from Galilee . . . a Jew who heals the sick and teaches love for one's fellowman.'

"'And what would the name of this Galilean be?'

"'Jesus of Nazareth.'

"The shopkeeper became very quiet, and when he finally spoke, tears filled his eyes. 'The one you seek is no more.'

"'Where has He gone? I must find Him. It is most urgent.'

"'No, brother, you misunderstand. The Nazarene was crucified this very day by the Romans — at Golgotha,' he whispered, then paused and quickly scanned the darkening streets.

"'Golgotha?'

"'The place of the skull, just outside the city.'

"'But —'

"Just then several Roman soldiers headed our way, and the proprietor glanced at them furtively, then added, 'I've said enough already, especially to one who's a stranger. Go now . . . I've work to do.' He disappeared into the recesses of his shop, taking the light with him."

"Is that all?" sighed Uriel.

Joseph stoked the fire to keep it going. "Not quite." Outside, stars danced a promenade across the heavens, using the black canopy as their stage, and a soft wind carried the scent of salt and fish into the cave. Below, on the marl beach at the base of the cliff, a fleeting tremor in the belly of the earth rearranged the pulverized limestone ever so slightly. Neither of the cave's occupants noticed.

"I asked questions of several and learned the place of the

Rabbi's burial. I arrived at His tomb well after midnight," continued Joseph. "There was a chill in the air that belied the normally warm nights. I stood before the great outcropping of rock and shivered. I couldn't cease looking at the huge slab of stone that sealed the entrance.

"Finally I collapsed in front of the sepulchre. Mercifully, the sweet release of exhaustion rescued me from my waking nightmare. Oddly, I dreamed of my time in Joppa.

"Suddenly an intense, almost blinding white light filled my head. Then, out of the light a voice spoke! And it was the same voice I'd heard at Bethel and Joppa! It was difficult understanding what the voice was saying because another voice was talking at the same time. 'Wake up, you!' the other voice said.

"I sat up and rubbed the sleep from my eyes, only to discover that I was surrounded by a contingent of Roman centurions led by a Praetorian. 'Who are you, and what is your business here?' the Praetorian asked me.

"I was terrified. 'My name is Joseph,' I told him as I stood up. 'I came seeking the man who is buried in this tomb. Who are you?'

"'I'm the commander of Pontius Pilate's Praetorian Guard. And I warn you, if you stay here any longer you will be subject to immediate arrest.'

"I knew enough about the Legion to know that one does not argue with a Praetorian. Inexplicably, in spite of the Praetorian's harsh words, I felt a strange kinship with him. Had we met under different circumstances, I believe we might have become friends."

"That's quite a story, my young friend. And now, because of what you've told me, I will share something with you that I've never spoken about to any man."

Joseph suddenly felt like he was being comfortably

immersed in a pool of warm oil. And, impossibly, the cave suddenly smelled as if it were filled with frankincense.

"We have not met by accident," Uriel said solemnly, fastening his gaze upon the younger man. "I've known for some time that a man such as yourself would come. I just didn't know when. I know now that my time here is nearly finished."

Joseph started to say something, but Uriel silenced him with a look. "The area around this cave was once known as the Vale of Siddim," he continued. "Many believe the name means 'Valley of the Fields.' However, the Vale Siddim is known to me, and others like myself, as the 'Valley of Demons.' Beneath the green expanse of water below this cave lies the plain of abomination, and beneath it lies the graves of giants . . . the *Nephilim*."

"'The fallen ones'?" muttered Joseph, translating the Hebrew.

Uriel nodded. "They are better known to you as the *Rephaim* — aboriginal giants who inhabited Canaan."

"'Spirits of the deceased.' The Anakim, the Emim, and the Zamzummin," whispered Joseph, remembering reading about them in Scripture.

Uriel frowned. "Cursed because of their lust for the flesh and the blood of men, they perished in the Great Flood."

Joseph's heart hammered. He knew from his studies that Sodom and Gomorrah were said to be buried under the great inland sea, and that the word *Gomorrah* actually meant "submersion." *Is it possible?* he wondered in amazement.

Uriel stood and went to the back of the cave, where he withdrew something wedged between two rocks. "What I'm about to tell you, Joseph, is covered in detail in these manuscripts," he said, holding up a linen-wrapped bundle.

"Are you the author?"

Uriel shook his head. "Merely a guardian." He handed the parchments to Joseph. "A time will come when you will know what to do with these. Trust your heart when that moment comes." The old man paused, a faraway look in his glistening eyes, then continued in a somber voice. "You know the phrase *wayigra*, of course?"

Joseph nodded. "It means, 'and He called.' It contains the opening lines of the third book of the Pentateuch."

Uriel smiled. "You learned your *bar mitzvah* lessons well. Yet, when the Greek scholars translated the books of Moses into the Septuagint nearly three hundred years ago, they named the book 'Leviticus,' because it contains the law of the priests, the Levites, and illumines the priestly approach to God."

"Atonement," interjected Joseph, wondering how this abrupt transition fit in with the information he'd been given about the *Nephilim*.

"Atonement as it relates to Aaron and his descendants, the Tabernacle, the brazen altar . . . the entire nation of Israel," pressed Uriel, skillfully guiding the conversation. "And the most important element throughout the entire book is —"

"The blood."

"Precisely. The *Torah* teaches that the life of the flesh is *in the blood* and that the blood is given to make atonement for the souls of men. That is why God admonished Noah not to eat the flesh in its life, the blood, and later instructed Moses to tell his people that anyone, even strangers who sojourned among them, who ate or drank of the blood of any animal would be forever cut off — not only from their people, but from Him."

"But how —"

"Shhh, let me finish, my impatient young friend. What I must tell you is this. The remnant of the *Nephilim*, although they no longer have fleshly bodies, are still very active. They can no longer operate in the natural realm as physical beings, but they still foment madness and perversion among the ignorant. Being offspring of angels and women, they are neither angelic nor human. Having once been flesh, they desire again to be flesh. But this is denied to them, except in rare instances. Nevertheless, they feed on fear, anger, strife, and perversions of the flesh. Ever consuming, never coming to fulfillment, they are eternally damned. They hunger for blood, because they know that there is life in the blood. Yet, they are spiritual bastards, so no matter how much blood they consume, it is *never* enough. For them, there is no *life* — only the torment of everlasting darkness."

Joseph was stunned. He was having a hard time comprehending all that the old man was telling him. True, he knew the basics — but the rest? Disembodied demons, thirsty for blood, searching for hosts . . .

His mind reeled with the implications. He felt lightheaded, like a marathon runner nearing the end of his long yet exhilarating ordeal. He gathered the bundle to his chest and wondered why he didn't doubt for a moment what Uriel had told him.

Uriel studied Joseph's face, then reached over and took his arm, patting it as a father would a child's who needed reassurance. For the time being he'd given Joseph enough information about the scrolls. God would do the rest. "It's time you slept," he said soothingly. "And tonight I promise your dreams will be peaceful. The demon has left you. He seeks more succulent prey."

Joseph's whole arm tingled when Uriel touched him, and the hairs on the back of his neck stood up. At the same time he felt lethargic, as if he'd been drugged. *No,* he thought, *it's more like a tremendous burden has been lifted from me.* He stretched out on the limestone floor, and a smile crossed his lips as he closed his eyes. His last thought was that in the morning he must tell Uriel of his decision: he would seek out the disciples of Jesus and join them, if they would have him.

When he awoke in the morning, Uriel was gone. Beside him lay the linen bundle. Joseph knew deep in his spirit that the old man would not return. He stood and stretched, feeling refreshed for the first time in weeks, then walked to the mouth of the cave and looked out. He took several deep breaths, savoring the salt air, and smiled as he watched the sun rise.

It was time he returned to Jerusalem.

IV

W hat would I do without you, Deucalion?" Pilate asked rhetorically, adjusting his toga as the two men walked through narrow, dusty streets in the heart of Jerusalem. Underneath the toga he wore a tunic, the *angusticlava*, with a narrow bordering strip of purple running the length of the garment, indicating he was a member of the *equestrian* order, a clan second only to the senatorial, which sported the *laticlava*, a wider purple strip. "You know, my young friend, there are pitifully few people one can trust these days. And there's a strange kind of madness in the world . . . "

"I'm not sure I understand what you mean, Pontius," replied Deucalion as he adjusted his own clothing. Unlike the Procurator's loose-fitting toga and tunic, the armor he wore weighed heavily upon his tall, muscular frame. The sun had only been up a short time, and already his body was complaining about the heat.

"It's in their eyes, my young friend," Pilate whispered, indicating a group of old men engaged in a heated discussion on their left. "Never doubt what you see exposed in those twin mirrors of the soul. Men hide their feelings in many ways, but few are able to control their emotions so that the truth of what they feel does not register in their eyes."

Deucalion, caught off guard by the moment of intimacy, stared first at the old men, then back at his superior. In the past few weeks Pilate's body had become gaunt, almost emaciated, and his deeply tanned skin had taken on the consistency of parchment. His cheeks were sunken, and there were deep, dark circles underneath his once bright, brown eyes.

A sudden, strange thought flowed into Deucalion's mind. He wondered if Pilate was suffering from some untreatable malady — perhaps a vicious parasite that consumed the Procurator's life-force from within. It would be like him not to speak of it to anyone.

"It is the eyes that record a man's life — and it is the eyes that provide a record of a man's sins. Words can deceive, but the truth of what is in a man's heart is found here," continued Pilate, tapping the spot to the right of one eye with a long, bony index finger. "If you look into the eyes of the people as we pass among them, you'll see the anger . . . the fear . . . and the desire to be free from the burden of Rome upon their backs."

Deucalion grew more and more perplexed as Pilate talked. He realized that something was bothering the Procurator; yet his superior was obviously finding it difficult to express what he truly felt.

"Did you know that the Jews have a unique way of dealing with a man who kills another without just cause?"

Deucalion shook his head in the negative, matching Pilate step for step as they entered the open square that was the central marketplace of Jerusalem.

"The dead man is securely fastened upon the back of his murderer. The guilty party must carry the rotting, decaying, maggot-infested corpse in that manner, until he succumbs himself to the filthiness of death. Sometimes, late at night, when the city is as quiet as a tomb, I dream that Rome is that decaying corpse and that her carcass rots upon the backs of the innocent."

The Procurator stopped abruptly in mid-stride and grabbed Deucalion by the arm. "Do you find my dialogue morbid?" he asked petulantly, a pained look in his tired eyes.

"The truth, Pontius?"

"Don't you always give it to me . . . whether I want to hear it or not?"

Deucalion managed a chuckle from his sun-cracked lips. He wanted desperately to banish the stifling heaviness that cloaked their conversation. "You know me all too well, Pontius . . . perhaps too well for my own good."

The intensity of Pilate's stare unnerved him, but he continued, "Yes, I find our conversation much too revealing for the light of day. These topics are better reserved for the emptiness of night, when a drunken man's tongue can speak freely of the demons that haunt his sleep."

The Procurator flinched.

Deucalion didn't seem to notice. "I too, as we have discussed on many an evening, am concerned about the course Rome's helmsmen have plotted," he said. "We who man the oars have little to say about our destination. I have learned, however, not to worry about the steering of the ship. I leave that to the captains."

"And what if *you* were captain?" asked Pilate, thinking he would be proud to have this man as a son.

Deucalion stared hard at Pilate for a moment before he answered, trying to read what he saw in his superior's eyes. *What is it that torments him so?* "Perhaps I would chart a different course," he answered solemnly.

Pilate arched his eyebrows, something he did when he was impressed with what he heard, which was not often. "You never cease to amaze me with your boldness, Deucalion." *And for one so young, you are quite a remarkable soldier*, he thought appreciatively. "If I had but a cohort of men such as yourself," he added, letting out a deep, unrestrained laugh, "I would seriously consider taking on the Empire."

Abruptly Deucalion realized that the source of the feelings beginning to crystallize within him was also the source of the

Procurator's torment. The revelation came as he remembered the conversation he'd had with Pilate's secretary, Antonius, two days ago.

"There is no one I can trust with what I'm about to say but you, Deucalion. Do I have your word you will not repeat our conversation?" Antonius had whispered.

He'd nodded his assent.

"My master is plagued by a demon. He wrestles with it nightly in his sleep."

The fear he'd seen in Antonius' eyes had startled him. "Sometimes I think I'll wake in the morning and find his chambers empty . . . his body having simply been swallowed up by the darkness."

"And what is the source of all this?"

"My master is obsessed," whispered the distressed slave, "with the death of the Jew from Galilee. He believes the man posed insufficient threat to Rome to warrant crucifixion. Although he hates the Jews, and especially their preoccupation with their God, he feels that Roman law, in this case, did not provide a just resolution. He believes there should have been a compromise."

Deucalion understood all too well what Antonius was saying. Ironically Pilate, defender of the sanctity of the State, had found himself in what was for all practical purposes a situation in which no victory was possible. Jesus had done nothing wrong as far as Pilate and Roman law were concerned; yet the Jews, whom he despised, insisted Jesus be put to death.

Pilate would have loved nothing better than to free Jesus, and in so doing spit in the faces of the priests who sentenced the accused to die. Yet, because of a quirk of the law, the Procurator had been forced to validate their mandate and carry out their wishes. Hoping for a way out, he'd sent Jesus to Antipas, who had in turn sent Him back to Pilate. Not only had the Jews successfully drawn blood with their ploy, but they twisted the blade in the wound as well.

"Enough of this talk of madness and death," Pilate said as he slapped Deucalion upon the back, exhibiting genuine affection for his attaché. "We have more pressing, and much less philosophical, matters to discuss."

In the blink of an eye Pilate's demeanor had changed dramatically. He was now the soldier planning his campaign. "Antipas has not responded to my request that he make an accounting for his actions in the case of Jesus of Nazareth."

"He seemed highly agitated when I gave him the scroll from Rome," interjected Deucalion, bringing his thoughts back to the conversation at hand.

"As well he should be," Pilate grunted. "Rome will expect me to provide them with some sort of justification for my actions in the matter. And as you are well aware, they want an immediate solution to the problem of the increasing insurgency among the populace." He did not add, for it went without saying, that was why Deucalion had been sent to Judea. The Procurator hated to be reminded of his shortcomings.

"With all due respect, Pontius, your problem is not Rome. Nor is it Antipas."

The older man winced. He did not take criticism well, even from Deucalion. "No? Who then?"

"Caiaphas . . . and the Sanhedrin."

"Aha! You've been doing some investigating on your own, haven't you? Do you think I should tighten the reins a bit?" He smiled sardonically. "Perhaps about the neck of Annas?"

Deucalion shrugged, squinting his eyes against the harsh glare. He had plans he dared not mention. "Perhaps," he echoed, "but not immediately."

Despite the breeze that had arisen while they talked, both men's tunics were soaked, yet neither seemed to feel it.

"Oh?"

"We need to know more about what is happening within

the Sanhedrin. I have a feeling there's more going on than we are aware of, even with the information your spies supply."

"And how do you propose to accomplish that task?"

Deucalion smiled. He was back in control of the conversation. "I've received an invitation from a dissident member of the Great Council. One who sent me a secretive, rather tantalizing note indicating he has certain information he wishes to impart to you through me."

Pilate was suddenly apprehensive. "Why you?"

"I'm not sure. Perhaps he feels more secure speaking with an intermediary. At any rate, he says the information could be most valuable in resolving what he circumspectly referred to as 'the dilemma Caiaphas has gotten us all into.'"

"Most interesting indeed." Pilate stroked his chin with his right hand, toying with the three-day stubble that further darkened his deep-brown coloring. "And this ferret's name?"

"Doras."

"You accepted, of course?" Deucalion smiled again, and Pilate slapped his shoulder. "Well then, by all means indulge him. We don't want to disappoint a member of the Great Sanhedrin, now do we?"

"As you wish, Procurator."

"If only I had a hundred men like you . . . " chuckled Pilate. "When is this, ah, meeting to take place?"

"Tonight. I'm to have dinner with him at his home."

"Excellent. This could be the answer I've been hoping for, gods be praised."

A shocked look crossed Deucalion's face. "I didn't know you favored the gods, Pontius."

"I don't," Pilate replied as he grinned expansively.

"I don't understand."

Pilate shrugged. "Destiny, Commander, destiny."

Deucalion grew thoughtful. He'd always found the Roman

preoccupation with gods somewhat foolish, but the idea that a man's fate was predetermined — even before his birth — was something else altogether. "Who determines a man's destiny, then, if there are no gods?" he asked.

"I didn't say there are *no* gods, just that I don't favor them. Only men who have no answers from within seek answers from without."

"Are you that sure of yourself then?"

Pilate flinched. "And why shouldn't I be?"

"What if we are *not* in control of our destiny? What if there is only *one* God, such as the Hebrews claim, who created everything and rules from His throne in Heaven?"

Pilate stopped walking and eyed his commander. "I listen to that rot from the Jews — I certainly don't expect to hear it from a Praetorian," he replied harshly. "Now, tell me about this Doras."

V

Deucalion arrived at Doras' house, located not far from the Temple, in the minutes just after sunset. As he approached the entrance to the small but prominent residence, he marveled at the sanguine complexion of the sky. *There is nothing to compare in all the world with the beauty of the setting or rising sun*, he thought.

He also thought about his mother, knowing she would approve of his musings. She was Greek and a student of Plato. Like her philosophical mentor, she believed in the love of the *Idea* of beauty, the doctrine that physical objects are merely impermanent representations of unchanging Ideas.

"It is Ideas alone that give true knowledge, Deucalion, not the imperfect *manifestations* of the Idea as they become known by the mind," she'd told him just before he left for Syria.

At the time her words confused him. But now, as he watched the sun disappear over the rim of the world, he felt as if he knew what she'd been trying to say.

If light were absolute, he reflected, *one might conclude it was the very essence of spirit. Being free from all impurity means it has the power to cleanse any lesser form simply by coming into contact with that form. The manifestation of that cleansing then becomes of secondary importance — an effect rather than a result.*

The intensity of his thoughts made him feel dizzy, and he

closed his eyes momentarily in an attempt to steady himself. When he opened them, the rich, vibrant colors of sunset had melted together into the soft yellow-bronze of dusk.

He started for the doorway when something caught his eye. He looked up and glimpsed the face of a dark-haired woman watching him from the portico above the veranda. He raised his hand to shield out the glare and blinked, then looked closer. The woman was gone, leaving nothing but shadows dancing across the gypsum-coated, sun-dried brick walls. "Must be the heat," he muttered and strode forward.

The first thing he noticed as he entered Doras' house was the cleanliness; there didn't seem to be a speck of dust anywhere. That was most unusual, even for a Jew, since Jerusalem was a very dusty city. The second thing he realized was that Doras was clearly not a poor man. The small home was filled with a variety of expensive rugs, brass and copper lampstands, and marble furniture.

Dinner was served in the main living area. He sat opposite his host upon cushions covered with very expensive carpets from Persia. Half a dozen large brass lanterns, overlaid in gold, provided light.

During the meal the two men enjoyed casual conversation covering a variety of topics. As the servants cleared away the last few dishes Doras said, "I must say, Deucalion, that you intrigue me. Previous to this evening I would have thought our conversation much too arcane for the Roman soldier's mind, preoccupied as it must be with military matters."

Deucalion smiled nonchalantly at the subtle way Doras sought to establish control of the conversation. "Not all soldiers are as pragmatically blind as our detractors would have you Jews believe. Some of us even fill our idle hours studying Hebrew history."

"Oh?"

"You Jews believe in a god called Satan, correct?"

"Satan is no god, Praetorian. He is consummate evil."

"Then why do your Holy Scriptures refer to him as a 'son of the morning fallen from heaven,' a god wrongly worshiped?"

"Surely you're not suggesting —"

"And did not the god you call 'Jehovah' promise in the Garden of Eden that the one who would 'bruise the head' of the serpent, Satan, would come through the lineage of Abraham?"

Doras grew agitated. "Where did you get this information, and why are you taunting me with it?"

"I assure you my intent is *not* to taunt you, Doras."

"What then?"

"Merely to make a point."

"I'm listening."

"You are an Edomite, are you not?"

Doras flinched. "So?"

"And the Edomites are descendants of Esau, the eldest son of Isaac?"

Doras nodded.

"Well then, you of all people should understand. The Edenic promise of the one who would crush Satan was fixed in the family of Abraham. Let's see, I believe the lineage should have been Seth, Shem, Abraham, Isaac, *Esau*. But that was not to be, was it, Doras? Esau sold his birthright — for a bowl of pottage, no less. And so his younger brother Jacob received the irrevocable blessing."

By now Doras was livid. "This is intolerable. I will not allow a Roman soldier to insult me in my own home."

"Forgive me . . . I thought we were discussing why you invited me here tonight."

Doras reached for his goblet of wine and said angrily, "I don't understand your point."

"My point? Esau's bitter hatred towards his brother Jacob

for fraudulently obtaining his blessing was inherited by his descendants. In fact, when the great Babylonian king Nebuchadnezzar besieged Jerusalem, the Edomites joined forces with the Assyrians. They took an active part in the plunder of this city and the slaughter of its Jewish residents. I believe you are a direct descendant of the man who led the Edomites."

Doras gasped. "But how —"

Deucalion smiled. "I have my ways, just as you in the Sanhedrin have yours. The point is, you are not happy with Joseph ben Caiaphas as High Priest. Knowing that Pilate is extremely unhappy with him as well as a result of what happened during the Passover, you wish to align yourself with us so that we might help you remove Annas' puppet. And you hope to convince me that your plan will serve *our* interests as well as your own."

Doras glared at Deucalion, but remained silent.

The Praetorian resumed his explanation. "Now that we understand one another, perhaps you'd care to elaborate on why you invited me here tonight."

"Out on the veranda," grimaced the flustered Jew, rising unsteadily. "I need fresh air."

The veranda wasn't large, and the only pieces of furniture were a small wooden table and two cushions. Both men chose to remain standing.

Deucalion gazed up into the clear sky and stared at the full moon. He was relieved to be outside; the atmosphere in the house had been cloying. Truth be known, he wasn't very happy with himself because of the way he'd berated Doras. Yet, he'd had to do it.

The older man would be stunned if he knew that a Praetorian with a gift for languages had mastered not only Greek and Aramaic, in addition to his native Latin, but Hebrew as well. It was a secret few knew, one that gave

Deucalion a tremendous edge in dealing with the Jews. There were times he almost believed he could *think* as they did.

That's why he knew Doras would be easy to manipulate. Although the aging Jew was a not a Pharisee, he thought and acted like one. He served the law of his people diligently only because he knew he could profit by it. Other Jews referred to men like him as *Shechemites*, so named after the son of Hamor who seduced Jacob's daughter, Dinah, only to be brutally killed by the girl's brothers, Simeon and Levi.

"Everything a man does depends on fate and God," said Doras after taking several deep breaths. "And *everything* that happens in the world takes place through God's providence. That being the case, it follows that in human actions — whether good or bad — the cooperation of God is implicit. So you see, your intimation that my blood is tainted because of my ancestry evidences your complete lack of understanding of our religion."

Behind them, inside, the servants extinguished the lanterns.

"And what about a man's will?"

Doras smiled. "God allows spontaneity. It pleased Him that there should be a mixture; that's why He added the will of fate to human will."

"As a sort of balance between virtue and baseness, no doubt."

"Exactly." Doras had regained his composure. "For one who is not a Jew, you are indeed quite perceptive."

Deucalion ignored the implicit arrogance of the statement. "Perceptive enough to know there are serious political problems within the Sanhedrin, and that is why you sent me that cryptic note." He also knew all too well that the Israelites went out of their way to avoid all contact with the heathen, lest they be defiled. This evening was indeed extraordinary.

Doras turned from his perusal of the city and faced

Deucalion. "Political problems, as you put it, are, for those who subscribe to the Pharisaic tradition, not political at all."

"Oh?"

"The Pharisees in the Sanhedrin are not a 'political party' as you Romans think of such. Their aim, that of insuring strict adherence to the law, arises from religious, not political, motivation."

Deucalion knew this, but he let his host continue as if his revelations about Jewish government were new.

"As a group, the Pharisees are comparatively indifferent to politics. However, there are others within the Sanhedrin who do not share these sentiments. Consequently, the Council is divided."

"In what manner?"

"The Pharisees, scribes, and other elders who support *me* agree with the idea of divine providence."

"Ah, the idea that we Romans occupy Palestine only because it is the will of your God."

"That's only a small part of it."

"Go on."

"Rome's power over us is a *chastisement* of God that must be submitted to willingly. Thus, so long as we are not prevented from the observance of the law, the harshness of your occupation must also be borne willingly."

"But why?"

"Because *that* is the will of God."

"That seems rather fatalistic."

"I suppose to the Roman way of thinking, it is. But we Jews know that one day the Messiah will come and set us free. You see, Deucalion, we believe there is *nothing* that cannot be accomplished by faith."

"Yet you crucified the one man in your whole history who claimed to be that Messiah."

"The Nazarene was a blasphemer," replied Doras angrily.

"Nothing more, nothing less. However, His death has produced some unexpected fruit." He grew suddenly pensive.

"You said there were two groups?"

"A few Pharisees and most of the Sadducees, among them Annas and Caiaphas, believe that Israel must acknowledge no other king than God alone and the ruler of the house of David whom God has anointed. For them your supremacy is both presumptuous and illegal. Therefore, the issue for them is not whether obedience and payment of tribute to Rome is a *duty*, but rather whether or not it is *legal*."

"I see. And how does all of this relate to your problem with the High Priest?"

Before Doras could answer him, they were interrupted by the most beautiful woman Deucalion had ever seen.

Because the veranda was lit only by a solitary lantern, the immediate brightness of the flame mellowed into a soft glow just beyond Deucalion's depth of vision. It gave the illusion that at the point of blending the light had no real ending and the darkness no real beginning. The raven-haired woman stepped into that dull glow as if she were stepping out of eternity and into time.

"Why have you disturbed us?" Doras asked in a gruff voice.

"I thought the two of you might be thirsty, so I brought a flagon of dandelion wine," the woman replied.

"Put the wine on the table and leave us. And do not interrupt us again."

The woman did as she was told. Then, without a further word or glance, she left them to their business.

Deucalion stared after her, watching her long black hair dissolve into the darkness. Her voice had sounded like silk rustling in a gentle breeze, and the appraising look he'd seen in her eyes made his heart pound. "Who is she?" he asked, amazed at the effect the woman had upon him.

Doras studied Deucalion a moment before saying, "She's a married slave."

Something in the abruptness of his tone warned Deucalion that Doras was lying, but he could think of no good reason to tell him so. Instead, he stared into the darkness that had absorbed the woman and wondered about the truth.

VI

Deucalion left Doras' house well after midnight, and his thoughts were like miniature ships tossed about upon a choppy sea of dandelion wine. Doras had shocked him with his revelation of the conspiracy between himself and Antipas. Yet, in spite of the significance of that piece of information, the Praetorian could not shake the vision of the incredibly stunning black-haired woman.

Who is she, really? he wondered. He did not believe for a moment that she was a slave. She was far too beautiful, too noble. Besides that, the look she'd given him before Doras had commanded her to leave had not been the glance of a married servant. She was no timid wife stealing a glance at an unusual house guest.

Her eyes had shone. They'd radiated a lustrous but soft light that seemed to push back the darkness. And in their few seconds of eye contact he'd seen interest and excitement in those sparkling eyes. His curiosity had been roused to the point of distraction. Or maybe it was simply the dandelion wine.

Suddenly his head exploded in pain. He was knocked to the ground, gasping for breath. In rapid succession he received several harsh kicks to his ribs. He tried to stand and fight, but was repeatedly knocked to the earth. The wine dulled his reactions and made him easy prey.

He tried to focus on his attackers, but all he saw were four blurred figures. The one detail he could see, however, caused him to gasp. They were centurions!

His mind raced. Why would members of the Legion attack *him*? What madness possessed them?

Once more he tried to stand and fight, but was again pushed off his feet. More humiliated than hurt, he rolled himself into a tight ball. He had to protect his head and ribs.

His attackers remained silent throughout the beating, although upon his submission to their punishment the blows became less pronounced, almost cursory.

As abruptly as it had started, the attack was over.

He lay in the dust, groaning. Blood trickled out of the corner of his mouth. His right eye was swollen shut, and he felt like he'd been kicked in the chest by a horse.

One of the attackers pulled out a small purse of gold and silver coins, then threw the bundle into the dust near Deucalion's face. The bag of money landed with a soft thud, sending a small puff of dust into the air.

Deucalion coughed and spit red saliva. One of his teeth was loose, and he felt nauseous.

From the darkness to his right came a harsh voice. "You will take the money, Praetorian, and you will not make trouble." A different voice, this one on the left, said, "All of us except you agreed to take the money and be silent. We do not want to hurt you further, but we will do what is necessary if you persist in challenging the inquest's findings." A third, muffled voice came from behind him. "There was *no resurrection*. You saw nothing unusual at the tomb. The body was stolen by thieves, perhaps even by the stranger you encountered when you arrived at the tomb."

The fourth assailant spoke, and his was the only voice that sounded vaguely familiar. "Enough! Remember, Praetorian, the investigation is concluded. You've been warned!"

With that, the four assailants disappeared into the night.

Deucalion sat up and vomited. *So much for the lamb and dandelion wine*, he thought. *Rich food and fine wine are not for the likes of this soldier's son.*

The weak attempt at humor did not ease the pain coursing through his battered body. What hurt worse, however, was the humiliation. And he knew that was what his attackers had most wanted to accomplish.

Physical scarring was one of the hazards of soldiering and was taken in stride by all who were in the Legion. In fact, among some it was a sign of status; the more scars, the more one had embraced death and lived to tell of the encounter. His assailants, however, had had a more devious intent in mind. They wanted to scar him emotionally and thought they knew him well enough to accomplish such a purpose. The sting of the beating he'd received lay in the lack of opportunity for him to defend himself with dignity, as befitted a member of Rome's elite guard. Fighting one's opponent in a fair match was even accorded to gladiators in the Colosseum, who were but slaves trained to fight and die heroically for the pleasure of Caesar and the crowd.

Well, his attackers had seriously underestimated him. Oh, they might have known the man who had been ordered to make sure the Galilean was dead, the same man who was then sent to guard the body. But what they could not know, because he'd only just begun to realize it himself, was that he was not the same man when he left the tomb three days later.

He'd gone to the tomb thinking only of accomplishing an important task assigned him by Pontius Pilate. Three days later he left the burial site thinking of nothing but the light he had seen when there should have been no light. Light that was brighter than fifty lanterns, yet was soft and shimmering as well. Light that had wrapped itself around him like a fine mist, reminding him of the spray of water surrounding a cascading waterfall.

And the sound! There had been music. *Singing!* It had enveloped him in a cocoon, blanketing out every sound but its own. The light was sound; the sound was light. He felt as if he were *hearing* the light and *seeing* the sound.

At first he thought he'd fallen asleep and was having a dream. Just as he was about to cry out to his men, a voice spoke to him out of the light. It was of the same character and quality as the music. Yet it was *different*. Something in the tone set it apart from the rest of the music and singing, almost as if the sound had become a living entity.

"Rejoice, for the light is come. The glory of the Lord is risen. The glory of the Lord is risen upon you."

And then, as abruptly as it had appeared, the light was gone . . . The music ceased . . . The singing stopped.

There was nothing save the eerie silence of dawn.

He'd blinked several times when he realized that the sun was only just starting to march upon the horizon. What then had been the light he'd seen? He watched in a daze as the fibrous, yellow-red tendrils of daylight crept upward from the purple-black horizon, seeking out the fastenings of darkness, burning them loose and collapsing the curtain of night.

On that fateful morning, the evening performance had come to an end *twice*.

When he regained his senses, he'd looked around at his men, curious whether they too had seen and heard. They had. He could tell, for they had the same look on their faces that he imagined he must have on his own.

Some were rubbing their eyes. Others looked at their companions in amazement. One asked if the sun had risen early. Abruptly Malkus had cried out in alarm, "Commander, over here . . . Come quickly."

The small contingent of soldiers gathered as a group behind him and his second-in-command and stared at him with questioning eyes.

The seal was broken on the tomb!

The stone had been rolled away!

There were murmurs of fear. The penalty for falling asleep on guard duty such as this was *death*.

"Shall I check the body, Commander?" asked Malkus.

He nodded woodenly.

Malkus entered the sepulchre while the entire company of men stood transfixed, their eyes fastened on the gaping, black entrance.

Malkus reappeared, his face drawn, a look of surprise — or perhaps anger — in his eyes. In his hands he held the blood-stained linen the Jews had used to wrap the body of Jesus. "The body is gone," he said in a hushed, trembling voice. Then, realizing what he'd said, he added, "A thief has stolen the body. Quickly . . . find him before he can escape. He can't have gone far."

They searched until noon and found nothing.

No thief. No body.

No, they don't know me at all, thought Deucalion as he sat in the dusty street gazing at the stars and remembering. When it was all said and done, he was not so sure *he* knew who he'd once been. But one thing he did know: the thought of "fighting for dignity" made him want to laugh. What a contradiction in terms!

He broke out into hysterical, wonderful laughter. "Fighting for dignity, indeed," he muttered, then laughed and laughed and laughed.

In the early-morning hours of the first day of June, Joseph Caiaphas sat quietly and contemplatively in the Hall of Hewn Stones, the apartment of the national Temple, the *lishkath haggazith*. Somewhere in the darkness outside, a cock crowed. The High Priest tilted his head and grunted, as if he'd just received a long overdue message from within the depths of the Holy City.

Jerusalem, the city whose name meant "foundation of peace," had been anything but peaceful for him lately — especially the past two weeks. He'd been preparing for tonight's meeting of the Sanhedrin, the most difficult task of his long career.

He'd spent the time since his conversation with Simon gathering as much information about the man from Nazareth as possible. Realizing there were members of the Council who would like nothing better than to see him disgraced and removed from office, he was determined to provide a thorough accounting for his actions.

To that end he had summoned Helcias, the keeper of the treasury of the Temple, the one who had given the informant, Judas, his payment of silver. He swore him to secrecy and charged him with the task of ferreting out as much reliable and provable evidence of Jesus' guilt as was available.

Much to his surprise, he found there were a great many unanswered questions about just who Jesus was and, not surprisingly, that there were several conflicting accounts of the circumstances surrounding His birth. One particularly odd story was that His mother, Mary, had been a virgin.

Nevertheless, the more information he'd accumulated, the more he'd become convinced he had acted properly. He was also certain now that Pontius Pilate, whom he detested, had not realized the true extent of the Nazarene's influence.

He sighed heavily, listening to Jerusalem awake from her slumber. Soon he would find out if he was right.

VII

June was being kinder to Pontius Pilate than May had been. And May was most certainly better than April.

In fact, the single worst month of Pilate's entire life had been April.

By the gods what a month, he thought as he looked out over Jerusalem, spread out before him, below and around the ostentatious palace Herod the Great had built.

From where he stood in the tower Herod had named after Mark Antony, he could look down upon the Temple. It was claimed by the Jews to be the greatest and most noble of the despot's achievements. Pilate had been told upon his arrival in Jerusalem that the Jews had a saying about the Temple: he who has not seen the Temple of Herod has not seen a beautiful thing.

"What unmitigated garbage," he mumbled.

Antipas, the only Jew Pilate could bring himself to associate with on a regular basis, in one of his drunken moments had confessed that although it was commonly rumored that his "noble" father had rebuilt the Temple in order to placate the people who despised the ruler they felt had sold them out to the Romans, that was not the case. No, Herod the Great was far too shrewd a man to have such a single-minded, benevolent purpose.

Pilate remembered the conversation well. He'd invited the Tetrarch to partake of his private stock of fine Sicilian wine, hoping the man would reveal his secrets.

Antipas had not let him down.

"Why is it you Jews are so preoccupied with your place of worship?" the Procurator asked, genuinely interested. "Your father spent a good portion of his treasury, and the better part of his life, rebuilding a decaying monument to a God who has turned His back on His people."

The aging Tetrarch did not answer immediately. He stood on the porch, looking down at the splendor below him. When he finally replied, his eyes held a glint of cruelty and satisfaction, as if by revealing the truth of his father's motive he was at once betraying a family secret and striking a posthumous blow against a demon that had ridden his back far too long.

"My father's intent," he snarled, letting loose a resounding belch, "was to possess all of the public genealogies collected in the Temple. Especially those relating to the priestly families."

"I don't understand."

"He intended to destroy the genealogy of the expected Messiah, to prevent Him from being born, and then to usurp His kingdom."

Pilate arched his eyebrows at the mention of a Messiah, but said nothing.

"To accomplish his purpose he went to extreme lengths to make our people understand he was doing them a great kindness. He funded the massive project from money taken out of his own pockets —"

"Which had gotten fat by the taxes he'd exacted under the guise of Roman mandate," interjected Pilate.

Antipas turned from the window, a malevolent smile accompanying derisive laughter. "Oh, yes indeed. My father was truly beguiling. He convinced the people that his magnanimous appropriation of personal funds for such a holy purpose would be atonement for the very abuse that made the gesture possible."

"And how did he accomplish such a fraud?" asked Pilate, impressed by the man's audacity.

Antipas filled his goblet with more wine and shrugged. "He promised the priests he would not attempt to build a new Temple, but would merely restore the ancient magnificence of the one built by David's son, Solomon. When the priests questioned him further as to his intentions, he told them that the restoration by Zerrubbabel, made upon the return of Israel from the Babylonian captivity, had fallen short in architectural measurement, according to Scripture, by some sixty cubits in height."

"I see " said Pilate, though in reality he was just beginning to understand. "And no doubt your father, being true to his title, promised to rectify that not insignificant oversight."

"Exactly. He pointed out that the entire structure evidenced substantial deterioration and compared it to rotting teeth, scarred with decay, then argued persuasively that a Temple whose purpose was to glorify God should not be allowed to remain in such a cursed state of disrepair. I believe his exact words were, 'A man's mouth feeds his body so that the flesh will not wither and die, and so it behooves him to keep his teeth in good condition, that he may partake of all the good things his Father has provided for sustenance. Similarly, the Temple is the mouth of the priesthood, the tithes of the people being the food on which it survives.'

"The priests agreed with his assessment, and the Temple was razed down to its original foundation. My father hired one thousand wagons to carry stones and ten thousand skilled workmen to teach the priests the art of stonecutting, carpentry, and metal-smithing. After eighteen months of continual labor the Temple proper was completed. Although the work still continues and although he did not gain possession of the public genealogies, my father believed he had accomplished his purpose."

Pilate snapped from his reverie as the six-week-old conversation died inside his head and looked out over the Temple grounds. The huge structure stood as a constant reminder of his calamitous and fateful appointment as Procurator of Judea.

The Temple proper, where the Ark of the Covenant was kept, was one hundred and eighty feet in length and thirty in height. A great white dome, adorned with a pinnacle of solid gold, sat atop the building. The first time he'd seen it, while he was still some distance from the city, it had reminded him of the snow-capped peaks of Mt. Hermon.

However, the view that commanded his attention of late was that of the avenue at the southwestern angle of the Temple. The bridge that spanned the intervening Valley of Tyropoeon was colossal. It was built upon huge arches, spanning twenty-seven and a half cubits; the spring stones measured sixteen cubits in length and were a third of a cubit thick.

He'd spent many a day during the last six weeks standing on this balcony, staring at the Royal Bridge. Below him, the city spread out like a map. Straggling suburbs, orchards, and seemingly ubiquitous gardens dotted the landscape. His gaze wandered to the horizon and became lost in the hazy outline of the distant mountains. Inevitably, however, his eyes were always drawn back to the bridge over which the Galilean had been led, in plain view of all Jerusalem, to and from the palace of the High Priest — the meeting place of the Sanhedrin. He shuddered with the memory.

"I wonder if Herod ever had an April as bad as I have had," he muttered.

"Probably ," came the voice of Deucalion from behind him, startling him.

"What did you say?" he asked, turning his back on the Temple of God and straightening his sagging shoulders.

"You were talking to yourself again, Pontius."

"Oh?"

"I said he has had much worse."

"Worse?"

"Of course, Pontius . . . the man is dead!"

Pilate chuckled. "I was thinking of the *son*, not the father."

Strange how one man's death could bring so much peace, and so much pain, thought Deucalion, noting that his superior seemed to have aged considerably in the past month and a half. There had been rumors that even though the Procurator had sentenced Jesus to death, something profound had passed between the two men. However, what exactly *had* happened during the time Pilate was alone with the Jew remained a mystery.

He'd questioned Pilate about the events of the Passover, but the Procurator refused to discuss it. Actually, it was more like he *could not* speak about what had happened; as if each word he spoke in recalling the event cut his *spirit* like the razor-sharp edge of a sword cuts flesh and bone.

"Antipas wants control of the Sanhedrin," he said, pushing thoughts of the Nazarene from his mind. "And Doras is his tool. The other activities he's been engaged in recently are camouflage. As we expected, he's no longer satisfied with the meager portion left to him by his father."

Pilate grunted his agreement.

"After talking with Doras, my guess is that Antipas is willing to do just about anything he feels he can get away with in order to achieve his goal."

"And how do we fit into this, ah, little game of political intrigue?"

"Antipas expects you to immobilize Annas, thus hemming in Caiaphas."

Pilate remained thoughtful and asked, "What information did Doras give you that we can use against the High Priest?"

"The trial —"

"What trial?" croaked Pilate, cutting off Deucalion's reply in mid-sentence. His whole body shook, as if it had been suddenly stung by the lash of the scourge.

"The initial interrogation of Jesus, and His final trial before the Sanhedrin," replied Deucalion softly.

Pilate turned abruptly and walked over to the portico. He stopped at the edge of the balcony and stared balefully down at the Temple.

Deucalion came up beside him. "What is it that disturbs you so, Pontius?" he asked, genuine concern evident in his voice. "I thought you'd be pleased with my information."

Seemingly having not heard a word Deucalion had said, Pilate replied, "Your hand . . . What happened?"

Deucalion glanced at his bandaged appendage. "Nothing to be concerned about, Pontius. I had a minor altercation with a couple of men in the streets last night, on my way home from Doras' house."

"Jews?" snarled Pilate, spitting the word instead of speaking it.

"No . . . they were not Jews, Pontius."

"You're certain?"

"Yes, I'm certain," sighed the younger man. "Tell me, why do you hate them so?"

Pilate turned and stared into Deucalion's eyes, his own eyes glistening with fear. "Because they are my death," he whispered in a scratchy, guttural voice.

As Deucalion walked the streets of Jerusalem in the early-afternoon hours, he remembered Pilate's words. *Death is not a subject with which I am unfamiliar,* he thought. He'd experienced its more violent forms firsthand in the service of Rome. "No, death is no stranger to me," he muttered.

Fortunately he did not need the constant memory of battle to remind him of how it sickened him. As much as he had reconciled himself to the necessity of killing in time of war, he'd never been able to steel himself to the brutality many members of the Legion, including some generals, seemed to inflict unnecessarily. And that was why he was so disturbed now.

Pilate had instructed him to take personal charge of insuring there were no outbreaks of rebellion among the disenchanted followers of the dead and buried Jesus, emphasizing "dead and buried" a little too forcefully.

When Deucalion had asked exactly what the Procurator had in mind, he'd been informed there was a Jew who had taken a personal interest in the religious "disease" that was festering like pus in an untreated wound. This Jew had taken it upon himself, with the blessing of Rome of course, to lance the wound as deeply as he deemed necessary in order to cleanse it — permanently — of all infection.

And Pilate had instructed Deucalion to provide "support as required," whenever this Jew deemed it necessary.

"I've already agreed to provide whatever judicial authorization is needed," said the Procurator with finality. "And I've further pledged the full support of the garrison. Because this is a religious and not a military problem, Rome's official position on the matter is that it is the responsibility of the Sanhedrin to insure that the fanatics are eliminated — preferably as rapidly and as efficiently as possible."

The thought of possibly having to participate in violent activities against an unarmed populace brought a rise of bile into the Praetorian's throat. *We have sold our souls to the god of power,* he thought miserably, *and we will pay for it with our blood. We lose our humanity as fast as the Jews lose their lives.*

Pilate had also informed him that he'd sent a message to Caiaphas. The Procurator intended to confront the High Priest in three days with the information Doras had supplied to them and to demand an explanation of his activities.

That was the only hopeful note. At least Deucalion would have time to do what he planned. If he was successful, perhaps he could prevent things from getting totally out of hand. In the meantime, he was to make his services, and those of the garrison, available to the Jew. On his way out he'd asked Pilate, "And who is this Jew who will wipe out this disease of Jesus' followers?"

"Saul of Tarsus," replied Pilate, dismissing him with a wave of his hand.

Now the Praetorian was on his way to see Antipas, needing to locate this Saul who was so anxious to persecute his own people. As he entered the marketplace to the south of the Herodian Palace, he experienced a moment of disorientation. Increasingly there were moments when he felt that were he to try and grasp hold of the events whirling around him, his life would be sucked into a vortex, like so much dust sucked into a whirlwind. This was one of those moments.

He looked around at the people, trying to make sense of what he felt, and was struck by the fact that the world in which he lived was vastly different from the world he had started seeing inside himself. That part of his mind he considered to be the old part told the new part he was thinking too much.

Perhaps that was his problem.

During his early days as a centurion, his instructors had literally beaten into him the idea that good soldiers have no time to think; their purpose is to hear and obey. Thinking during battle was distracting, and distractions meant death.

One of his commanders had said, "If you are lucky enough to achieve the rank of general, Deucalion, then you can think. But remember the price . . . " Here he'd laughed sarcastically. " . . . you will have to answer to Caesar for your thoughts. In any case, centurion, remember this: we who serve the Empire are not required to exercise any profound moral restraint; fortunately we are free from the burden of such esoteric considerations. On the battlefield there is nothing except the fight . . . and survival."

The memory brought to mind his father. And he wondered if he would end up the same way — lying dead in the dust of a foreign land, his grey-blue, Greco-Roman eyes staring blindly at the setting sun.

He shook his head to clear it of the depressing thoughts and headed for the palace. The marketplace was crowded with a throng of people engaged in afternoon bargaining, and he scanned the mass of bodies out of habit. He wasn't looking for anything in particular, just looking.

His heart skipped a beat when he saw the beautiful and mysterious dark-haired woman he'd seen at Doras' last night. She bobbed in and out of his vision as she shopped at the various stalls, carrying a straw basket filled with a variety of foods and fruits. He watched, fascinated, as she moved from vendor to vendor with the ease and self-confidence of one accustomed to getting exactly what she wanted for exactly the price she had decided to pay beforehand.

Instead of rushing forward to ask her who she was and if she remembered him from the previous evening, he found himself rooted to the parched ground beneath his feet. Last night he had only noticed her hair and eyes; now he had the opportunity to observe her more completely. Even though she was unusually tall, that did not catch his eye. Her skin did, or rather the golden tint of it. The color reminded him of the amber coloring of olive trees. And he could swear that she seemed to radiate light, as if she were glowing from within.

As she moved among the people she spoke to those around her, and it was obvious she was not dispensing perfunctory greetings. He could tell by the look on their faces she was saying something special to each one.

He tried to remember where he had seen those looks before. Suddenly he had it. At the tomb — on the morning he had seen music and heard light. The expressions he saw on the faces of the people, though not as intense, were similar to the looks he had seen on the faces of his men.

What in the name of the gods can she be saying to have such an effect upon complete strangers? he wondered, observing her.

He must get closer, so he could hear.

He jostled and elbowed his way through the crowd and managed to find a spot just ahead of her progress, but out of her direct line of sight. He strained to hear her voice, but it was too noisy.

Suddenly she changed direction and headed straight towards him.

His heart started to beat rapidly, and he felt lightheaded. "What is happening to me?" he muttered, surprised at the intensity of his emotions. This was not like him at all.

She stopped short of where he was standing, distracted by a vendor who sold dates and olive oil. He watched her from a bare twenty feet away, mesmerized.

Almost as if she could hear his thoughts, she stopped what she was doing and turned to look in his direction. Their gazes locked together for an instant, and Deucalion realized now that it had not been her words that had so overwhelmed the people. It was rather what they saw in her eyes. They were luminescent, as if they shone with the soft light one catches a glimpse of in the moments between night's end and daybreak.

A wisp of wind brought a stunning fragrance to his nostrils. A sweetness, like a tingling vapor, suddenly enveloped him — as pure a fragrance as he'd ever smelled. Like frankincense, yet not like frankincense.

The moment passed. She disappeared into the throng of people as quickly as she had dissolved into the night.

He scanned the crowd frantically, but she was nowhere to be seen. He was not disgruntled, however. He knew somehow that they would meet again. Soon. And he wondered what he would say when they finally met.

VIII

The meeting of the Great Council was called to order as usual, Caiaphas presiding. However, due to the somewhat unusual purpose of this particular session, he would immediately relegate presiding authority to Annas, the titular head of the Council.

Before he spoke, the High Priest looked out over the semicircle of faces within the Hall of Hewn Stones. Sixty-nine pairs of eyes stared at him with nervous anticipation. There had not been a formal inquiry into the actions of a High Priest within recent memory.

In challenging the behavior of the highest representative of their God, the Council was challenging the efficacy of the very institution of the priesthood. Fundamentally they believed that no matter how much time one spent in preparing to become High Priest, if God's hand did not guide, and if His voice did not confirm in the hearts of all who voted that indeed the man they'd chosen had been called to the position, whomever sought the office would not prevail.

Although a man was not infallible, there was an inherent bias in the thinking of those who served in the priesthood: because of their constant communion with the Father, they were less likely to err; the High Priest, being at the top of the hierarchy, was the least fallible of all.

The tension in the room was palpable, and when Caiaphas settled his eyes upon Doras, it was with a great deal of restraint that he showed little of the raging anger simmering inside him. During his reign as High Priest, there had never once been any suggestion that he had acted without proper authority. Until now.

As a result of the challenge to his authority, he'd prepared for this moment with all the expertise his tactical, legal mind could muster. And he had but one purpose: that of convincing one man, and one man only, as to the validity of his actions — Annas.

If he could not convince his father-in-law that he was in complete control of the Council, and if he were unable to demonstrate once and for all that he had acted wholly according to the requirements of Scripture and not out of any personal dislike for the Nazarene and what He represented, Annas would be forced to call for his removal. Annas would then select the next High Priest. Thus the door would be opened for Doras, and that was something Caiaphas could not allow.

"Members of the Council, greeting," he said in a loud, commanding voice. "In obedience to your request that I account for my actions in the case of Jesus of Nazareth, and in defense of my handling of His arrest and trial, leading ultimately to His crucifixion at the hands of Rome, I submit the following report for your consideration.

"Before I begin, however, I would preface my statements by sharing my heart with you."

The Council members settled in for what they correctly perceived was going to be a long afternoon.

"It has come to my attention that there are particular members of this Council who, given the opportunity, would undermine our autonomy by submitting to pressures brought to bear by the Romans. And there are even some who have developed rather questionable associations with Rome."

The barest ripple of murmuring disturbed the veneer of attentiveness in the great hall.

"In assessing my report," continued Caiaphas, "I would remind you that you are judging a Jew who represents Hebrew interests, and not a Jew who, shall we say, perhaps has two masters."

The High Priest smiled, warming to the task before him. "I state for the record that I, Joseph Caiaphas, am first a Jew, subject to the same laws that I am pledged to administer; second, as High Priest of this Council, I am charged with the maintenance of our Faith; and lastly, like all Jews, I am yoked unequally to Roman law, by conquest rather than by choice. Therefore, I am limited to specific conditional authority.

"During the fifteen years of my tenure as High Priest, no one has seen fit to question with such audacity and such obvious personal motive my rationale in the administration of my duties as protector and example of the Faith. It is unfortunate, especially in these times of political unrest, that there are those among this august body who would put self-interest and personal gain above the pressing needs of our people. An attitude, I might add, that stands in direct contradiction to one of the most basic requirements of character necessary for consideration for selection to this Council."

Caiaphas scanned his audience, finally focusing on Doras, and the two men locked eyes. "It is and has always been my avowed and heartfelt aim to serve the ends of Almighty God first, the needs of His people second, and my own personal interests last. Nothing has occurred in the past few months, as far as I am concerned, which has altered that vow."

The Council remained quiet as Caiaphas paused. Annas' face, as usual, was set in a perpetual grimace, as if he were forever scowling when anyone but himself was speaking. Yet behind that façade, Caiaphas knew all too well, there was a finely honed, highly polished political mind, ever weighing and balancing words, just as the tax collector constantly weighs and balances silver and gold.

Doras seemed unusually calm, and Caiaphas made a mental note to be on guard for the moment when his adversary would strike. His immediate intention, however, was to keep the members of the Council, particularly the Pharisees, focused on the legality of his actions, while sending a subtle yet dramatic message to Annas: he had not lost the ability to deal with vipers in the nest.

The majority of the predominately Sadducee Council, including the Pharisees, were aware of the threat Jesus had posed. Thus they accepted the fact — although not without disagreement on the means employed to accomplish the end — that he had to be dealt with decisively. That is why the Council, with but a few exceptions, had so readily agreed to the High Priest's initial proposal just weeks before. It was only *after* the trial and crucifixion that protesting cries had been raised.

And it was Doras who had cried the loudest. He knew that the only way he would have a chance of becoming High Priest was to produce a scandal of such magnitude that the Council members, in a fit of passion and unreason, would banish the one responsible for the scandal and elevate the one responsible for uncovering it.

The whole mess smelled of Herod Antipas. Caiaphas knew, as did most of the other men on the Council, that Doras cared nothing about the death of a blaspheming Jew. What he desired was recognition. The High Priest didn't doubt that it was Herod who had created out of the death of the Nazarene an opportunity to drive a wedge between Sadducee and Pharisee. He intended to disrupt the delicately balanced coalition of power and usurp Annas' uncontested control of the Council.

"As you all are well aware," Caiaphas continued authoritatively, "there was no love lost between the Sadducees, the Pharisees, and Jesus of Nazareth." There were nods of assent from the Pharisees. "Yet we did not challenge Him because of His lack of respect for tradition, neither for His claims of holiness, as some have suggested, nor because He prophesied and ignored the sanctity of the Temple.

"No, it was not any one of these reasons that brought about His demise . . . Yet in a way it was the result of all of them.

"We Sadducees do not hold to the idea that a man's fate determines the outcome of events in his living. Instead we favor the idea that it is man's will which decides success or failure in God's plan.

"I submit to you that there was a cause, a substantial motivation behind the behavior of the Galilean — one other than the simple message he is purported to have preached — one that threatened to shred the very fabric of our Faith. And it was my understanding of this motivation that guided me in making my final decision. Therefore, in making *your* final determination, I adjure you to confine yourselves to the legal basis for my behavior and to judge me accordingly, even as I judged Jesus."

He paused, then struck a lightning thrust. "In order for me to best state my case, and remembering the responsibility I shoulder as the highest administrator of the laws of our nation, please indulge me in a few moments of oral tradition."

An excited murmuring spread rapidly through the chambers, like a brushfire out of control. Even old Annas had lost the grimace from his face and was sitting forward in his chair. Doras shifted uncomfortably and began rapidly assessing the situation. He did not like what he was hearing. Caiaphas was striking for the jugular in a most unconventional manner.

It was well known that the Sadducees gave little or no respect to the oral tradition. For them, the *Torah* was the final word. The Pharisees, on the other hand, accepted all of the explanatory and supplementary material produced and contained within the oral tradition that evolved during the time of the Babylonian exile. To them it was inspired and therefore equally authoritative.

No one on the Council could have anticipated that Caiaphas would utilize references to tradition as it related to matters not specifically covered in the *Torah*. This meant he could argue by extension, something the Sadducees loathed doing. The tactic would appeal to the legalistic thinking of the Pharisees and thus allow him to argue that there was in fact legislation covering his behavior, an argument arising from analogy or inference.

This line of reasoning would give a much broader scope to the High Priest's already extensive reach of power and was not something Doras had anticipated him using. Such a frontal attack, coming from one so thoroughly entrenched in the aristocratic concept of the social and religious hierarchy, meant Doras would have to revise his own plan of attack.

The High Priest continued as if he had said nothing unusual, ignoring the questions forming on the lips of his surprised audience. "First and foremost, we believe in one living and true God. Our God never changes. Not only is He beyond our comprehension, but He, with one exception, is indescribable and unnameable.

"That exception, of course, is that it pleases Him to allow us to define our relationship to Him in terms of His several names. These are found nowhere except within His holy Temple — in the Ark of the Covenant. And no one may approach Him in this earthly place of strength and power save those who have been sanctified according to the law.

"Each of the several names He gives us is a complete element of His divine presence unto itself, and the combined grouping presents us with the majesty of the Hebrew God, *Elohim*.

"*Eloi* means 'mighty in strength'; He accomplishes the most difficult of tasks with the same ease He does the least.

Elaah signifies eternal existence; He has no beginning and no end — he simply is. *Hhelejon* demonstrates His unchangeable character; His will is perfect, and therefore no contradiction exists concerning His purpose. *Jah* is knowledge that understands without being understandable. *Adonai* stands for His sovereignty, His supreme rulership exercised as a prerogative rather than being an attribute.

"Individually and together these are *Jehovah* — the God of Abraham, Isaac, and Jacob — the Hebrew God.

"My point in reciting what is well known to all of you is threefold. First, God spoke to the father of our nation, Abraham, and made covenant with him that all who are circumcised by the cutting of the foreskin and the shedding of blood shall be saved. We do not merely view the act of circumcision as ritualistic. Each act of cutting binds us to our God. Circumcision is the seal of our covenant.

"If this is false, then God has violated Himself by annulling the contract. The Nazarene taught that baptism and *not* circumcision is the seal of God, and that *all*, regardless of their lack of physical circumcision, could receive the blessings of Abraham. He even went so far as to associate with the unclean — the lepers, the prostitutes, the poor and wretched souls — that segment of humanity who do not fast and who pay no tithes in support of the Temple and the priesthood. It's no wonder that His teaching appealed to their unsanctified flesh. His teaching led them to believe that every man could be his own priest, worshiping as he chooses.

"There is further evidence that His teachings appealed to the very weaknesses of human nature which our strict adherence to religious custom seeks to overcome. Though He preached for less than three years, he had more followers at His death than Abraham has today. Indeed, had it not been for the Roman soldiers keeping the multitude contained on the day of His execution, we very likely would have had a blood-bath to contend with."

There were nods of agreement and grunts of assent from the audience. However, Caiaphas noted with satisfaction that Doras was growing increasingly agitated.

"Secondly, according to the Book of Leviticus, God told Moses that we should offer the bullock, the ram, the oil and flour after having fasted seven days, in order that the sins of the people would be atoned. Every year, in the seventh month, on the tenth day of the month, the High Priest must select two unblemished goats, one for the Lord and one for *Azazel*, the scapegoat. After casting lots upon the goats, the one for the Lord is to be offered up to Him as a sin offering and the blood taken within the holy Tabernacle and sprinkled upon the mercy seat.

"The goat upon which the lot falls to be the scapegoat must also be presented to the Lord. The High Priest must lay both hands upon the head of the live goat, confessing over him all the iniquities of the children of Israel, putting them on the goat. Then he sends the goat into the wilderness."

Now Caiaphas looked straight at Doras and smiled confidently. His next words were chosen with the care with which the *sicari* chooses a dagger.

"Either Moses was deceived, and thus deceived us, or Jesus of Nazareth was a false teacher, for He taught that repentance is sufficient restitution for sin. Were this the case, a man could sin as he wished; remorse for his crimes would be sufficient restitution unto the offended party. This teaching contradicts the mode of atonement ordained by God and revealed by Moses."

He'd been gradually raising his voice as he spoke, and the deep, bass resonance of it echoed off the polished marble walls of the hall. He raised his right hand dramatically. His palm faced the Council, and his index finger pointed to the heavens as if it were an adder poised to strike. At the same time he moved his great bulk to and fro, gliding almost hypnotically over the dulled lustre of the dust-covered, pinkish-white marble floor.

"Who was this man?" he asked deprecatingly, his molten, ebony eyes seeking out dissent in his audience. "Who was He that He should so perniciously refute fourteen hundred years of tradition?"

The stillness of the hall was marred only by the raspy breathing of old men seeking to fill burning lungs with much-needed oxygen as quietly as possible, lest the High Priest turn his attention to them.

Abruptly the High Priest turned his back on the Council and, facing Annas, addressed his last point to his father-in-law. "Thirdly, Jesus claimed that He was *almah*, born of a virgin; that He and His Father were one — that is, that They were one and the same. That being so, where is He today? Why doesn't He stand before us and repudiate all I have said?"

He paused dramatically for effect, turned to stare at the semicircle of faces once again, and answered, "Because, my learned brethren, *He is dead!* His body was hung from a cross so all might witness the payment for blasphemy. As it is written: 'Cursed is he who hangs upon the tree.'

"The Galilean was no more the Son of God than you or I; perhaps less, considering all His heresies. Indeed, if He were what He claimed to be, why were His teachings not of God? If His teachings were true, then God's must be wrong. At the very least, absent are those perfections in Him that are evidenced by the names which comprise the holy name of *Jehovah*.

"Had we allowed the man to continue teaching His falsehoods, we would have in effect been saying to the Romans — indeed to all the world — that the Hebrew God is without any power but that which His subjects allow Him to exercise.

"We would, in fact, be rendering Him incapable of the perfection that is worthy of our honor and obedience. Thus we would demonstrate to the world that we are not a people to be taken seriously. In doing that, we would say to the world, 'Our religion has no authority behind it, no power in it.'"

Here he sighed heavily, as if he were purging himself of a terrible burden, and he noted the effect on his audience. "It would not have been long before our nation's bulwark against the rampant moral pollution infecting the world would have deteriorated into nothingness. We would be left unprotected against the madness and decadence of the heathen population engulfing us. More importantly, not only would the way to Heaven be blocked off for *all* Jews, but we would also be cut off from the very God who has delivered us from our captivity in the past. Who, then, would deliver us from our present enslavement?

"Had we followed the teachings of Jesus, we would be required to love our enemies and accept the domination of our people." Caiaphas was now obviously incredulous. "Is it not enough that we are required against our will to support their wretched conquest and enslavement of the world with the taxes we give like blood to Caesar?

"The man would have had us believe it matters not who rules or governs, saying it is better to convert the Romans than to have them as enemies. It would not be hard to imagine His being an agent of the Romans, employed to keep the Jews in submission to their tyrannical rule, were it not that the Romans too feared His seditious behavior.

"Most assuredly, you men of the priesthood must realize that the more divided we become, the more the Romans see an excuse to slaughter us and confiscate our property and possessions. If we become cut off from our God, so too our forefathers — who obeyed God in all His ordinances, had faith in

His promises, and praised the triumphs of holy living for more than three hundred and fifty generations — are cut off."

Caiaphas paused. The hall was silent, but he was not quite finished with his audience. "I give you another thought to ponder. What will become of our children . . . and our children's children . . . and their children, if we do not keep the hedge in good repair?"

At the far back corner of the hall, deep in the shadows, a pair of grey-blue eyes watched the proceedings in fascination. No one in the huge room had seen him. He willed the shadows to wrap themselves about him and held his breath. He'd come too far to steal away now. No, he must watch the drama below him play out, knowing full well that if he were caught, he would die on the spot.

IX

The Council was beginning to warm to the High Priest's presentation, and Doras realized that if he were going to maintain the support of those he had so meticulously courted these past few weeks, he would have to act soon and with decisiveness. He knew he was walking a taut rope. If he was going to defeat Caiaphas, and block Annas from filling the void left by his son-in-law's demise, he would have to be every bit as strong as David and act with the wisdom of Solomon. Otherwise, he might end up like old King Saul — a crazed madman bereft of power, dignity, and his God.

When one risks as much as I am risking, it is wise to wait for the perfect moment to strike, he thought smugly. *After all, David slew Goliath with but one stone.* As he concentrated on what Caiaphas was saying, his eyes narrowed with cunning.

"Perhaps the greatest insult Jesus indulged in was His attack upon the holy Temple of God," said the High Priest pointedly, following up his earlier train of thought. "He ignored the holy Temple as a place of worship, and even went so far as to accuse the priests, who diligently serve God on a daily basis, of being a 'den of thieves.'"

There were rumblings of assent from the audience.

"Is there a man here today who doesn't believe the holy Temple was built under the direction of God Himself? I think not. We in the priesthood understand all too well that the House of God is a place of refuge, a haven where men can hide from the turbulence of persecution and sin. *All* men may come and be blessed, clothe their naked souls, feed their hungry bodies, and learn the wisdom of Almighty God.

"In short, my brothers, the holy Temple is the focus of our entire relationship with our God. It is the cement which binds Jews together. It is the grandest of all the grand gifts from our Father. Yet, the Nazarene scoffed at the Temple. And with a pettiness common to those who would seek to usurp rightful authority and gain favor for their own personal beliefs and doctrines, He insisted that the Temple would be destroyed — almost as if He would be glad to see such an occurrence — and raised up by Himself in three days."

Caiaphas smiled, knowing by the looks on the faces before him that he had not lost his skills of persuasion. *I am like the great leviathan of the ocean,* he thought. *I have no fear of my enemies; they are impotent against me.*

His moment of private, prideful exaltation was cut short, however, as the memory of his dream intruded into his thoughts. Suddenly his mouth was as dry as the sand of the Negeb. And in the space of a heartbeat it was as if a blistering summer wind swept through his spirit like a Syrian *sirocco* sweeping in off the desert, scalding his soul.

He gasped as a quiet, firm voice inside him said, "Remember Job . . . and be not deceived." He scrutinized the faces staring at him expectantly and realized that no one but himself had heard the rebuke. Flustered, he gathered the bulk of his priestly apparel about him, like a shepherd gathering together his flock, and regained his composure.

Until this moment he had been directing his statements to the Council in general. Now it was time to reach down deep into the hearts of the Pharisees and, like Gideon, strike a decisive and conclusive blow in the heart of the enemy camp, where Doras had found succor and encouragement.

Caiaphas knew that the Pharisees, being primarily the

merchants and tradesmen in the business community, had no formal education in the interpretation of the Scripture. They relied heavily upon professional scholars, the scribes, for their information regarding legal tradition. This led to an attitude of excessive rigidity and intolerance, especially where the practical application of the law was concerned. To the Pharisees, the orthodoxy of the Sadducees was a cumbersome weight inhibiting spiritual growth. Consequently, the emphasis of their teaching was moral rules rather than the theological aspects of the Scriptures.

He intended to pluck at that ethical cord by appealing to that side of their personalities which led them to champion human equality. At the same time he intended to portray Jesus as a man who would have eliminated their oral tradition — thus destroying the "hedge" against unbelief — and as one who viewed them as "vipers," unfit for salvation.

"Who among you would deny that should the Temple be removed or forsaken by the Jews, our nation would be destroyed utterly, disappearing in the blink of an historical eye?" he asked as he lifted both arms and spread them wide. The resplendent colors of his robe shimmered in the subdued, dusty light of the hall.

Annas' eyes darted back and forth between Simon, Caiaphas, and Doras. He was fascinated by the unorthodox approach of his son-in-law. His face remained stolid, but his mind raced as he tried to unravel the mystery his son-in-law had set before the Council.

"We have endured hardship and slavery our entire lives," continued Caiaphas, "but we have never been alone, without God as our guide. I ask you, if there were no Temple, what then of the priesthood? How would our people know that which is right in the sight of God? It is only our religious tradition that separates us from the idolatrous worship of the unrighteous.

"Is there one among you who would advocate returning to the idolatry of the time of Noah? I think not," he answered and shook his head balefully, inwardly congratulating himself. As a silkworm weaves silk by ingesting dead and decaying mulberry leaves, he too had constructed his own silken net of rhetoric from the mulch of information he'd gathered on the Galilean. And now it was time to draw tight his finely woven web of logic around the minds and hearts of the Council.

"Before I conclude, I offer one final point. Scripture tells us that there can be but one God. The Nazarene's contention that He too was God, that He was *the* Son of the Most High God, not only is incompatible with reason, but with our Faith. God's Holy Word tells us unequivocally that He is the one living God: 'I am the Lord your God, which have brought you out of the land of Egypt, out of the house of bondage . . . The Lord your God is one God; there can be no other.'

"Whenever Israel has turned away from her God, the people have suffered. As long as we have kept His commandments and have not given ourselves over to idolatrous worship, we have not succumbed to the pollutions of the world. God, through the mouth of Moses and now, I might humbly add, through my mouth as High Priest, warned us what would happen if we did not abide under the protection of the law: utter desolation. Who among you would deny that the history of our people has borne witness to the words Moses spoke so long ago?"

Silence filled the great hall, punctuating his point.

"In summary, let me remind you that as priest of the Most High God I am charged by God Himself with the upholding of the holy ordinances of our blessed religion. The law was given to us by God that Israel might secure salvation and escape the penalty of spiritual death reserved for those who forsake Him, the one who created all. I could not stand by idly while an imposter sought to pervert all that is good and pure and righteous before God, having only the authority of John the Baptist, who himself could give no authority save the one who sent him to baptize.

"It was I who stood between our God and our people, being made responsible for the protection of our blessed doctrines and the preservation of our government. If I have erred, it is for God to judge, not man."

The recitation was finished. The meeting had been called to order in midafternoon, but by now the sun had set and candles had been lit in the great hall by the scribes in order that they might continue recording all that transpired. Three of these specially educated men were present. One was seated on the right of where Caiaphas had positioned himself, and it was his responsibility to record the arguments upon which acquittal was grounded, as well as those judges who voted for the same. On the left sat the scribe who was responsible for recording those arguments in favor of condemnation and the judges who supported such a position. The third scribe sat in the center of the hall, keeping an account of the entire proceeding, with his record serving as a check and balance for the other two; in the case of dispute or a contention of error, his record overrode the independent records of the other two.

Caiaphas had presented his argument well, and it was to his credit that the silence among the members of the Council was not broken for several minutes.

Doras had not taken his eyes off of Caiaphas during the whole time he'd been speaking. He had, near the very end of the speech, begun to waver in his certainty that tonight would be his opportunity to outfox the fox. However, to his great relief he realized with a flash of insight that the High Priest had indeed shown his weak spot, even as Hector had at the battle of Troy.

Like Achilles, he was about to bring down the mighty warrior who had until now been invincible. He smiled to himself, the glint in his brown eyes like the sparkle of light reflecting off the cold steel of an assassin's dagger, then stood to his feet. The fulvous light in the great hall gave his skin a grey pallor, so that at first blush he appeared to be but a spectre of a man.

He clapped his hands together in a cadenced, metronomical fashion, and the sudden sound reverberated off the polished marble walls. The act of defiance was a parody of applause, and it sliced through the silence, stunning the members of the Council.

"I commend you, Joseph," he said insincerely, making his way to the front of the hall. "It seems you've regained the ability to humble your audience with your words. One might even liken the ability to that of the cobra; the snake that flattens its neck into a hood-like form when disturbed or threatened, thus distracting its intended prey before striking with its lethal venom."

He knew he had their attention, just as he knew he'd managed, by virtue of precise timing and execution, to appropriate the momentum of Caiaphas' climax and divert command of the audience into his own hands.

The left scribe began to record his words after a moment of phlegmatic inertness.

"In spite of your eloquence, I for one am not convinced." He paused upon reaching the speaker's position, then turned to face the Council, keeping his back to Caiaphas. "Especially since you neglected to mention the issue of the *validity* of Jesus' arraignment before you on the *evening* of His arrest," he added, inferring that Caiaphas had neglected to deal with the salient issue of legality.

"Surely you haven't forgotten that it is a well established — and I might add, inflexible — rule of Hebrew law that proceedings in capital trials cannot be held at night."

He turned abruptly to face Caiaphas and saw the High Priest glance furtively in his father-in-law's direction. Annas remained pensive, but said nothing, his eyes hooded, his mouth tight-lipped.

Satisfied he was on the right track, Doras pressed his point. "Why was it that you saw fit to question the Nazarene the same night He was arrested? And why wasn't that questioning done here, before the members of the Council?"

The murmuring began anew, and Annas was starting to scowl. His bushy, jet eyebrows had come together at the top of the bridge of his nose, and his jaws were clenched tightly together. Had he been a wolf, he would have been snarling.

Doras was unaware of these changes and seemed unperturbed by the potential for disaster. "I submit to you that the trial of the Nazarene was a sham, merely a formality to appease the Roman sense of justice, and that the guilt of the accused had already been determined — not by the Council, but by Caiaphas himself!"

Several members jumped to their feet, protesting loudly.

The only person unaffected was Caiaphas. He remained silent, observing the tactics of his opponent with calm reservation. Like a Roman centurion, well heeled in battle, he sat unruffled at the first lunge of Doras' figurative sword. He waited and watched, trusting his inner sense to tell him when the feint of his adversary would become the killing thrust. For now he was content to use silence as a shield.

Annas called for order. "Explain the legal basis for your accusation," he growled.

All three scribes wrote furiously, diligently recording the proceedings.

Doras, surprised at Caiaphas' failure to respond as he had planned, wondered if he'd misjudged the strength of his opponent among the Council members. Unfortunately, he was now deeply committed; he had no choice but to continue. He hoped he had not misread the tone of the Council's request to the High Priest two weeks ago, and he prayed he hadn't seriously underestimated the depth of his own support.

"It is clear to all of us that a trial before the Sanhedrin was necessary because of the nature of the offense," he continued, keeping his voice steady even though his legs had suddenly gone weak. "Rome refuses to recognize our religion and demands that we settle all internal religious problems ourselves. Ironically, a second trial before Pontius Pilate became necessary because a conviction involving the death sentence was secured. Thus, in the name of Roman sovereignty the Roman Tribunal was convened to review our decision. Which brings me to the point of my intervention in this matter.

"It is a peculiarity of our law that in a case where none of the judges defends the accused and all pronounce him guilty, the verdict of guilt becomes invalid. Because the culprit has had no defense in the court, no sentence of death can be handed down.

"I ask you, then, Why the exception in the case of the Galilean?" He let the question hang, intending for it to become a source of agitation in the minds of the Council. "As my learned brother has so aptly pointed out, Hebraic jurisprudence is founded upon not only the Pentateuch, but upon the *Talmud* as well. The Mosaic code, embodied in the first five books of the law, furnishes us with the necessary platform of justice, while ancient tradition and rabbinic interpretation supply the needed rules of practical application.

"Nowhere, however, are we given leave to *create* that which suits the needs of a particular moment.

"The man from Galilee stood accused out of the mouth of one of His own disciples, a man named Judas, whom it appears hung himself shortly after his former master was executed. If this man Judas was initially a co-conspirator with Jesus, and became His chief accuser only after receiving thirty pieces of silver, then we also have a situation in which accomplice testimony was used to convict prior to trial.

"Surely the High Priest is aware, having spent many years studying our legal traditions, that accomplice testimony is forbidden. If Judas was an accomplice, Jesus was innocent. Thus, his arrest was not only an outrage, but illegal as well."

The members of the Council exchanged glances. Few at this point were willing to risk eye contact with Caiaphas. Doras was presenting his case well. Even those inclined to support the High Priest did not want to commit themselves until they were absolutely certain Caiaphas would be triumphant.

"Before you ask the obvious question of why I waited until now to voice my dissent, let me finish my point," continued Doras, his voice resolute. "If the capture of a supposedly seditious rebel was *not* the result of a legal mandate from a court whose intention was to conduct a legal trial for the purpose of reaching a righteous judgment, then we have not only left ourselves open to the wrath of the Romans . . . but more fearfully, to the wrath of God Himself."

He turned to face Annas and was startled by the look he saw on the older man's face: disgust and anger. He faltered momentarily as he realized dismally there was nothing he could do but finish what he'd started.

He put everything he had into his words. "Testimony in trials such as the one under discussion is given under the sanction of the Ninth Commandment: 'One shall not bear false witness against one's brother.' It is a well settled maxim of Talmudic law that whosoever will not tell the truth without an oath will not scruple to assert a falsehood with an oath.

"Indeed, many among us," he added, glancing out of the corners of his eyes at Caiaphas, "assert that swearing is injurious in itself, and that one who consents to swear should *ipso facto* be suspected of lacking credibility. The three witnesses who testified against Jesus were given the following adjuration in the presence of all assembled:

"'Forget not, O witness, that it is one thing to give evidence in a trial as to money and another in a trial for life. In a money suit, if your witness-bearing shall do wrong, money may repair that wrong. But in this trial for life, if you sin, the blood of the accused and the blood of his seed to the end of time shall be imputed unto you . . . Therefore was Adam created one man alone, to teach you that if any witness shall destroy one soul out of Israel, he is held by the Scripture to be as if he had destroyed the world; and he who saves one soul to be as if he had saved the world.

"'For a man from one signet ring may strike many impressions, and all of them shall be exactly alike. But he, the King of kings, he the Holy and the Blessed, had struck off from his type of the first man the forms of all men that shall live, yet so that no one human being is wholly alike to any other.

"'Wherefore let us think and believe that the whole world is created for a man such as whose life hangs on your words. But these ideas must not deter you from testifying to what you actually know.

"'Scripture declares: "The witness who has seen or known, and does not tell, shall bear his iniquity." Nor must you scruple about becoming the instrument of the alleged criminal's death. Remember the Scriptural maxim: "In the destruction of the wicked, there is joy.'"

"The two elements of this preliminary caution are generally sufficient to bind the witness by the sanctions it represents. However, in view of the events which allegedly transpired at the tomb of the accused — three days *after* His death — and in view of the increasing hostility of the people towards the priesthood, I find it necessary to question the validity of the trial of the Nazarene before this Council."

Doras turned to his right and stared straight into the smoldering eyes of the High Priest. "I submit that because of his personal hatred of the Galilean, the High Priest was blinded to the possibility of another solution, one which would not inculpate the entire Council of wrongdoing." With great effort he shifted his gaze and turned to face the Council. "If Rome decides that the Council acted not only rashly, but illegally as well, or that we are no longer able to uphold the laws of our ancestors, having invalidated our authority by disobeying our own doctrines, we will be required to submit to a final blasphemy — the Roman administration of our religious affairs.

"The likely outcome of such sacrilege could well be the destruction of our nation."

Here comes the killing thrust, thought Caiaphas.

"In view of this possibility, brought about by the carelessness and shortsightedness of our current High Priest, I recommend to this Council —"

"Enough!" bellowed Annas.

The pair of eyes in the shadows at the back of the hall blinked furiously several times, and there was a muffled gasp.

Fortunately no one in the room noticed.

"I have heard enough," repeated Annas, shaking with rage. "I will not listen to this political bantering any longer. It has become painfully clear to me in these last hours that we are a divided Council. Devastatingly divided. And divided, we cannot stand. Not against Rome, not against the world, not against sin."

He stared menacingly at Doras. "We are the governing body of Israel and are supposedly above the pettiness of personal aggrandizement. It is clear to me that you, Doras, do not have the best interests of this Council in mind. Further, your preposterous allegations offend me. Your insinuation that the High Priest — who has faithfully served his people and our God for fifteen years — has suddenly suffered a loss of credibility is not only objectionable but laughable."

He rose to his feet, scowling, and spoke directly to the Council. "Is there anyone here who is willing to formally accuse the High Priest of a breach of the sacred oath of the priesthood? Is there anyone who will stand before God and declare that Caiaphas has acted without restraint in the case of the Galilean? If so, let him do it now."

Doras scanned the stormy sea of faces, seeking contact with those who earlier, behind closed doors, had agreed to support him. Now none would look him in the eye.

The hall remained quiet. The scribes, poised with pens in hands, had nothing to record save the interlude.

Doras realized he'd failed. The trembling in his legs moved up his body to his hands as he stared at Caiaphas with the look of a defeated animal and relinquished his position. Without looking back and with no further word he left the hall.

Caiaphas stood, approached the dais upon which Annas sat, and formally resumed his position of authority. The session was over. There would be no formal charges, no further investigation. Yet, he knew he'd won nothing but time. Doras had struck a powerful blow, and the wound would fester in spite of temporary suturing by Annas.

There's nothing to be done now except ride the horse until it collapses, he thought miserably as he watched the members of the Council depart from the debacle. *I hope the animal does not fall upon me and crush me in its death throes.*

He exchanged glances with Simon and noted with sadness the look of resignation in his former teacher's eyes. It was evident that Simon also realized that no matter how it might seem to the other members, something of vital importance had been lost here this night. Even as the tides of the great Mediterranean subtly altered the contours of the surrounding continents day in and day out, the ebb and flow of the tides of change would slowly erode the power of the Council. The only remaining cordon separating the nation of Israel from the desolation and darkness of the unrepentant would gradually dissolve until nothing remained. Even as water had the power to dissolve the land masses holding them captive and reducing them to grains of sand, so too words had the power to unravel the fiber of faith woven into the heart of a nation, dissolving it into strands of unbelief.

The ensuing two hours, after the last of the Council members had left the Great Hall, passed Caiaphas by as if he were a tiny ship adrift in an ocean of time. He felt lost and disoriented, and he wished desperately that he could free himself from the quagmire of impotency.

Now, as he sat in the darkness of doubt, his mind replayed a scene from the past. The thoughts ran through his brain, over and over again, like a herd of wild horses loosed unexpectedly from captivity. Try as he might, he could not get the accompanying thundering echo of words out of his head: "*Ecce homo*. Behold the man."

Pilate had spoken those words to the crowd as the Nazarene stood before them. Embedded upon His bloodied forehead was a crown of thorns. His back was flayed so badly that His shredded skin looked like the blood-red pulp of grapes squeezed through a winepress.

Caiaphas had been standing among the crowd of screaming, belligerent people, and even he had been sickened by the brutality of the Romans. Yet he could not bring himself to cry for mercy. The maddened crowd of mostly Jews had screamed for justice. "We have a law, and by our law he must die because he made Himself the Son of God." Then the Procurator paraded the bloodied and torn lump of flesh before the multitude saying, "Take you Him and crucify Him: I find no fault in Him."

The High Priest had moved to the front of the crowd then, and there had been a brief moment in which he and Pilate had locked eyes. In that instant each had looked into the depths of the other's soul, each had seen the intent of the other's heart.

Caiaphas had seen fear in the heart of the Roman. Not the

fear of the unknown, but of the known. Now he realized that Pilate knew what he, High Priest of the Most High God, refused to believe.

The man who stood before the crowd in the purple robe and crown of thorns the soldiers had draped about His broken body in mockery of the priesthood stood not as a man condemned to death, but as the last scapegoat offered up for the sins of man. Neither Caiaphas nor Pilate had any say in the matter any longer. The players no longer read their lines; they had *become* their lines.

And what of the High Priest himself? What did Pilate see in the heart of the man ultimately responsible for the death of the Nazarene? A black cloud of uncertainty, no doubt — the dark force of doubt that feasted upon the tender morsels of rotting truth become lies. The same dark hole that threatened to swallow him up now.

What if the man was indeed the Son of God? he wondered. *Ecce homo.* "May God have mercy upon us if we were wrong," he mumbled as he looked out into the blackness of the night.

X

Herod Antipas, a sophisticate of the Hellenistic East, did not think of himself as a man who achieved the extraordinary through the use of guile, as his enemies would most certainly reply if asked, "To what do you attribute the overwhelming success of the son of Herod the Great?" Instead, he viewed himself as a man with vision, not only for himself, but for the dynasty he represented.

Although he was the appointed "ruler" of his people, he held the position only because of the esteem the Romans still held for the name *Herod*, a result of his father's tremendous political acumen and foresight. Because the nation of Israel functioned as a theocracy, the real power lay with the priesthood. And because of the sacred status of Jerusalem and its environs — a status recognized by the Romans — the Sanhedrin was given control over all national matters, so long as public order was maintained and tax revenues continued to flow into the Empire's war chests.

He sat in his chambers, in the palace his father had built, the Palace of the Hasmoneans, and reviewed the parchment he'd received from Rome. It had remained intentionally unanswered for two weeks now, pending the outcome of his manipulation of certain members of the Sanhedrin.

Rome was displeased, as he'd suspected, with his handling of the matter of Jesus of Nazareth. However, Tiberius Caesar relied upon Lucius Vitellius for information about what was happening in Palestine. The Syrian Governor, in turn, received his information from Pontius Pilate. And it was precisely because of this fragmented dissemination of data that Herod had been able to devise a plan to wrest power from Annas.

After months of meticulous planning, he'd carefully instructed Doras on the final details two weeks earlier. "We must create a situation in which Pilate finds it expedient to apply some firm political pressure on Annas. At the same time, you must convince key members of the Council that the High Priest made a tremendous mistake in arresting and convicting the Nazarene.

"Once Caiaphas is disgraced, Annas will have no choice but to accede to your demand that his son-in-law be removed from his office — and from the Council. And if what you tell me about the Pharisees is true, you should have no problem getting enough votes to become the next High Priest.

"The Procurator, in turn, must be made aware that such an occurrence will give him indirect access to the Council, through you. Not only will that get Rome off *his* back as well as mine, but Pilate will have what no other Roman has ever had — a conduit into the heart of the nation of Israel."

Doras had been reluctant and skeptical, but he'd agreed to the plan, and so far everything had gone as intended. *It's time my ferret came to report*, Antipas thought gleefully, letting the parchment drop to the floor.

Caiaphas and Annas walked silently through the darkened streets of Jerusalem. The High Priest was drained from his encounter with Doras. He offered a sidelong glance at his father-in-law, who had not spoken to him since they'd departed the Hall of Hewn Stones. He was reluctant to begin a conversation with Annas for fear of where it might lead; yet he felt a compelling *need* to speak.

"I've been having a disturbing dream, Annas," he said finally in a hoarse voice.

The older man stopped abruptly and stared at him intently. After several moments he replied, "Well, are you going to tell me about it or not?"

Caiaphas sighed heavily, then told his father-in-law about Joshua and the sun. When he was done, Annas grunted and started walking again. After a moment's hesitation Caiaphas hurriedly followed. When his son-in-law reached his side, Annas said, "According to Scripture, man is a spirit, has a soul, and lives in a body. And the background of man's existence is a dim, sometimes occluded region of knowing that labors forth into the daylight through the realm of thought, especially in times of sleep. Often the knowledge of this realm comes to a man only in retrospect, upon waking, and only after the content of the dream is scrutinized."

"You're referring, of course, to the Book of Job," interjected Caiaphas.

Annas nodded and quoted the exact Scripture:

"'For God speaks once, yea twice, yet man perceives it not. In a dream, in a vision of the night, when deep sleep falls upon men, in slumberings upon the bed; then He opens the ears of men, and seals their instruction, that He may withdraw man from His purpose, and hide pride from man.'"

"I'm familiar with the passage, but I don't understand the meaning it has for *me*."

Annas grunted, then continued, "The life of genius, awakened in sleep, has produced many artistic creations, scientific solutions, and spiritual perceptions. The soul, selfish and restless, uses the arena of dreams as a means of holding its true nature up to scrutiny in the hope of finding it valid. More often than not, remorse is the dream's reply.

"The soul, in return, seeks to redefine its impulse towards self-preservation in terms of rejection of the obvious source of its discomfort: the spirit. Thus, we see why the Scriptures hold man accountable — if not for dreaming, at least for the *character* of his dreams."

Caiaphas wasn't sure if Annas was rebuking him or not. Nevertheless, he was impressed with his father-in-law's adroit analysis. Annas was not known for his loquaciousness where such arcane matters were concerned; the language of his world was politics, not the analysis of mental states, although he freely employed the latter to excel at the former.

The older, crafty man was trying to tell him something. Caiaphas only wished his mind could grasp it.

When Doras arrived at the palace, just before midnight, he found Antipas lost in thought. There was a flagon of wine in the Tetrarch's right hand, and he was wearing a half-smile that added another crease to his deeply lined and prematurely aged face.

Doras stood in the candle-lit room, just inside the entrance to Antipas' chambers, and shivered despite the fact that it was warm. For an instant he imagined the darkness was a cloak that would shield him from the penetrating, intimidating gaze of the man with whom he conspired. *There is something decidedly unnerving, even unnatural about him*, he thought miserably, wishing for all the world that he didn't have to tell the man he despised what had transpired. *He might be a Jew, but we definitely don't serve the same God.*

He pushed the unsettling thoughts as far down into his mind as his conscience would let him, then went forward wearily, knowing that the information he brought would eradicate the smile stretched tautly across Antipas' face.

XI

During June days in Jerusalem the temperature could approach 100 degrees. But at night, because the city was situated on a rocky plateau some 1,700 cubits above sea level, the temperature dropped rapidly after sunset.

As Deucalion waited for his initial meeting with Saul of Tarsus, he wondered how history would record the events about to take place. He speculated upon what a scribe would pen were he allowed to accompany the group of soldiers, led by a fanatical Jew, on their raid upon a group of "believers" holding a nighttime meeting somewhere in the city.

He found it somewhat contradictory that the Jews referred to the followers of Christ as *believers*, especially since the Jews considered *themselves* the chosen of God.

He looked out over the city and took a deep breath, filling his lungs with the cool breeze that refreshed his armor-clad body. The day had been a particularly hot one. But the dust had remained reasonably dormant, almost as if it were waiting for the right moment to spring from the parched earth and frustrate the intents of any who thought they could be free from its ubiquitous presence.

The Praetorian knew his men were on edge. There had been a substantial undercurrent of resistance when they'd been told the purpose of their nocturnal duty. Most of those he'd selected had seen more than their share of battle in the last few years; some had even fought at his side. None of them were looking forward to serving a zealot intent upon dealing with a group of religious dissidents.

Rome had always been relatively tolerant in the past regarding the religious beliefs of its populace, particularly where conquered peoples were concerned. It was common knowledge that there were many besides the Jews who chose not to worship Caesar. So why all the fuss over *these* believers? Was it possible Pontius was not telling them the whole story?

Perhaps the Procurator's descents into depression were starting to affect his thinking. This whole arrangement Pilate had negotiated with Antipas smelled foul to Deucalion. Suspicions of why Rome was involved reminded him of the deceit which had become part of the investigation of the events surrounding the alleged theft of the Nazarene's body from the sepulchre.

The Praetorian had testified before the Tribunal, convened to determine if there had been dereliction of duty by anyone assigned to the guard detail. Unfortunately, he had not been supported by his men. Even Malkus had turned against him, remaining silent as to the truth.

The only thing that saved Deucalion from a severe reprimand, perhaps even a demotion, was that none of his men had lied. They had abbreviated certain important details and remained silent when questioned about specifics, but none actually denied the veracity of his account of the event.

The Tribunal concluded that the body had been stolen by persons unknown for the purpose of inciting the insurgent populace. As far as Rome was concerned, the matter was closed. And Pilate had made it clear that it was never to be discussed again.

There was one problem, however. Deucalion knew there had been no theft because he'd been there. He had seen the light and heard the music. *He knew the truth.*

And only now was he beginning to understand the magnitude of the deception offered to hide the truth. After the ambush, he'd begun his own investigation and learned that of those present on that fateful morning, all had accepted money to hide the truth except him. They tailored their stories so they would fit the predetermined findings Rome wanted to hear. At the time of the inquiry he did not believe Pilate would be involved in such a gross subversion of Roman jurisprudence — upholding the law was what he lived for. But now the Praetorian was uncertain.

"Where is the man called Deucalion?" came a gravelly voice out of the night, breaking his reverie. A chill coursed up and down his spine when he heard his name spoken, and he had a sudden premonition of impending doom. Shaking off the melancholy thought, he strained to see the man behind the voice.

"He stands over there, at the edge of the light," one of his men answered, pointing in his direction.

The disembodied voice carried with it an intensity he found disconcerting. He had no idea what the man from Tarsus looked like and therefore did not know what to expect. All he'd been told by Antipas was that he should not let Saul's appearance deceive him.

As the sepulchral figure approached from the far side of the campfire his men had lit to break the evening chill, Deucalion rubbed his eyes. The salty stinging seemed to be a constant companion. Abruptly he remembered his dream. *The light. The voice. The sound of his own scream waking him.* Why couldn't he remember the whole thing?

"Deucalion Cincinnatus Quinctus?"

He nodded and pushed his own unanswered question into the recesses of memory, then focused on the Jew standing before him.

His first impression was that Saul looked as if he'd been

sewn together from mismatched body parts. He was short and squat, and his legs, like his arms, were crooked and very thin. Both pairs seemed to have been cut from the same mold and looked as if they belonged to one much taller than he. Oddly, his skin seemed rather pale, almost luminescent in the firelight. And his head was almost bald. There were, however, a few wisps of light-brown, stringy hair above either ear, both of which seemed overly large and out of proportion to his head. The most distinguishing features of his entire countenance, however, were his eyebrows; the hairs were long and bushy, of a jet-black color like that of purest obsidian, and they grew together slightly.

As Saul stepped closer, Deucalion stared into his eyes and was immediately struck by the explosive force of the man's gaze. Here was a man driven by a hatred which ran deeper than that of even some of the men he had fought against in battle. The rage he saw in those glistening hazel-brown eyes suggested that Saul would be capable of a viciousness that might well exceed his own ability to curtail without the use of deadly force. And that was something for which Antipas would not sit still.

"So you are Deucalion," said Saul petulantly. "I am Saul of Tarsus, and I'm told you're one of the best Rome has to offer. We shall see."

"Are you Jews always so blunt and disrespectful? I've dealt with only a few of you educated in the ways of the priesthood, and none of you seems the least bit humble to me. I thought it was you who served your God, and not the other way around."

Saul smiled a crooked half-smile, the first glint of respect shining in his eyes. "It's my understanding, Centurion, that you've been instructed to cooperate fully with me. Is that *your* understanding?"

"This is the second time in as many days that one of you

Jews has erroneously, and discourteously, referred to me as 'Centurion,'" replied Deucalion, his voice steady and without any suggestion of malice. "I'm a Praetorian in the service of Rome, not in the service of you Jews, and I'm quite proud of my position and my country. As proud, I might point out, as you Jews are of being called 'Rabbi.'

"While we do have different measurements of status, I might also point out that I am well studied in a variety of subjects, speak three languages fluently, and yet manage to communicate with the common people I meet — including Jews — without resorting to the use of intimidation. I think you would be well advised to remember that it is we Romans who occupy Palestine and not you Jews who occupy Rome."

"You and I will get along just fine," chuckled Saul. His voice held no sarcasm, and it was clear from his tone that he acknowledged the mild rebuke.

"Don't be so sure. I'm not in agreement with this decision."

The wily Jew sobered abruptly. Remembering his task, he spoke curtly. "It's time we were off; we've much to do before dawn."

Deucalion gave the order, and the small contingent of men, under the leadership of Saul, headed for the inner section of the city.

"Tell me, Saul, why do you fear these 'believers' we are going to arrest?" asked Deucalion as they walked.

"Arrest? Oh yes . . . of course," mumbled the enigmatic Jew. "In order to answer you properly, and since you seem to have a genuine interest — unlike most Romans, I will endeavor to give you a brief education about what it means to grow up as a Jew.

"Jewish law prescribes that a boy begin his study of the Scriptures at age five and the study of the legal tradition at age ten. My first recollections are of my father repeating words from the *Talmud* to me over and over again. When he finished the daily ritual he would admonish me by saying, 'Saul, you must never forget you are a Jew. We serve *Jehovah* only. Our life is dedicated to His service. You must endeavor constantly to learn His Word. In so doing you will learn what it means to be a people apart.

"'Never forget that we are different; the circumcision of our flesh is done in furtherance of the blood covenant God struck with the father of our nation, Abraham. Never let the sun set upon your face without your having memorized a portion of the *Talmud*.'"

"Was there no time to be a boy?"

"Rarely. The focus of my childhood was a curriculum of study involving every aspect of Jewish life."

Deucalion was amazed. "Nothing else?"

Saul shrugged. "There was always work. My father also agreed with the prevailing sentiment that manual labor was a noble manifestation of our love for God. He advised me repeatedly that intellectual prowess and physical activity go hand in hand. And he often quoted the saying, 'Excellent is *Torah* study together with worldly business, for all *Torah* without work must fail at length and occasion iniquity.'"

Saul turned toward Deucalion, curious to see if the uncircumcised soldier was following what he was trying to tell him. The Praetorian seemed to be listening intently. "As you can see," he added, "we Jews are not at all like what the world thinks of us."

Saul pulled his plain white robe tighter about him and shook off the fine coating of dust that had settled upon it. "The primary goal of Jewish education is to produce a man who can both think *and* act," he continued. "Preferably one who is neither lost in the clouds with his thoughts, nor clumsy in matters of everyday living."

"What does all that have to do with what we're doing tonight?"

"Patience, Praetorian. At thirteen, boys become *bar mitz-vah'd* — a 'son of the covenant.' At that time we're expected to take full responsibility for the obligations of the law. Those like myself who show special talents are encouraged to study further under a Rabbi or teacher, in order to become fully educated in the ways of God. That is how I came to be in Jerusalem."

He paused for a moment and gazed at the stars before finishing his thought. When he continued, there was no anger in his voice; yet though his tone suggested he had accepted the circumstances, it was clear he was not resigned to them.

"Although I'm a tentmaker by trade, I've spent the better part of the past seventeen years studying under various teachers. For me, the law is of paramount importance; without it, we Jews are nothing. God commanded, through Moses, that we uphold our portion of the covenant by keeping His law. He admonished His people not to turn to the right or the left, and told us in no uncertain terms that if we did, we would perish and our nation would die in desolation. The history of my people stands as obvious testimony to the truth of God's Word. And you Romans have played no small part in the fulfillment of that prophecy."

"I'm surprised to hear you speak about Rome with such a lack of antagonism. I have yet to meet a Jew who doesn't resent our presence here in Palestine."

"Perhaps that's because even though I am of pure Hebrew descent, from the tribe of Benjamin, I also inherited Roman citizenship."

Deucalion was surprised, but said nothing.

"Shall I continue?" asked Saul rhetorically.

"By all means."

"The Nazarene claimed He was the 'Word made flesh'; that He was *the* Son of God. His teachings, rejected by learned Jews such as myself, were designed for the ears of the uneducated and therefore gullible populace. Even after His death the heresies spread epidemically, infecting even the most religiously faithful among our nation.

"I am one of the few who knew His death would fail to purge the infection. We waited too long to act, and His inflammatory words had already taken root. Like pernicious weeds in a garden, they are now choking out the life of our Faith. Now it is imperative that the blasphemous teachings of His followers be stopped, before any more damage is done."

"But the man was a Jew like you," interrupted Deucalion with consternation. "Many called Him Rabbi. He healed the sick and raised the dead." He stared at Saul incredulously. "Has any man, Jew or Gentile, priest or not, ever done what witnesses claim they've seen *Him* do?"

Saul scrutinized Deucalion. "You sound as if *you* believe," he growled. "That kind of thinking is dangerous."

Deucalion ignored the rebuke. "From what I've learned about the Nazarene," he replied, "He preached against no man and held scorn for no one save those who refused to believe what their own eyes, ears and heart told them was truth."

"Ah, therein lies our dilemma. If what he said is *truth*, then the Holy Scriptures are false. And if they are false, what then of God? If God is not who He has revealed Himself to us to be, there is no covenant. If there is no covenant, we have no law. And without the law, there is no Jewish nation."

They didn't speak again for quite a distance. Deucalion was relieved. It gave him time to think.

Finally Saul broke the pensive silence. "I hope you understand now why I don't take the spread of this false religion lightly. Not only *my* existence, but the very existence of my people is being threatened."

"And what about Rome? Why do you require our participation in a purely religious matter?" asked Deucalion, not sure he really wanted to hear the persuasive Jew's answer.

Saul smiled. "The answer to that, Praetorian, should be quite obvious. You yourself observed not twenty minutes ago that it is Rome who occupies Palestine, and not the reverse. The Legion is responsible for the safety and well-being of loyal Roman subjects. Individuals who engage in seditious activities cannot expect to be included in that category. I am merely acting as, shall we say, a concerned citizen who fears not only for the welfare of his own people, but for the welfare of Rome as well. Since we Jews have no military authority, you Romans must assume the burden of cleaning the wound of the poison that rots the souls of the lost. If the infection isn't dealt with at its root and the disease spreads, Rome will also suffer. No doubt Tiberius Caesar would be most unforgiving should that happen."

"No doubt . . . " was all Deucalion managed to reply before they arrived at their destination.

XII

Esther sat quietly upon the dusty floor in the back of a woodworker's shop and listened to an anonymous speaker telling about the power of love. Gradually she became aware that tonight, unlike the other nights she'd been in this same place, there was an unexpected undercurrent of tension in the room.

Her companion, a man she'd known only a few days, suddenly gripped her hand in his, squeezing it hard. Several people around them began to stir, murmuring to one another, but before she could ask the question that had formed in her mind, she was touched by a strange sensation. She *felt* rather than heard a still, small voice inside her say, *Fear not, for I am the Lord your God; I am with you always. Trust in Me. I will never forsake you, nor leave you. I am the Way, the Truth, and the Life; he that believes in Me shall not perish, but shall have everlasting life.*

Instinctively she looked around to see who had spoken. When her eyes found those of her new friend, he was staring at her in amazement.

"What's happening, Joseph?" she asked, surprised at her lack of fear.

A look of understanding spread across his face as he replied, "The Lord has spoken to us, Esther."

"All of us?" she asked, looking at the rapt expressions on the faces of the people around her.

"Yes. We must trust in Him. Evil is upon us."

"But how do you know?"

"Because I've heard that same voice before."

"Here? Tonight?"

"No." He sighed, his eyes glistening in the subdued light. "It was some time ago."

The speaker raised his hands and spoke to the group, cutting off their questioning murmurs with his words. "Brethren, the Lord is with us. Do not be afraid. We must pray together that we do not fall prey to the snares of the wicked one." He scanned their faces unhurriedly, then began to lead them in prayer. "Our Father who lives in Heaven —"

At that instant the wooden door separating the storage area from the rest of the shop burst from its leather hinges. It crashed to the dirt floor with a sickening thud, sending sawdust and splinters of wood flying into the small, windowless enclosure.

Esther coughed repeatedly and rubbed her burning eyes. She was dazed and disoriented, and she felt a sharp, stinging sensation on her right cheek. When she touched the spot, her hand came away stained with blood.

Joseph grabbed her by the arm and pulled her from the center of the room. He dragged her towards the corner, to the right of where the door had been, out of the direct line of sight of the squat, bald-headed man who stood resolutely before them, scowling.

The heat of anger that flamed in the man's eyes chilled Esther. His flushed face looked like that of a wild, maddened dog.

The room went deathly quiet, but as the dust began to settle, there were intermittent fits of coughing from the small group of believers.

The man addressed the huddled gathering, mockery evident in his voice. "I am Saul of Tarsus. And you, it seems, are a group of rebels engaging in treasonous activity."

The speaker, unruffled by all the commotion, challenged their accuser's assessment without rancor. "Brother, we conspire against no man or government. Our only desire is to worship God and to honor His Son. If fellowshiping with Him who was, is, and always will be is a crime, then we are indeed guilty —"

"So you admit your guilt," interrupted Saul.

"You didn't let me finish, brother. I was about to say that if we are guilty, it is only of seeking to deny death the tax He levies upon the unregenerate soul."

Esther began to tremble uncontrollably as she watched Saul's face turn almost purple with rage. She tried to push herself further into the corner, but could not. She stared at the doorway behind Saul, wondering if she could squeeze through without him seeing her, but what she saw lurking in the shadows turned her blood to ice. Centurions!

"How dare you lecture me, blasphemer!" yelled Saul, his voice filled with loathing and disgust. "You are indeed mad if you think it is I who am at risk and not yourselves. You speak as if you are drunk with wine. If this is indeed a gathering for the purpose of worshiping Almighty God, why are you not at the Temple? Surely you don't believe you can edify God *here*?"

"Brother," continued the leader patiently, "it is not necessary that we go to the Temple in order to fellowship with God. We see and honor God in everything we do and say. It is only by the power of His grace that we live and breathe, and it is through His mercy that we are able to return to Him like lost children to be cleansed when we are fouled by sin. We who have lived for so long under the sentence of death are now free. And we gather here tonight to give thanks unto Him who has unlocked the gates which held us captive. We praise the holy name of His Son, Jesus of Nazareth, who died that we might live."

Saul started to interrupt, but Deucalion stepped forward

from the shadows and grabbed him by the arm, then said firmly, "Let him finish."

"He who knew no sin became sin that we might live forever. His sacrifice has restored us to our rightful place as priests and kings unto God. The shedding of His holy blood upon the cross and His resurrection from the dead were prophesied by the prophet Isaiah. They are the seal of His covenant with us."

"Stop!" bellowed the man from Tarsus. "This has gone far enough. You are like a rabid dog. Your words infect and inflame. I will listen to no more of this blasphemous talk." Catlike, he moved towards the front of the room. His robe was held closed by a cord, securing the garment at his waist, and from it hung a scabbard holding a long dagger. As he moved towards the speaker, he reached down and drew forth the blade.

Behind him a woman screamed. Pandemonium followed on the heels of its dying echo.

Oblivious to Deucalion's cry for order, Saul rushed forward, raised the dagger over his head, and with a sickening *swooosh* plunged it deep into the chest of the speaker. Blood spurted from the gaping wound, staining both the victim's and Saul's white robes with ruby-red death.

The old man crumpled to the earthen floor. His body twitched spasmodically in the dust.

Nausea consumed Esther. She felt as though she was trapped at the bottom of a deep, dark well, with no way out. She glanced at Joseph and realized he must have been struck by a flying piece of wood, for he was slumped over and there was blood on the floor.

Everything that was happening seemed to be unfolding in dreamlike slowness. When she saw Saul move towards the old man with his dagger raised, she screamed. Immediately four centurions entered the room with swords drawn. Several members of the gathering rushed towards the door in an attempt to escape. In their haste they impaled themselves upon the swords. Blood splattered everywhere, and a strong odor now filled the room.

Other people began to scream and cry out. The small enclosure had become a slaughter-house of death.

Abruptly Saul turned and stared at Esther with a cold, heartless gaze that was darker than the darkest night she'd ever experienced, then began to move purposefully in her direction. She could not move. She was paralyzed by the brutality she'd witnessed and by the cruel look she saw in Saul's eyes.

Deucalion tried unsuccessfully to restrain his men, but inexplicably they had caught Saul's contagious madness. More centurions rushed into the small room, and in the ensuing chaos the Praetorian was knocked to the floor from behind.

Fighting against the crush of bodies, he struggled to his knees. It was then that he noticed the raven-haired woman he'd seen at Doras' house cowering in the corner.

"No!" he shouted, shocked to see her trapped in the midst of this madness. Then he saw Saul standing over her, his dagger raised, a malicious, demonic look in his eyes. "Saul, don't!" he commanded, desperately trying to free himself from the mass of broken and bleeding bodies surrounding him.

Joseph sat up, holding one hand over his right eye. Out of his left he saw a short man with bushy black eyebrows standing over Esther with a bloodied dagger in his right hand. Galvanized into action by Deucalion's shout, he struck the man as hard as he could in the stomach. The man gave a grunt and staggered backwards. Mobilized by instinct, Joseph stumbled to his feet, grabbed Esther, and pulled her through the crumbling doorway.

Deucalion struggled upright, pushing aside the body of a believer, unconsciously wiping his bloody hands on his tunic.

All thoughts of controlling Saul were now replaced by thoughts of how he could help the dark-haired woman escape the carnage. His sword lay on the floor, covered by blood and dust, forgotten as he fought his way to the opening and stepped out of the madness.

At the front of the shop, Joseph leaned in a daze against a large pile of birch. Blood trickled from a gash above his eye. Esther stood by his side, her eyes vacant.

Deucalion rushed forward and grabbed her by the shoulders, then roughly grasped her chin in his right hand and turned her face to his. "You!" he demanded. "What are you doing here?"

She did not reply.

Frustrated, he slapped her. Not hard, but not gently either. Her eyes fluttered, and he saw recognition. He tried to get through to her again. "You can't stay here. I can't control my men. We must leave now."

"Where . . . ?" came the soft-spoken, hesitant reply.

"We must go outside."

"My friend . . . Joseph . . . You must help him . . . He's hurt."

Deucalion grasped the wounded man, supporting him with his right arm, but did not let go of the woman. "Stay close to me, and say nothing when we step into the street," he whispered in a strained voice.

Outside the shop a crowd was beginning to gather. Many of them had been awakened from slumber by the screams of those being slaughtered inside the woodworker's shop. Most were Jews, and they argued violently with Deucalion's men. The centurions had their hands full maintaining order as more and more people, both Roman and Jewish, began to fill the small street.

As Deucalion and his two charges emerged, one of his men approached them hurriedly. "The crowd is becoming unmanageable, Commander," he said, staring at his superior with consternation. "What in the name of the gods is going on in there?"

"The Jew has gone mad," Deucalion replied, his body trembling noticeably. "I'm taking two prisoners to the garrison for questioning."

The centurion stared at Deucalion, covered as he was with blood and dirt, and then at the man and woman he supported. "But —" was all he said before Deucalion's stern gaze silenced him. He saluted stiffly and said, "Hail Caesar."

Without looking back, Deucalion moved towards the shadows, with Esther and Joseph stumbling along at his side. He pressed through the growing crowd, ignoring their shouts.

Unknown to Deucalion, an expressionless pair of eyes watched the whole scene from the darkness of a doorway a short distance away, making note of his conversation with the centurion. As soon as the Praetorian and his two charges had disappeared into the night, the eyes blinked twice and were themselves gone.

XIII

Before they'd gone very far, Joseph moaned. Deucalion, fearful the groanings would attract attention and not wanting to encounter any of the stray groups of centurions who might be wandering through the city, decided it would be best if he found a spot where they could rest. Also, he needed time to think.

There was a small meadow just outside the western gate, on the outskirts of the city. It would be safe there, temporarily at least; the Roman patrols did not venture outside the walls of Jerusalem at night unless there was specific reason. And it would be a good place to question the woman.

He maneuvered them through the darkened streets without incident. When they arrived at the meadow, he gently eased his burden to the ground, then examined the man's wound. The cut was superficial, but because the wound was just over the eye, it had bled profusely. Deucalion tore off a piece of his tunic and wrapped it tightly around Joseph's head to stanch the flow of blood.

Joseph groaned again, less loudly this time, and Deucalion knew he would be semiconscious for some time. He finished tying the makeshift bandage, then turned his attention to the woman. Darkness shrouded the meadow, though the moon did give some illumination. Even though she was standing several feet away, there was just enough light to allow him to see her face clearly.

She was dazed and disoriented, and she had a glazed look in her eyes. It was a look he'd seen many times in the eyes of soldiers on the battlefield and one that he knew had been in his own eyes on more than one occasion.

He also knew from harsh experience that the glaze mirrored not only pain, but fear and denial as well. There were some things human eyes were not meant to see.

Sensing this strikingly beautiful woman's silent agony caused him a moment of almost overwhelming grief. Simultaneously, he felt an intense desire to comfort her. "Would you like to talk about it?" he asked. "Sometimes it helps."

She shook her head and said warily, "You must be a man of some importance in the Legion."

"How can you tell?"

"Because of the way you spoke to the centurion outside the woodworker's shop."

"So you *were* paying attention. What in the name of the gods were you doing at that meeting?"

She ignored his question and asked one of her own. "Why have you risked your commission, and perhaps your life, to save us?"

"You mean because you're Jews?"

The woman nodded. "We cannot even claim the protection of the Sanhedrin, because —"

"Go on," he insisted.

"Because we believe that Jesus of Nazareth was the Messiah spoken about in the Holy Scriptures." She paused, and her eyes suddenly cleared. She seemed to stand a bit straighter at the mention of the name of the Galilean, and she held her head high. Deucalion was caught off guard by the amazing change in her expression. He didn't know what to say.

"Well?" she pressed.

"What are you asking?"

"Why did you rescue us?"

"I'm not sure I'm ready to answer that question just yet."

"Why not?"

"You ask too many questions for someone in your predicament."

"Then at least tell me your name, so I'll know who my benefactor was."

Deucalion frowned, puzzled by her words.

"Before they take you away and put you in prison for treason," she finished quietly.

In spite of the circumstances, he laughed. "You're very beautiful when you're so serious," he chided as he sat down on a large rock, leaning back on his elbows. "Deucalion Cincinnatus Quinctus, at your service. And I doubt I'll be arrested for treason for merely questioning a slave."

Esther frowned, then whispered, "What a nice-sounding name. Deucalion . . . Cincinnatus . . . Quinctus," she repeated slowly in a strong, resonant voice, emphasizing the syllables of his name as if she were testing each upon her tongue.

"Most people, when they first hear it, tell me it's an odd-sounding name."

"I don't find anything odd about it at all," she replied with finality, as if that settled the matter once and for all.

"I was named for a Greek god and a Roman hero of the fifth century," he continued, wishing desperately they had met under much different circumstances.

"In that order?" she asked, feigning disbelief, hoping he could hear the amusement in her voice.

"In that order," he replied, smiling. He was grateful she was not behaving as he'd expected — fearful and timid. He admired her strength. "You're a very entertaining woman when you're not being chased by a fanatical Jew."

The barest trace of a smile quivered on her lips.

He asked her name. She told him and said, "Perhaps you're wondering how someone as plain as I was given such a beautiful name."

"I don't think you're plain at all," he replied, suddenly sobered by her modesty. He looked at her intently and added, "In fact, I can't imagine a woman being any more beautiful than you are at this very moment."

Esther felt shy and awkward, and she allowed the silence of the night to cloak her thoughts with its quietness. Oddly, she wasn't embarrassed by Deucalion's unabashed expression of emotion, just surprised. Doras had always spoken of Romans as if they were incapable of any emotion save arrogance.

Deucalion was also surprised at his outburst; he'd never spoken to, or even about, a woman in such a manner before.

Finally Esther broke the silence. "My name means many things to many people, but to Jews it is a name that signifies loyalty, compassion, strength and, most of all, love. Not of self, mind you, but of others. Esther was one of the Jews' greatest heroines. The Festival of Purim is dedicated to her."

"The casting of lots or *tabernacle*," said Deucalion knowingly.

"You know Hebrew?" she asked amazed.

"A bit," he replied, understating his fluency, knowing it was the soldier in him that prevented him from being entirely candid, yet wanting very much for it not to be the case.

"Tell me, what else do you know about my name?"

Deucalion sat forward and shrugged. "Nothing."

Esther cast him a doubtful look.

"Really, I don't. Please continue," he said, flustered. "I like listening to the sound of your voice. It reminds me of the sound a young bird makes when singing in the trees."

Although Esther was flattered by his compliments, she wondered if he was toying with her. She thought it over and decided that it didn't matter if he was; she'd already made her decision about him the night she'd seen him with her father.

"Perhaps my voice sounds like birds' song because the proper Hebrew form of my name, *Hadassah*, means 'myrtle'; birds are drawn to the starry, white flowers of the bush."

"How interesting."

"That's not all. The Persian rendition is derived from the name of the great Babylonian goddess Ishtar."

Unable to resist showing off, Deucalion interrupted her again. "In Greek your name means 'star,' from the word for Venus."

"How nice to be compared to a star," she said and smiled appreciatively, then looked up and admired the star-studded night. "There's nothing more beautiful than twinkling stars," she added with a sigh. "They shine against the black canvas of the heavens, reminding me that no matter how dark it is, love can blossom — and sometimes live."

Deucalion was captivated by the poetry of her words, and, oddly, he felt lightheaded, like the night he'd consumed too much dandelion wine at Doras' house. He didn't want to break the spell, but he was also aware that certain matters must be dealt with immediately. The Praetorian in him took charge. "Your master will be concerned if you don't return soon," he said, pushing all other thoughts from his mind. "We'd better get you cleaned up and back to Doras' house."

"What about Saul?" she asked, suddenly fearful. "I've heard my father speak of him. He's a very persistent man; he won't rest until he identifies and deals with all who were at the meeting tonight." As soon as she'd spoken, she realized she'd confirmed something Deucalion had been wanting to ask her. She could tell by the look on his face.

"I thought you didn't have parents — that you were a slave."

"Is that what he told you? That I'm his *slave*?"

Deucalion felt as if he'd been kicked in the stomach. "Is he your husband?" he asked, fearing the answer.

Esther began to weep, her whole body shuddering. Between sobs she managed to speak. "I . . . am . . . not . . . a *slave*. And . . . I . . . am . . . not . . . *married*."

Deucalion wanted to comfort her, but didn't know how. He felt awkward and therefore made no move to hold her.

After several minutes, Esther regained control of herself. "I'm sorry," she said, wiping the tears from her cheeks with the back of her hand. The wet was stained pink, and she remembered the stinging sensation she'd felt on her face, and the blood on her hand, just after Saul had kicked down the door at the meeting.

Deucalion noticed the bleeding cut for the first time. He tore off another piece of his tunic, then stood up and gently wiped the bloodstained tears from her face. "If I have to do this much more this evening, I won't have a tunic left," he said, trying to make light of the situation.

This time Esther managed a smile.

"There. I hope I didn't hurt you. The cut isn't deep, and in a few days you won't even know it was there." When he finished, he let his hand linger on her shoulder for a moment.

A tremor ran through her body at his touch. She looked up into his smiling face and shivered. Her heart seemed to have broken loose from its moorings and came to rest in her throat, where it lay throbbing.

Deucalion thought she might be getting cold. "It's time we got you home," he said softly, glancing briefly at the eastern horizon.

"I *can't* go home," she whispered, wondering if the longing she felt inside was written all over her face. "That's what I've been trying to tell you."

"I don't understand," he said, realizing for the first time

that her eyes were a magnificent jade-green color, with variegated specks of blue, like an agate.

"Doras is my father," she replied softly, running the words together, hoping he wouldn't hate her. "I can't disgrace him, no matter what might happen to me."

Moved by her plight, Deucalion grasped her by the shoulders and stared deep into her eyes. He was immediately lost in the jade-green ocean of her doubt.

"In spite of his love for me he won't be able to forgive me this transgression," she continued, feeling weak in her legs from Deucalion's touch. "His Faith is all he's ever really possessed."

"But he's your *father*. Surely he'll understand."

Esther hesitated. Should she tell him? She'd only just laid eyes on this man two nights ago, yet already they were talking as if they had known each other from childhood. And now she was about to tell him a secret she'd never told anyone.

Deucalion was also thinking. And his thoughts disturbed him deeply — for several reasons. Although he barely knew this woman, he was fascinated with her. The fact that she was a Jew and he a Roman was of no consequence to him; he'd never allowed himself to slip into the rhetoric of bigotry, much less the hypocrisy of self-worship. And even though she had ventured into extremely dangerous waters by associating with the disciples of a man whom both Rome and the Jews feared, the difficulty, if handled properly, could be overcome.

But the fact that she was the daughter of Doras was something else all together.

"I knew you'd hate me if I told you the truth," she whispered, pulling away and turning her back on him.

"I don't hate you, Esther. I barely know you," he replied, turning her around with soft words.

"Then why are you so quiet all of a sudden?"

"Because I'm thinking."

"About what?"

He smiled. "Why do women always do that?"

"Do what?"

"Demand to know what a man's thinking?"

"Because we're not as unintelligent as men seem to believe, and we often have some very good solutions to problems men assume only *they* can figure out."

"Oh?"

"Have you ever heard of a woman named Rahab?"

He shook his head.

"But you *have* heard of Joshua?"

"Of course. He led the army that defeated Jericho. And you Jews believe that he caused the sun to stand still for a whole day."

"No," Esther corrected, "we believe *God* made the sun stand still for a whole day; Joshua simply heard and obeyed God."

"So what does this woman have to do with Joshua?"

"See, I'm already proving my point. Rahab was a harlot who lived in Jericho at the time the Israelites entered Canaan, and she was responsible for saving the men Joshua sent to spy on the great city. She hid them among flax stalks on her roof, then told the officers sent to find the spies that they'd left the city before the great gates were closed."

"And the rest is history, as they say."

"Please, I'm trying to make a point."

"Sorry. Go on."

"The story is important to Jews because it illustrates that when confronted with the choice of submitting to the King of Jericho or obeying God, Rahab, a woman who was looked down upon by all in her city, chose to serve God. Because of her faith, she became part of the genealogy of the *Christos*."

Deucalion flinched. "Who?"

"The *Christos*. It means 'the Anointed One' in Greek."

"I know what it means, but who was this 'Anointed One'?"

The harshness Esther heard in Deucalion's tone caused her to tremble. She swallowed hard and forced herself to answer him. "Jesus of Nazareth. The man you Romans crucified two months ago," she replied, amazed at her boldness.

Deucalion's head spun, and he staggered backwards, as if he'd been struck. *What was going on here?*

"What's wrong?" she asked.

"Nothing. Just a moment of dizziness. It'll pass." He couldn't believe how both of the conversations he'd had tonight had ended up with the mention of the Galilean. Earlier with Saul, and now with Esther. It had to be more than coincidence. There was no way either of them could know what he'd done, the horrible truth behind his nightmares.

Esther watched Deucalion intently, certain he wasn't telling her everything. Oddly, she was no longer fearful.

"Listen to me," he finally whispered. "If I tell you something, will you promise never to reveal it to anyone? It could mean both our deaths."

"I — I don't know," she stammered.

"Please . . . I need to talk to someone about it. But there's no one I can trust."

Esther both heard and felt the pain in his words. In spite of her earlier fear, she found herself wanting desperately to help this lonely Praetorian. "I'll listen."

Deucalion began to pace, wrestling with his conscience. He felt trapped, hemmed in. He had to be certain he could trust this woman; there was too much at stake. "We don't have much time," he muttered more to himself than to her. "It'll be daylight soon." Should he tell her about what happened at Golgotha, and later at the tomb? Would she believe him?

Suddenly he stopped pacing. He'd made his decision. It would be safer, for now, to stay out of those murky waters. "Did you know your father has been conspiring with Herod

Antipas to remove Joseph ben Caiaphas from his position as High Priest?" he asked, pushing the other thoughts from his mind.

Esther was surprised at Deucalion's formal tone, then realized suddenly she was seeing the elite Roman mind in operation. "Not exactly," she replied. "I mean — yes, I know he desires more than anything else to be High Priest; that's all he's spoken about for some time. But I wasn't aware he was conspiring, as you put it, with anyone. I thought he was merely making himself available for the position," she finished softly, hoping he would believe her.

Joseph moaned.

Deucalion's mind raced. He knew he had to make another important decision — immediately. And he had precious little time to weigh the consequences of his choice. "Is there someone you can trust — someone with whom you can stay until I can make sense of the situation?" he asked abruptly.

Esther thought for a moment before she answered, pulling at the strands of her long, dark hair nervously. "Perhaps. I have a friend, a Jew who like myself is a believer. She lives alone, just east of the city, off the road to Bethany."

"Good. Help me get Joseph to his feet. I'll take both of you there."

"But what about you? Your men will surely want to know what has happened to you. You told the centurion you were taking us to the garrison for questioning."

"I'll worry about that later. First I have to get you and your friend someplace where you'll both be safe."

XIV

Pontius Pilate held Deucalion's sword in his left hand and gestured vehemently at Antonius with his right. "What do you mean no one knows where he is? He's the Commander of the Garrison. Praetorians do not simply vanish into the night, never to be heard from again!" he yelled, furious with his cowering servant.

Antonius stepped backward, out of the reach of Pilate's shaking fist. "He hasn't been seen since he left the woodworker's shop," replied the servant. "One of his men spoke to him during the melee, and he told that centurion he was taking two prisoners to the garrison for questioning. But he never arrived."

"Prisoners? What kind of prisoners?"

"An injured man and a woman."

"Jews?"

"The centurion didn't say, master. He only indicated that they disappeared into the night."

Pilate's initial rage began to subside as he considered the possibilities. "Disappeared, you say?"

Antonius remained silent, shrugging his shoulders in reply.

"Find Malkus immediately, and tell him to report to me at once," said the Procurator, walking over to the balcony and staring down at the Royal Bridge.

Antonius didn't move, alerting Pilate that he had a further message for his master.

Without turning around, Pilate asked, "What else?"

"I would remind you that you have an appointment with the High Priest this morning. He'll be here shortly."

Under his breath, Pilate cursed. He'd completely forgotten about Caiaphas. He'd gone to great lengths to arrange a surreptitious meeting with the High Priest. His predecessors had set precedent by dealing directly with Antipas, letting him be responsible for the conduct of the members of the Sanhedrin. He'd grudgingly acceded to that precedent, although not out of any sense of loyalty or duty. Antipas' weakness was his lust for power, and it was precisely because of that lust that Pilate was able to control the Tetrarch.

The meeting he'd arranged for today, however, was an additional safeguard. He considered the irony of the situation. Not only was he using Antipas to subjugate the priesthood, but he was also using the priesthood to insure that even if Antipas failed, Pilate would have a scapegoat. *Rome is not going to crucify me as it did the Rabbi from Nazareth*, he thought. *I've ruled this cursed mote of dust and death for seven years, and what have I to show for it? Nothing. Nothing, that is, but nightmares. It's time these Jews return some of the blood they have leeched from me.*

He stared morosely at the soft haze cloaking the distant mountains. The thick, grey-white mist reminded him of the vaporous heat that rises up from the surface of a stilled lake as the chill of dawn caresses the warm, languid water. His gaze kept straying, however, and he had to force himself not to look at the bridge. He feared the madness he found within himself whenever he remembered what had happened there.

Nevertheless, the memory flooded his mind unbidden, as it had done repeatedly for the past two months. In his mind's eye he could see the blood that flowed unceasing from the Nazarene's wounds. The ruby-red river had permanently stained the white marble stones that made up the long walkway over which Jesus had been paraded before the jeering mass of people. His body battered beyond recognition, His back flayed by the scourge, the Nazarene had struggled mutely under the back-bending weight of the heavy wooden cross.

Even now, the Procurator imagined he could hear the blood of the Rabbi calling out to him from the ground. Strangely, the voice was not one of retribution, but of forgiveness.

But in his heart he knew he didn't want forgiveness. He wanted to be in Rome, living as a Roman, preferably as a retired General — not here in Judea, living as a tortured shadow of the soldier his father had raised him to be.

"Thank you, Antonius," he said finally with uncharacteristic politeness. "Inform me when the High Priest arrives, but don't send him in immediately." The glaze of hardness in his eyes stood in marked contrast to the soft, controlled timbre of his voice as he added brusquely, "I want him to squirm."

"You want whom to squirm?" asked Deucalion, his voice tired and fractured with resignation.

Pilate turned and gasped. "What in the name of Caesar happened to you?"

"What happened may have been ordered in the name of the Emperor, but it's not something a Roman soldier can be proud of," replied the younger man wearily, sitting down at the marble table Pilate used for his desk. His tunic was torn and shredded in places, as if he had been attacked by some sort of wild beast, and there were copper-colored stains smudged with sawdust and dirt, remnants of the spattered blood of dying believers.

"It was a bloodbath, Pontius. Saul is mad! He slaughtered helpless men and women — people who'd done nothing more than gather to worship their God."

"Get hold of yourself, Deucalion," Pilate snapped. "You're

babbling." He studied his commander briefly, knowing there was something he was holding back. "Where have you been since you left your men last night? And why am I in possession of this?" he asked angrily, holding up Deucalion's sword, "instead of you?"

Deucalion watched Pilate's rage with a detachment he wouldn't have thought himself capable of two months ago. Normally he would have made a concerted effort to calm his superior, perhaps even to interject a joke to lighten Pilate's intensity. Today he was too tired, more fatigued than he could ever remember being.

The sight of his sword, its sharp-edged lustre dulled by the coating of dried blood smeared along its length, made him sick to his stomach. *What is happening to me?*

"What is all this talk of madness and slaughter?" berated the Procurator. "I expected you to report to me early this morning, but not in this condition," he continued, gesturing futilely at Deucalion. "I sent Antonius to find Malkus. I thought the Jews had *murdered* you!"

As if he'd just become aware of the fact that he must indeed look horrible, Deucalion stood up and examined himself. He grimaced, then walked over to a table next to the arch leading to the balcony and poured some fresh water from the alabaster pitcher into a gold-rimmed basin. As he washed his face and hands, the clear, tepid water turned a deep rust-brown color.

Pilate stood silent, waiting for Deucalion to make himself presentable.

The Praetorian finished washing as best he could with the limited facilities, then turned and walked past Pilate wordlessly. He stood on the balcony and looked down at the Temple, wondering how men who professed to serve God could engage in the kind of brutality he'd witnessed last night.

"I've served Rome faithfully for fifteen years — since I was twelve," he said absently. "I've traveled wherever she wished and fought whomever she declared to be her enemy, and I've never concerned myself with politics." He shook his head wearily. "I've chosen to develop my skills as a soldier instead, leaving politics for Caesar, the Senate, and the Generals. Yet, never have I been a party to such cowardice and such bloodthirsty hatred as I was almost forced into participating in last night."

"What do you mean *almost*?"

"I've seen women and children killed in the course of battle, and I've wept over their corpses," he continued, ignoring the question. "But last night I could not weep. Had I loosed my true emotions, I would have killed Saul, and perhaps even turned upon my own men." He turned from the window and added, "I'm not sure why I'm explaining this to you, Pontius, or even if I'm making any sense, but it's something I must say.

"It was almost as if once we entered the woodworker's shop, a blackness deeper and darker than the night descended upon Saul. I was standing beside him, and I felt him *change*. We'd been talking civilly to one another as we walked, and I thought I was beginning to understand what it was that drove him so." He stared into Pilate's sullen eyes. Without condemnation, but with the realization of one who has probed the hearts and souls of two seemingly dissimilar men and found a common scarlet thread binding them to madness, he said, "He has the same passionate, narrow-minded love for Hebrew law that you have for Roman jurisprudence.

"But I was totally unprepared for what happened when we arrived at our destination. Saul became a man possessed. He ripped the door leading to the back of the shop from its hinges with one blow. My men and I were stunned. He exhibited the strength of several men.

"Once inside the room, he harangued the small group of people unmercifully, attempting to antagonize them into a foolish act so he could justify what he'd planned to do from the start. The fact that they did not respond as he intended seemed to cut loose the last tie binding him to reason. That's when the slaughter begin. And that's when I lost my sword."

Pilate listened without expression and without comment. It was evident that Deucalion's attitude had changed dramatically in the last few days. The Procurator realized now that by refusing to acknowledge the chasm growing between them, even as he refused to accept the implications of his actions on the bridge over the Tyropoeon Valley, he had doomed their friendship. He wanted to weep, but knew he could not.

Now, more than ever, he realized the truth of the matter. He was a man who because of his intellect could not plead ignorance. Yet he was one who, because of pride in that same intellectual ability, could not help but make decisions that were contrary to his own best interests. In many ways he was as much addicted to power as Antipas.

That bit of introspection startled Pilate. He'd thought himself incapable of such stark honesty where his own motives were concerned.

Overcome by a rare moment of compassion, he opened himself up to Deucalion. "Listen to me," he pleaded, catching the Praetorian off guard. "I'm a man plagued by the demons of unjust decisions, most of which I found not merely unpalatable but abhorrent to my sense of ethics and morality. And I've been forced to make those types of judgments in order to survive in a world I no longer understand. The memories of those decisions resurrect themselves inside my head at will. I have no control over them. A sight . . . a sound . . . sometimes the touch of another human being — all open the door to the pit and unleash the power of evil.

"In those terrifying moments of darkness, I imagine that my deeds are so foul, so repugnant, that even though I hold a ticket of passage on the ferryman's ship of death, I am an unwanted guest. I ride Charon's demonic frigate endlessly as it glides over the putrid sea of misery — the one the gods call the River Styx. I sit apart from the lost souls who are my fellow passengers and, like a leper, pray that no one will look at me. Yet I desperately want one last moment of recognition, one look to assure me that at least there was a time when I was one of them, even if only for a moment."

He rubbed his temples, trying to massage away the pain that had become a constant companion. "I'm no longer the proud citizen of Rome I once was, Deucalion. I'm no longer sure of my destiny, no longer certain of my ability to survive no matter what the odds. And I'm even less certain of the institution I worship like a god.

"Rome has failed her people. And I, once a true son of the Republic, have failed Rome. I have given up on my adopted mother. Oh, there was a time when, like Oedipus, I courted her, blind to the fact that she was *who* she was and *what* she was. Now, however, my conscience robs me of my ignorance."

Although the Procurator's suddenly placid eyes were dry, Deucalion thought Pilate might weep. With unwavering voice the superior continued, "You are the closest thing to a son I've ever had. Claudia has given me only prophecy — illegitimate prophecy to boot. The idea of losing you to a woman is understandable; the possibility of losing you to an ideology that is beyond my ability to comprehend is unbearable."

He twisted his hands together. "I fear losing your friendship," he croaked, his voice almost a whisper. "No, that's not exactly true. I fear the loss of the *sense of belonging* that you've given me. I dread that more than I dread losing my appointment as Procurator."

Realizing what he'd said, he grew suddenly quiet. His face became an expressionless mask.

Outside Herod's palace, a bird sang merrily. When the

sound of its fluttering voice reached Deucalion, he glanced at the city spread below them, a sprawling metropolis of contradictions, and thought about Esther. He wondered if there were myrtle trees nearby, and if the bird was frolicking with a potential mate, wooing her with music, singing to her of his love as she sat upon the starry-white flowers.

At the same time, he was intrigued by Pilate's unusual behavior. He was also stunned by the Procurator's confession. Maybe there was still hope. "You never mentioned anything about prophecy to me before, Pontius," he said with compassion. "Certainly not in reference to Claudia. Tell me, what prompted her to speak to you in such fashion?"

Pilate stared at Deucalion with sunken eyes, the pale skin beneath them stained by the dark smudge of too many sleepless nights. "Claudia visited me only hours before I sentenced Jesus to die and told me she'd had a vivid dream. She warned me I was making a serious mistake. I argued with her, but she wouldn't be moved."

"What exactly did she say?"

He recounted Claudia's exact words, then said, "I didn't listen to her — or my conscience. And the price I've paid for my foolishness is beyond measure. If the *Gehenna* of the Jews is real, I don't want to face it. Surely it's worse than the hell I live in now — and that is almost more than I can bear."

"But, Pontius, you just told me that many of the decisions you've made have been forced upon you. Obviously you've honored Rome by being a faithful servant, as well as a loyal soldier."

"Ha! You're too young and far too naive to understand what soldiering in the service of Rome is truly like. My father, Marcus Pontius, was a native of Seville. He gained fame in the service of Rome during the wars of annihilation waged by Agrippa against the Cantabrians.

"Some say he was a renegade to the cause of his countrymen, the Spaniards. When Spain was conquered by Rome he received the *pilum*, a reward for his service and a mark of distinction. Shortly thereafter he changed the family name to Pilati, in honor of the javelin he had received from Caesar." He forced a smile. "My father used to tell my mother that our new name would bring us luck because it was the weapon favored by many in the Legion. Since the Legion represented Rome, which was invincible in his eyes, he would be an extension of that invincibility.

"He was quite a visionary, my father," Pilate added, chuckling, turning his back on Deucalion and the balcony. He walked inside, and when he reached the marble table he rubbed the fingers of his right hand along the polished surface. "After leaving Spain, I entered the service of Germanicus on the Rhine and served throughout the German campaigns. Not long after, I found myself in Rome. It was there I decided that I must make some crucial decisions if I wanted to get where I believed I belonged."

Deucalion flinched at Pilate's choice of words; they echoed hauntingly in his ears.

"I made what I thought at the time was a prudent and far-sighted decision — I married Claudia."

"I don't understand."

Pilate turned and let his tired eyes linger upon Deucalion, then looked past him, staring outward again at the distant mountains. He thought he could hear a bird singing, out beyond the balcony. "Your youthful naiveté keeps raising its honest head. Claudia is the youngest daughter of Julia, daughter of Augustus."

Recognition glowed in Deucalion's eyes, and they widened considerably at the mention of *Augustus*, the imperial title of Octavius, the successor of Julius Caesar.

"I assumed at the time I would find favor with the Emperor, stay in Rome, become a member of the Senate, and retire. I'd be a happy, not to mention wealthy, landowner. But the gods had other plans," he added resignedly shrugging his shoulders, as an old politician will do when a weight he has been carrying for too long becomes too heavy to bear.

"It is indeed ironic how the fates have manipulated my life. Augustus ordered an enrollment, for tax purposes, that caused two undistinguished Jews to go to Bethlehem, where a son was born to them. He in turn eventually upset two nations: one worshiping a supposedly benevolent god of love, the other serving a relentless and uncompromising god of war.

"He alienated and incensed His own people, the Jews, by claiming to be the Son of God. And by refusing to behave as the treasonous rabble-rouser His accusers labeled Him, He placed the greatest empire the world has ever known in one of the most disastrous predicaments it has ever been in.

"Now *we* must help our enemies eradicate the very infection that threatens to accomplish what all the might and power of the Legion could not. What irony!"

Pilate's face sagged as he spoke. He looked like he was wearing a wrinkled mask left over from a long past bacchanalian party. "So you see, my young and innocent Praetorian, Charon's frigate is large enough to carry nations as well as people. And that, of course, is the final irony. Rome's blindness has brought her to the brink of oblivion. She is slowly dying, and her citizens don't even realize that the rot they fear from without has already taken root and spreads from within. The fecundity of the once invincible empire has been destroyed by one too many abortive attempts at self-preservation."

Deucalion could not believe what he was hearing. Pilate had never spoken to him with such passion before. That such a razor-sharp, pragmatic assessment of Rome's predicament should come from the lips of a career soldier was astounding. It was obvious that in spite of all he'd said, Pilate still loved Rome, just as an unhappy but very married man loves his mistress. It was equally obvious that Pilate had misinterpreted a key piece of information — an error which on the battlefield would inevitably prove fatal to a field commander.

It wasn't Rome's *blindness* that fueled the fire voraciously consuming the rotting infrastructure of the Empire. It was simply *momentum*. Rome was like a wounded leviathan. Thrashing and howling in her death-throes, she'd turned upon herself and was desperately trying to tear the source of pain from her body. In the process, she was unwittingly ripping herself apart.

"If you see all this so clearly, Pontius, why don't you try to do something about it?" he asked.

The Procurator frowned. "Oh, but I am. I made a serious mistake by allowing the Jews to involve me in the Jesus incident, and I don't intend to make another."

Deucalion's sympathy for his superior rapidly began to dissipate. Deep inside, the disgust at what he'd witnessed the night before still burned hotly, like a live coal simmering in his belly. "So you make use of men like Saul," he said sarcastically. "Men who are not tormented by their conscience."

Pilate's eyes narrowed, and Deucalion knew he was stepping into dangerous territory.

"Don't take that tone with me, Deucalion. I'm fully aware of my responsibilities as Procurator. Men like Saul are a necessary evil. Unfortunately, they have a way of getting out of control. That is why we must be careful how we use them. So long as we avoid any direct involvement, we remain in control."

"There is no controlling what I witnessed last night," countered Deucalion with a conviction that disturbed Pilate but also reminded him of why he'd asked that the Praetorian be assigned to him. "If Saul's fanaticism is allowed to continue unhampered, and if he has the support of the Legion, there is truly little hope for Rome. We cannot participate, even nominally, in such madness and remain unaffected."

"You know, there are those, my young friend, who accuse me behind my back of being self-seeking and cowardly," replied the Procurator, barely controlling his anger. "Others argue that although I'm able to perceive what is right, I lack the moral strength to follow through with what I believe rather than simply executing my orders. Well, last night's undertaking should convince even my staunchest detractors that I have Rome's best interests at hand, no matter what my own beliefs may be."

"What are you talking about?"

"I was ordered by Vitellius to 'remedy the dilemma in Judea.' And that is exactly what I'm doing. If that is self-seeking, I admit to it. Who among us is not? As for cowardly," he shrugged, "I leave that for the historians to decide."

Antonius reappeared, interrupting the conversation. "The High Priest has arrived, Procurator," he announced.

Angered, Deucalion asked, "What is *he* doing *here*?"

"Have you forgotten? Last time we met I told you that I'd arranged a meeting with Caiaphas to find out what is happening within the Sanhedrin. I've heard strange rumors —"

"What kind of rumors?"

"I'll tell you about them later, after my meeting with the High Priest."

Deucalion ignored the attempted dismissal. "Does Caiaphas know you're once again on speaking terms with Antipas?" he asked, determined to find out as much as he could before leaving.

"I doubt it. He wouldn't be here if that were the case. That would be a bit like walking blindly into the lions' den, would it not? At any rate, even if he suspects something, the information you obtained from Doras should distract him."

Deucalion fought the nausea churning within his belly. He knew that Pilate would find out from the High Priest that the information from Doras was old news. And he knew it would do no good now to tell the Procurator that he'd spied upon the meeting of the Great Council. That information would only serve to make him more suspect than he would already be when the truth of last night's events became known.

And the truth *would* become known. Of that he had no doubt. Once Pilate had the scent of a scandal, he would ferret it out. And if it had the potential to affect his chances of retiring to a villa outside Rome, he would eliminate the problem — permanently.

"I don't want Caiaphas to see you here," said the Procurator. "Wait outside on the balcony and listen. I want your opinion of what's said."

XV

The hot season had already made its debut in Jerusalem by the time *Tam'muz*, July, made its appearance on the Hebrew calendar. The air was still and clear, the heat intense.

The sky was as brass, the earth as iron. Wind, when it came, usually heralded from the northwest, although sometimes it blew from the east. On rare occasions, a *khamseen* blew in from the south.

The wheat harvest was in full swing in the mountain districts. Time was precious to the barley farmer; springs were drying up, and vegetables were withering and dying on the vine. Bedouins left the steppes for the more succulent mountain pastures as Judea rapidly became dry and hard, a dreary wasteland of withered stalks and burned-up grass.

Thank God for the morning dew, thought Esther. Without it there would be no relief from the heat. She worked the sticky dough between her hands vigorously. She loved to bake, and now she had plenty of time to do just that. Deucalion had been gone for almost a week, and during the time he'd been away she'd heard nothing from him. She wondered if he would ever return.

Part of her was fearful because he was, after all, a Roman Praetorian. And yet, in spite of her fear, she was drawn to him. There was something *different* about him. Something that touched her spirit.

She didn't have the same feelings about Joseph, though he

149

was a Jew. She wondered why. Joseph was a good man, and she cared about him, but not in the same way she cared about Deucalion. Now that her friend was fully recovered, he'd been spending more and more of his time in the company of the apostles of Jesus. He'd also left behind a number of leather scrolls, wrapped in linen; scrolls he said belonged to an old man he'd met in the caves on the shores of the Great Salt Sea, just a few miles east of where she was now. He'd asked her to watch over them until he decided what to do with them.

Outside the small house a pair of swallows sang a cheerful tune. "What an impossible situation," she muttered, adding leaven to the dough so it would rise when heated. She began to hum to herself, keeping tune with a previously unknown melody that suddenly filled her head, trying to push thoughts of Deucalion from her mind.

Abruptly, she heard a muffled *rap! rap! rap!* at the front door. Startled, she wiped her hands on her apron, then smoothed her hair.

"Who's there?" she asked, uncertain what she would do if it were centurions.

"Deucalion."

Relieved and excited, she unlatched the door and opened it, then hugged Deucalion fiercely. Tears of joy slid down her face and left tiny tracks in the flour that had settled there like a fine coating of dust.

Surprised by Esther's greeting, Deucalion returned her hug, then suddenly realized how much he'd missed her while he was in Jerusalem.

"I thought you'd forgotten about me," she said, her face buried in his chest. "Or worse."

"Worse?"

"You could have been making some sort of arrangement with my father —"

Deucalion grasped her by the shoulders and pushed her

away from him so he could look at her, then laughed. His eyes danced with pleasure as he soaked up the sight of her. In the light of day her jade-green eyes shone like crystal. They reminded him of the perfect pair of oval emeralds mounted in gold that Claudia, Pilate's wife, wore as earpieces.

"You find that amusing," she said with mock indignation.

"Not at all. It's just that you've either aged considerably since I last saw you, or perhaps I simply failed to notice the streaks of grey in that beautiful black hair of yours."

"It's the flour," she said and used a clean corner of the plain white apron she wore to wipe her face. "Tell me, what did you find out while you were in Jerusalem?"

The smile on Deucalion's face vanished. He stepped inside the clean, well-kept house and closed the door behind him. "I'm afraid I've some bad news, Esther," he said wearily.

Esther walked over to the small table she'd been working at and sat down, pushing the dough and flour to the side. From the sound of Deucalion's voice and the look in his eyes, she wasn't sure she really wanted to hear what he had to say.

"Your father," he began with a sigh, "once I was finally able to talk with him, was convinced something horrible had happened to you. When I told him you were alive and safe, he was relieved. I told him I knew you were his daughter, and that shocked him. He asked me how I knew and I told him the truth, but only part of it. I left out the details of what happened at the woodworker's shop, saying only that I managed to get you away from the meeting before Saul could harm you."

Esther stared at him with glistening eyes. "And his reaction?"

"His whole expression changed in an instant. One moment he was relieved, the next he was subdued and pensive. He listened quietly, then was silent for some time before he spoke."

"You must tell me what he said."

"Esther —"

"Tell me! I must know!"

"He said that you had disgraced him, that he could no longer call you by his name. He finished by saying you would never be allowed to set foot in his house again."

The silence in the room was thick, almost suffocating.

Esther stared out the window, a blank look on her face. Her body was so rigid that Deucalion immediately thought of a *Shit'tah* tree, standing resolute in the midst of a raging wind.

Realizing she wasn't going to respond to what he'd said, he continued, "Before I spoke with him, your father knew nothing of the incident at the woodworker's shop. That surprised me; I thought for sure Caiaphas would have informed him immediately, if for no other reason than to gloat."

Esther's head snapped around. "Why do you say that?"

"Because the High Priest had you followed."

"How do you know?"

Deucalion told her.

When he finished she said, "So it's true, then. My father *is* conspiring with Herod Antipas to unseat Caiaphas as High Priest."

Deucalion nodded. "The two of them have been subtly manipulating the Sanhedrin for some time. The crucifixion of the Nazarene gave them the perfect opportunity to make their move. Your father was supposed to garner enough support from the Pharisees and dissident Sadducees to unseat Caiaphas and wrest control of the Sanhedrin from Annas. Three weeks ago he openly challenged Caiaphas in a special meeting of the Sanhedrin. But he failed."

"And how is it *you* know what happened in the Sanhedrin?"

Deucalion remained silent.

Esther raised her hand to her mouth, unbelief registering

in her eyes. "You were *there*?" she exclaimed, stunned. "No Gentile has *ever* been present at a meeting of the Council. But yes, I can see the truth in your eyes —"

"I disguised myself as a Jewish merchant and hid inside the Hall of Hewn Stones. Had I been discovered and caught —"

"You would have been killed on the spot," she interrupted, astounded at his accomplishment. "The inner Temple Square, around the sanctuary itself, is a consecrated area. It's holy ground."

Deucalion shrugged. The incredible feat seemed unimportant now, in light of recent events. "It was something I had to do. I needed firsthand information."

"But how did you understand — ?" Esther stopped, suddenly remembering. "Of course! The night you rescued me I spoke Hebrew, and you answered me in my own language." She stared at him intently, debating with herself. Finally she made a decision. "There's something I must tell you," she whispered, "something I tried to tell you that night in the meadow, but couldn't — because I was afraid."

"Of me?"

"No. I was afraid of what you might think. But now. . . " She paused. She desperately wanted to trust him, but it wasn't easy. "Doras is not my father."

Deucalion frowned.

"That is, he's not my *real* father," she continued rapidly, praying he would understand.

"How could you be so stupid!" Antipas bellowed at Doras like a cobra-spitting venom. "Your own daughter a believer — infected with the damnable blasphemy that is spreading like a plague among our people!"

Doras stood mute before Antipas' rage, seeking refuge in

silence. His face was drawn and haggard, and his whole body seemed on the verge of shaking uncontrollably. *Oh, how bitter the sweet water has turned,* he thought, fighting nausea. *Curse the day that Persian bedouin, with his ebony eyes of fire, came into my life.*

"This is just the sort of thing Caiaphas needs to solidify the support of the Pharisees," continued the Tetrarch as he gathered his robes about him and paced nervously. Even though it was the middle of the afternoon, the room was dark and foreboding, like the lair of a wild animal. After several minutes, he stopped abruptly and whispered in a trembling voice, "The sins of the father . . . "

"What?"

Antipas turned and glared at Doras. There were dark circles beneath his sunken eyes. "Just before my father died, rumors circulated that he in fact was already dead. Believing the rumors to be true, two Pharisee teachers of the law incited a group of their students to climb to the Temple roof, in the middle of the day, and remove a large, solid gold eagle that had been affixed to the front entrance.

"My father had commissioned the huge bird, representing the Imperial Roman Eagle, as a political gesture to Augustus, his benefactor. However, the extremists among the Pharisees decided that the Temple had been desecrated. They claimed that the eagle, being an image of a living creature, violated the Second Commandment forbidding graven images."

"But that's foolishness," interrupted Doras. "The commandment only forbids the *worship* of graven images. Even Solomon's Temple was adorned with figures of bulls, lions and *eagles.*"

"Of course, you idiot, but my father was extremely disliked, and offense was easily taken whether it was justified or not," Antipas said as he walked over to a small table upon which sat a flagon of wine and two leaded goblets. He filled one of the goblets to the top and drank half of it. Some of the wine spilled onto his robe, staining it red, above his heart.

"What happened?"

"The fools hacked the eagle to pieces, while a crowd on the street below cheered them on. My father demanded that the perpetrators present themselves before him. The two teachers and their students, along with a group of notables from the community, appeared before his sickbed."

At this point Antipas did something unexpected: he assumed the role of his dying father, speaking with the voice of a demented, bitter, arrogant old man. "You ungrateful cowards! Not only did I rebuild the magnificence of Solomon's Temple for you, adding to its splendor by reconstructing it as it was in the time of Zerrubbabel, but I also kept the Romans off your backs in the process. I've done more for you in a few short years than the Hasmoneans did in a century. And *this* is how you repay my diligence? What have you to say in your defense?"

Doras was mesmerized, and unnerved, by the performance.

Antipas altered his voice and assumed the role of the two accused teachers. "We agree, Your Majesty. The culprits should be punished, severely. However, it was not us who committed this act of sacrilege against God. It was the students."

The Tetrarch paused and moved close to Doras, then cackled. "Can you guess what happened?" he asked.

Doras shook his head.

"He had them *all* burned alive. Then he dismissed the High Priest. A few days later he died. But it didn't end there. You see, my father had a grander plan — one that was truly worthy of his madness — one that was almost as brilliant as when he ordered the slaughter of every child under the age of two because of a Magi's innocuous inquiry.

"On the eve of his death, he commanded the most important men of the entire Jewish nation to come before him. Then he sealed them up in the Hippodrome and ordered them executed after his death, saying, 'The death of so many important men commensurate with my own passing shall at least afford a respectful mourning at my funeral.' It's no wonder Augustus said of my father, 'It is better to be Herod's hog than his son.'"

Doras' face was white with loathing, and his knees were trembling so much he could barely stand. Reaching the limit of his endurance, he vomited all over the polished marble floor.

Antipas laughed derisively, then retreated to the far corner of the suddenly chilled room.

Doras wiped his mouth and staggered to the table. He poured himself a goblet of wine and drank half of it greedily. "Go ahead and laugh, you wretched excuse for a Jew," he said, setting the half-empty goblet down. "You think I don't know what you are?"

Antipas glared at him, glassy-eyed.

"You're a demon from the pit of *Gehenna*, trapped in a man's body. You cut off the baptist's head because he dared speak the truth — and because you were drunk with passion. You are as vile as your father was, and no amount of circumcision will cleanse you of the poison that rots your soul. How could I have been so blind as to think that you were sincere in your concern for the well-being of our nation? I see now that you harbor an insatiable lust for that which you cannot have. You have given your soul over to darkness; you are beyond any hope of salvation."

"What about you, my power-hungry protégé? Did *you* not seek *me* out? Did you not prevail upon me to join with you in restoring the bite to the toothless Council?" Antipas pointed a plump finger at Doras as he taunted him. "You fool, I was the man who stopped the slaughter my father ordered to elevate his funeral arrangements to a level of worship!" Antipas stumbled around the room, waving his arms as he talked, as if he were fending off an unseen tormentor.

The man is completely mad, thought Doras. *He's talking to the walls.* He refilled his goblet and took several gulps, praying the wine would help his hands stop shaking.

Abruptly Antipas stopped shouting. The sudden quiet was unnerving. Simultaneously the chill in the room deepened, as though it were night and the middle of winter, not day and the height of an unusually hot summer.

Doras shuddered as a sudden, sharp pain racked his chest. He felt lightheaded and weak. His knees buckled, and he crumpled to the floor with his back resting against one leg of the table. The half-filled goblet tumbled from his hand, forgotten in the midst of a sudden realization. He was on the edge of the abyss; he'd waited too long before trying to secure the door to his own soul.

Antipas walked to him and stood over him, gloating. Doras whimpered when he looked up and saw twin ruby-red eyes, like two fiery coals from the white-hot center of a blacksmith's furnace, staring at him. He cried out in agony as something ancient, something horrendously evil, forced its way into his mind. He gagged, then choked, on the stench that filled his nostrils. The stench was worse than the putrefying odor that rose up from the Valley of Hinnom on days when there was no breeze to carry off the smell of burning refuse.

He heard Antipas' words as if from a distance. They were like the dry wind that is the harbinger of a Syrian *sirocco*. "A Jew ruined my marriage. A Jew ruined my relationship with Rome. And by all the gods, a Jew shall restore to me what has been stolen. You will help me or you will die, as the two before you have died — alone and without God answering your plea for mercy. Do you hear what I am saying?"

At this point Doras was willing to say anything to get

whatever had entered his mind out of it. He nodded, not trusting himself to speech.

Antipas stepped back and, as if nothing out of the ordinary
had occurred, said, "Now, where were we in our planning?"

Esther took a deep breath and plunged into her story. "I
always felt there was something special about me, but I never
realized what it was until the night before my twelfth birthday."
She smiled wistfully and played with several strands of her hair.
"Doras sat me down and reminded me that if I were a boy I would
be but one year away from my *bar mitzvah*, one year away from
becoming fully responsible for my behavior under the law.

"He seemed nervous, and that surprised me because he'd
always been in total control of his emotions — except when my
mother died. I asked him if something was wrong. He smiled and
hugged me, something he didn't do very often, and said, 'No,
precious one, there is nothing wrong. I'm just having difficulty
explaining to you that you must be more aware of yourself now
— you must be careful how you behave in public.'"

"I can understand why," interrupted Deucalion. "You're a
very beautiful woman." He reached out and cupped her chin,
then added, "And those eyes of yours — I've never seen eyes
so crystal-green. They sometimes seem to glow."

Esther felt her face color. "I must have gotten them from
my mother — my real mother — because Doras told me that
my real father's eyes were ebony with specks of gold." She
pulled away, suddenly shy, then continued her story. "I told
Doras he had nothing to worry about, that I had no intention
of doing anything to make him ashamed of me. I believed God
had something special for me to do, and I wouldn't let him
down. The next day, for my birthday my father took me to
Tiberias, where we sat for hours in a private hot-water bath."

Deucalion's mind raced. He knew that city was situated

atop the cemetery of the ancient town of Hammath. Strict Jews never went there.

"I know what you're thinking," she said, seeing the shocked look on his face. "But Antipas built the city, and as you know, the Tetrarch and Doras are close friends. It was also before Doras was appointed to the Sanhedrin. Once my father became a member of the Great Council, he became more circumspect in his private life.

"As we sat in the bath, Doras told me how I'd come to be his daughter. I was given the name Esther because I came to be their daughter during the Festival of Purim, on the 13th of Adar, the Fast of Esther. Doras and Rachel had been married for many years, but had remained childless. Finally, in desperation Rachel dedicated herself to fasting before God and asked Him to bless her with a child. She began praying in earnest during the Feast of Weeks."

"When is that?"

"Seven weeks after Passover."

"Ah, Pentecost."

"You know it?"

"Only by name. But I am fascinated by the Hebrew preoccupation with ritual. Tell me about it."

"According to custom, Doras adorned his home with flowers and herbs. He also purified himself by immersing his body in the baths at the Temple and confessing his sins before God. After the evening prayer, he and Rachel went to the synagogue, where the cantor blessed them. Later, when they returned home, they prayed further, and Doras read from the Holy Scriptures throughout the night. The following morning the two of them recited the great Hallel, and Doras read the lesson of the law — the *Maphtir* — from Exodus and the lesson of the prophets from Ezekiel. They repeated the same process again on the second day.

"After the *Musaph* Ritual, just about twilight, Rachel told

Doras that she'd heard from God . . . and that God had promised them a child. They were both overjoyed, and even though they didn't know how or when this would happen, they *believed* and waited patiently for God to fulfill His Word.

"It wasn't until autumn that Rachel announced she was with child. Doras was so certain it was a boy that he decided to name the child Samuel and to dedicate him to the service of God, as Hannah had done with her son."

"Why was he so anxious for a son?"

"Because the firstborn son of a Jew is the priest for the whole family. Also, because of the preservation of the firstborn of Israel, and the death of the firstborn of Egypt, all the firstborn of Israel, both man and animal, belong to Jehovah."

Esther paused, thinking. She remembered something she'd heard at the meeting the night Deucalion rescued her from Saul. The speaker had called Jesus "the firstborn of many." The insight hit her with great impact.

"Go on," prodded Deucalion, returning her to the present.

"Doras purchased an ephod for his son to be, and Rachel set about weaving him a mantle. The Feast of Tabernacles was an especially joyful time for them. It is a time of celebration, of *haq hassuccoth*, the Festival of Tents. Jews give thanks to God in remembrance of the fatherly care and protection of Jehovah while Israel was journeying from Egypt to Canaan. It is also *haq ha'osif*, the Feast of Ingathering; the collecting of the threshed flour and the product of the winepress are symbolic of the labor of the field and the fruit of the earth. Doras and Rachel thanked God for *their* harvest, but their joy was short-lived."

"What happened?"

"Rachel became very sick. She lost the baby in the sixth month of her pregnancy."

"So far along?"

Esther nodded. "They were devastated, Rachel more so

than Doras. She stopped eating and lost a great deal of weight. Finally, fearful for her life, Doras fasted for eleven days and begged God for help."

"Did God answer?"

"Not immediately. Rachel began to eat again, but she never fully regained her strength. Doras decided they needed to leave the city for a while, so they went to Caesarea. That's where they met the bedouin."

"The bedouin?"

"My real father. He was a nomad, and his wife — my real mother — had died giving birth to me. It's an extraordinary story —"

"Wait!" Deucalion interrupted as he looked out the window. "Someone's coming!" In the distance he saw a woman approaching the house.

Esther moved beside him and smiled. "It's only Abigail."

"Your friend?"

She nodded.

Instead of entering the house immediately, the woman went over to her garden and began working in it. Deucalion watched her as she deftly used a hoe to clear away the weeds from her vegetables. As she went about her tasks, selecting fresh cucumbers, leeks, and onions from the garden for dinner, Deucalion said, "Tell me about her, Esther."

"I met Abigail one day when I'd gone to hear Jesus speak. She was standing at the edge of the crowd, with her hands and face covered. I felt drawn to her and decided to introduce myself. As I approached her, I realized why she'd been hanging back. Her body was completely covered with huge white lesions. She was a leper."

Deucalion was stunned. He glanced out the window and stared at Abigail. "But that's impossible! Her skin is like that of a baby's."

"That's true."

"But how — ?"

"Let me finish. Although she was in no physical pain, she was emotionally ravaged. The ostracism from her family and from other people had brought her to the point of total despair. I convinced her I wasn't afraid of her, wondering all the time why I wasn't fearful of catching her disease.

"When she finally allowed me to hold her hand, she wept deeply. Between sobs, she told me that no one, not even other lepers, had touched her in five years! I bought her food and as she ate ravenously, she told me she believed Jesus would heal her. That's why she'd come to see Him."

Deucalion grew pensive at the mention of the Nazarene. He turned from the window and asked, "And was it He who healed her?"

Esther nodded. "With merely a touch. Not long afterwards, he was crucified. I helped Abigail find this house, and I've been paying the rent with money Doras gives me to buy clothes."

"Why doesn't she return to her family?"

"She tried. They want nothing to do with her."

The door opened, and Abigail stepped inside. The straw basket she carried was filled with a variety of plump, juicy vegetables. She eyed Deucalion suspiciously, noting the Roman uniform, but there was no fear. When Deucalion looked into her eyes, he saw the same strength he'd seen on the faces of the men and women at the woodworker's shop before Saul went berserk. What was it about the Galilean that inspired such calmness in the face of the unknown, even after His death?

"This is Deucalion," said Esther.

"The Praetorian who rescued you and Joseph from Saul?"

"Yes."

"Well, he looks like he needs a decent meal," said Abigail, setting down her basket. "If he'll bring me some water from the well, I'll make us a stew."

XVI

Joseph ben Kohath sang to himself as he walked down the road from Bethany. He was on his way to hear the Apostle Peter speak. Filled with joyous expectation, he praised the Lord as he thought about how dramatically his life had changed in a few short weeks.

Pentecost had changed his life forever; he was no longer the confused, tormented man he once had been. Although he had denied the *Christos* once, and although he had been unable to find Jesus in time to tell Him he was prepared to give his life in order to get life, in the end Jesus had found him — through His disciples. He'd sold the land his father had given him and dispersed the funds among the poor and needy. What he had been unwilling to do that day in Bethel, he had later done gladly and with joy in his heart, knowing that the gift he had received far outweighed any gold and silver he could ever acquire.

"Praise be to God," he sang softly to the heavens. "Glory to Him in the highest. Blessed be the rock of my salvation."

So absorbed was he in his worship that he almost missed the old man standing silently and unobtrusively on the side of the road. Moments before the road had been empty. Where had the man come from? Joseph eyed him from head to toe. The stranger appeared to be part of the landscape, and yet oddly the lamb-white robe he was wearing was free of dust and dirt. Further, there wasn't a dwelling within sight, yet the

163

man's feet were as clean as his robe, as if they'd just been washed.

Joseph stopped and wiped the sweat from his brow. The harsh afternoon sun beat down upon the rock-strewn road, and the cloudless, crystalline-blue sky offered no protection from the intense July heat. The stranger didn't seem to notice. In fact, he looked as if he'd just stepped from the pool at Bethesda.

Joseph noticed something else. The man seemed to be *glowing*. The soft, subtle radiance that covered him like a silken cocoon diminished but didn't overpower the natural light. When the man spoke, Joseph gasped. He knew that voice!

"I see the Potter's kiln has dried the glaze perfectly . . . and, as always, the result is magnificent," came the soft, melodious words.

Joseph smiled and chuckled, then walked forward to greet his friend. "You're always speaking to me with words that hold double meaning," he replied affectionately. "For once, however, I think I understand."

Uriel returned the smile but remained silent.

"He *has* done a mighty work in me," continued Joseph, amazed at how different Uriel looked. "I am not the same troubled young man you so patiently and lovingly cared for two months ago."

Uriel's eyes glistened with the same light that permeated the rest of his body. "Indeed you are not, Barnabas," he said.

"You know?"

Uriel nodded.

"But how — ?"

"Does it really matter?"

Joseph shook his head, then blurted out, "Who *are* you?"

Uriel laughed and replied, "Just think of me as a historian of sorts, my young friend."

"What are you doing *here*?"

"Waiting."

"For me?"

Uriel nodded. "Do you have the manuscripts with you?"

"No, but I've left them in good hands," he replied, wondering how Uriel knew he would be on the road from Bethany on this particular day at this particular time. His mind raced, trying to solve the riddle. The seed of an idea had been planted in his mind the morning after their last conversation, when Uriel had disappeared from both the cave and his life. Even though it was almost too incredible to be true, there was no other explanation. And he knew it was *possible*.

Uriel sighed, and Joseph had the feeling he was disappointed. However, when the older man spoke, his voice contained no hint of anxiety, only concern. "The parchments are very important, Barnabas. The chronicle of events has tremendous significance for mankind. They must not fall into the wrong hands." Uriel paused, then added cryptically, "I had hoped you would be the one to make use of the information, but now I realize the Lord has other plans."

"I don't understand."

"Never mind, my young friend. All is as it should be. The Lord will guide you to whomever He has prepared. He will insure that the knowledge isn't lost." Uriel glanced up at the sky and nodded, as if listening to a conversation only he could hear, then looked at Joseph and said with finality, "Good-bye, my friend . . . We shall not meet again."

More words with double meaning, thought Joseph as the air around Uriel began to shimmer with a stronger, more powerful manifestation of the same soft radiance that had flowed from his body. Even though there had been no breeze for several days, the air and the *light* around Uriel began to grow in intensity. It was almost as if the light was *alive*!

Suddenly Joseph was engulfed in a whirlwind of dust. He rubbed his watering eyes, trying to clear them, but to no avail. He could hear music, faintly, but he had no idea where it was

coming from. He strained to see and hear better. No, not music
— singing!

Then, in an instant, the whirlwind was gone, and he was
alone. Dazed, he turned a full circle.

Uriel had vanished!

Joseph's heart began to pound as sudden understanding
flooded his mind. He had his confirmation; he knew who the
old man was.

Smiling with the knowledge, he continued his journey to
Jerusalem, all the while singing "*Hosanna, hosanna, hosanna,*
blessed be the rock, blessed be the rock of my salvation . . . "

In the moments just after sunset, Joseph Caiaphas stood
quietly in the garden of his father-in-law's residence, resting
his back against the trunk of the acacia. The hard, finely-
grained, orange-colored wood felt reassuring against his tired,
aching body.

There were times, and this was one of them, when he felt
as if the weight of authority resting upon his shoulders was a
burden he could no longer bear. Were he Greek or Roman, he
might have likened himself to the mythical Atlas, standing resolute in the heavens, stoically carrying the weight of the
entire world upon his back. Being a Jew, he knew better. The
weight that rested like one of the Alps upon his body was his
conscience.

"I have truly failed them," he sighed aloud to the tree, then
paused and waited patiently, as he'd done in the Hall of Hewn
Stones, listening for a reply. When none came, painful understanding washed over him like a flood: he had no one to blame
for his demise save himself.

On the street below, a child's wail of fear penetrated the
quietness, and the mournful sound triggered something deep

Abigail glanced first at Esther, then at Deucalion, and replied, "The heat has scorched *both* your brains. I just pray we don't run into any centurions who recognize Deucalion."

"Tonight is the last night of the full moon," whispered Pilate to Malkus as they stood together on the balcony of Herod's palace. "Soon the nights will be darker than dark." He paused and sighed, then continued, "The moon is like a fickle woman, Malkus. She gives us the fullness of her beauty but three or four nights out of thirty, and then only from an untouchable distance."

The Procurator stared at the flawed, celestial pearl with sunken eyes. The dark circles under his eyes were so pronounced, he looked bruised.

"How like a chaste yet seductive woman that mysterious orb is," he crooned, as if his words could massage the pain from his aching soul. "She tantalizes us with bits and pieces of her beauty, then disappears and remains hidden from sight just long enough to make us weak with thirst for her return. The process repeats itself again and again, and we, love-starved suitors that we are, hunger for the completion of the seduction. We willingly court destruction, as if ignorance is an elixir that erases memories of unrequited passion. And we hope each time that we shall not be denied the beauty of her silken lustre."

Malkus stood mute, and Pilate watched his eyes flicker with uncertainty. "Come, Malkus, have you nothing to say?" he pressed.

"I await your orders, Procurator."

"Ah yes, my orders." Pilate stroked his chin, then offered a bitter smile. How unlike Deucalion this one was. "Tonight you and I are going to find out what it is about these 'people of the Way,' as they refer to themselves, that has my Commander of the Garrison in such a confused state of mind."

inside the High Priest. He began to weep. Tears cascaded down his cheeks. But there was no wind to dry his face.

When Annas returned from the meeting with his son Jonathan and a small, loyal group of Pharisees, he noticed his son-in-law standing in the garden, slumped against the acacia.

"The time has come . . . " he muttered, watching Caiaphas unnoticed. *I must move carefully, however*, he thought. *There's too much at stake. I cannot allow the Nazarene to achieve with His death what we worked so hard to prevent Him from accomplishing when He was alive.*

After a few moments he turned and silently climbed the stairs to his room, leaving his son-in-law alone with his thoughts and the acacia.

Caiaphas felt a sudden tingling at the nape of his neck and sensed he was being watched. He turned and searched the veranda, straining his eyes in the deepening dark, looking for the eyes he felt watching him from the shadows, but he saw no one. The chimes that hung above the archway were tinkling softly, but there had been no wind for some time. "Ah, the vagaries of power," he whispered. "One is never truly alone, especially in misery."

Esther helped Abigail clear the table and clean up after dinner. Deucalion was outside, drawing another bucket of water with which to wash the bowls and utensils. "There's a special meeting tonight," whispered Abigail to Esther, keeping her eyes on the door. "The Apostle Peter will be there."

Esther frowned. "Why are you whispering?" she asked.

"Deucalion may have rescued you from that madman Saul, but he's still a Praetorian."

Esther walked to the window and stared out into the darkness. "I think I'm in love with him, Abigail. What do you think about that?"

"I think you'd better let me call a physician because you've got to be out of your mind."

Esther laughed. "You're probably right. But whenever he looks at me with those grey-blue eyes of his, I feel overwhelmed with love."

"The heat has gotten to you, Esther. The only permanent mistress a Roman soldier has is the Legion."

"I don't want to be his *mistress*, Abigail."

"What then? His wife?"

"Perhaps."

Abigail shook her head. "You're a Jewess, and you're without a covering now that your father has disowned you. Believe me, you have no idea what it's like being cut off from everything you once took for granted."

Esther grew pensive.

"Until you met me and provided the money for this house, I lived off whatever scraps of food I could find in the Valley of Hinnom. I had to fight other lepers, and wild dogs, just to survive." Abigail shuddered with the memory. "Fortunately, even though you're an outcast, at least you're not a leper. But it's still going to be difficult."

"I know, but —"

"No, you *don't* know. What about money? How are you going to buy food and keep paying the rent on this house now that Doras is no longer giving you money?"

"I — I hadn't thought of that," stammered Esther, sobered by the harsh reality she heard in her friend's voice. She suddenly felt like a foolish child. "I suppose I could find work . . ."

Abigail sighed heavily. "I'm sorry, Esther. I didn't mean to attack you. After all you've done for me, I had no right talking to you that way." She began to weep. "It's just that I'm frightened, Esther. What's going to happen to us? I can't go back to living the way I was when you met me. You have no idea how horrible it was."

Esther walked over and put her arms around Abigail in comfort. In spite of her own momentary fear and confusion, she was suddenly calm. She heard a still small voice inside her, speaking to her, telling her not to fear. It was the same voice she'd heard the night Saul had tried to kill her. "All's well, Abigail," she said confidently. "The Lord will provide. He will not forsake us."

"How can you be so sure?"

The door opened, and Deucalion stepped into the room, carrying a bucket full of water. "Be sure of what?" he asked, setting the bucket down.

"That everything is going to be all right," answered Esther, wiping away Abigail's tears with the corner of her apron.

"Oh?"

"There's a meeting tonight in the city. Abigail and I are going, and we'd like you to come with us."

Abigail stared at Esther as if she'd truly gone insane.

"What kind of meeting?" asked Deucalion, frowning.

"The people of the Way are gathering to listen to one of Jesus' disciples speak. A man called Peter."

"I've heard the name before." Deucalion stared hard at Esther, then glanced at Abigail. "You realize, of course, that Saul might well show up again," he added, wondering why he wasn't vehemently arguing against such a foolish proposal. "And I can hardly escort two believers to an illegal meeting dressed as I am," he finished, softening his tone.

Esther smiled, realizing that Deucalion had just said yes. "The Lord will protect us against Saul if he shows up, just as he did the other night," she said. "And as for your clothes, I'm sure we can find something that will fit you, can't we, Abigail?"

XVII

Deucalion, Esther and Abigail worked their way to the front of the crowded courtyard, where perhaps a hundred people had gathered to listen to the tall, heavy-set man with thick, callused hands.

Abigail had found an old tunic and a cloak that fit Deucalion rather well, and he was certain no one would recognize him from a distance. He also wore a girdle around his middle so it would be easier to walk. It had a pouch on the inner seam in which he'd placed the small bag of money that had been thrown at him the night he'd been ambushed. He'd yet to spend any of it, however. But now he knew what he was going to do with it. After the meeting he would give the money to Esther; she would need it now that Doras had disowned her.

He wondered if Esther was as conscious of his presence as he was of hers. She stood to his left, and whenever her bare arm brushed against him, he felt a tingling sensation ripple through his arm. Also, he could swear that she smelled of frankincense.

A number of lanterns had been placed around the perimeter of the courtyard, and the flickering light shone in the faces of the crowd. Esther saw Joseph clearly and waved at him. When he saw her, he smiled and motioned for her to find him when the meeting was over. She nodded her agreement.

Deucalion had been extremely nervous at first and had constantly searched for any sign of trouble. But the man called Peter had been speaking for almost an hour, and nothing out of the ordinary had happened. Even though the apostle was obviously unschooled — a fisherman, someone had said—his words held power. No one in the audience seemed restless, and now Deucalion too found himself captivated by Peter's forceful words.

" . . . no doubt some of you are familiar with the story, but I'd like to share it with you anyway, because it holds special meaning for all of us.

"Jesus had a close friend named Lazarus, and there seemed to be a spiritual bond between the two of them that transcended the flesh.

"Not long before our Lord was crucified, He was ministering outside of Judea, somewhere beyond the Jordan, when He received news that Lazarus was sick . . . on the verge of death. Instead of leaving immediately for Bethany, as we who were with Him expected him to do, He waited a full two days before returning to Bethany. Thomas questioned Him about this, and Jesus answered by saying that Lazarus' sickness was not unto death, but would be for the glory of God."

Deucalion realized that Peter's story was tugging at his soul, pulling him to memories of another tomb. *What is it that is so compelling about this man's words?* he wondered, then shook his head and again focused his attention on the disciple.

"When Jesus finally decided it was time to return to Judea, some of us tried to talk Him out of the journey. We were fearful because there were Jews who had tried to stone Him to death on previous occasions and would most likely try again, given the opportunity. Jesus was unconcerned and rebuked us for our fears.

"When we pressed Him to tell us why He insisted on returning, He said Lazarus had died and that He was glad for our sakes, because we would now have yet another opportunity to exercise our faith and believe that He was who He said He was. Thomas again spoke up and said, 'Let us also go, that we may die with You, Lord.'

"By the time we arrived in Bethany, Lazarus had been dead and buried four days. His corpse was beginning to stink in the sweltering heat, and we could smell the stench ten cubits away from the stone sepulchre. His sisters, Mary and Martha, were beside themselves with grief. Jesus wept."

Peter was overcome with emotion at this point and struggled to keep his voice from wavering. He regained his composure and continued, "I saw Jesus stand before the tomb of His friend and heard Him pray to the Father. Then He called out in a loud, commanding voice: *'Lazarus . . . come forth!'*

"The mourners stopped their weeping and gasped." Peter's voice rose with fervency. "I tell you now that Lazarus — still wrapped in burial linen — stepped from the darkness of the tomb into the light of day."

Deucalion felt the hairs on the back of his neck rise. A tingling sensation surged through his body. All around him, people murmured and began crying and praising God.

The apostle scanned the gathering with penetrating brown eyes and concluded by saying, "Brothers and sisters, I fervently beseech you to gird up the loins of your minds; be sober, and hope to the end for the grace that is brought unto us at the revelation of Jesus, the Anointed One. We can all partake of the divine nature and escape the corruption that is in the world because of lust. Even as He who has called us is holy, so we also must be holy, because it is written, 'be holy, for I am holy.'

"We are not redeemed with corruptible things, such as silver and gold, from the vain citizenship we inherited by tradition from our fathers. We are redeemed with the precious blood of the *Christos*, the Lamb without spot or blemish.

"It is through Him that we believe in God, who raised Him

up from the dead and gave Him glory, that our faith and hope might be in God. Purify your souls, obey the truth through the Spirit, and love one another with a pure heart, fervently. All flesh is as grass, and all the glory of man is as the flower of grass. The grass withers, and the flower falls away. But the Word of the Lord endures forever. And this is the Word which, by the spreading of good news, is preached unto you."

Deucalion suddenly felt lightheaded. Could it be so simple? Could there be one, eternal God who cared so profoundly for man that He'd sent his Son to die for man? Peter's words struck a chord that lay tautly strung within the Praetorian. Instantly guilt assailed him, and it was all he could do to keep from weeping. Again he saw a vision of the tomb. *What have I done?* he asked silently, remembering that fateful afternoon.

Beside him, Esther asked, "Are you feeling ill? You don't look well."

"I've got to get out of here, Esther. I feel like I'm suffocating."

Esther searched his eyes and recognized the same look she'd seen on his face that night in the meadow. She knew that something horrible, something he couldn't speak about, was tormenting him. "Abigail and I must talk with Joseph. We can meet you later. There's a stable not far from here."

Deucalion nodded, then grasped her hand in his. "Be careful, Esther. I don't want anything to happen to you."

"We have to hurry, Esther," whispered Abigail, tugging at her arm. "Peter and Joseph are leaving."

Esther's heart was fluttering. She wanted to say something more, but Deucalion had already disappeared into the thinning crowd. She watched him go, certain that she cared about him. But how much? Abigail's stinging words lingered in her mind: "*The only permanent mistress a Roman soldier has is the Legion.*"

She realized she would just have to be patient and trust

the Lord. "Yes, Abigail, let us go," she said, pulling her veil over her face so she wouldn't be recognized.

Unnoticed, Pilate and Malkus observed the gathering of believers from the shadows. Malkus appeared bored, but Pilate seemed almost hypnotized.

"He sounds just like the Galilean," mumbled the Procurator.

"What?"

Pilate snapped from his daze. "I said the speaker sounds just like the Galilean."

Malkus grunted. "If you ask me, I think the whole thing is a hoax."

"What are you talking about?"

"I was at the tomb, with Deucalion, and I inspected the sepulchre the morning the body supposedly disappeared. The only evidence that the Nazarene's body had actually been there was a bloodied piece of linen."

"So?"

Malkus shrugged. "We never actually saw the body placed in the tomb. The sepulchre was already sealed by the time we arrived."

"But what about the stone? And the light? Deucalion told the Tribunal that the stone had been rolled away and that there was an odd, almost blinding white light *before* the sun came up."

"I don't have answers to those questions; but I do know that I watched Deucalion pierce the Nazarene's side with a spear while He was still on the cross, and I saw blood and water come from the wound and splatter him. The man was dead, Pilate — of *that* I am certain."

Pilate watched the crowd, then gasped and stepped forward in order to see better.

"What is it?"

"Quiet! Do you want us to be seen?" Pilate motioned for Malkus to step up beside him and pointed. "There, near the front, between those two women   Tell me, do you recognize the man?"

Malkus strained to see in the flickering light. "Deucalion!" he whispered.

Just then the man with the bushy black beard stopped talking and the crowd began to disperse. Pilate and Malkus watched Deucalion talking with the two women he'd been standing between. When the Praetorian turned to leave, Pilate said, "You follow the women . . . I'll take Deucalion."

Malkus nodded.

"And, Malkus, not a word of this to anyone."

"As you wish, Procurator."

"Good. Report to me in the morning."

"Hail Caesar," replied Malkus as he turned and melted into the night.

Pilate watched him go, a resigned look on his face. He mumbled, "Hail Caesar."

Deucalion waited anxiously for Esther at the stable, wishing he'd stayed with her. There was no telling what might happen with that madman Saul roaming about the city. While he waited, he thought about the events of the past two years, the chain of circumstances that had brought him to Jerusalem and to this place in time.

He'd been a member of the personal staff of guards assigned to Lucius Vitellius, Governor of Syria. Because of Deucalion's dedication to the Legion, Vitellius had given him the responsibility of selecting exceptional soldiers from among various auxiliary units to be trained as Praetorians. Then, just over a year before, he'd met the man who'd irrevocably

changed his life. He remembered the day as if it were only yesterday.

Lucius Aelius Sejanus, Commander of the Praetorian
Guard, stood stoically next to Vitellius in the hot Syrian sun
and watched Deucalion training his men, then finally called
out in a gruff voice, "Deucalion Cincinnatus Quinctus, stand
before me."

He'd complied, sweat dripping off his bare chest and arms,
while Sejanus scrutinized him. The commander said, "You
have a rather unusual name, young man. Greek, isn't it?"

"My mother was Greek, sir, and she favored the gods.
Deucalion was the son of Prometheus, King of Phthia."

"Aha, I see," Sejanus said. "How like a mother to wish her
son to be a king."

"Actually Prometheus was the first champion of mankind,"
continued Deucalion, brashly ignoring the jab. "Not only did
he beat old Zeus at his own game, which caused the angry god
to hide the knowledge of fire-making from mankind, but he
stole fire from Heaven and brought it back to earth."

"And what about your father?"

"Roman — and a soldier, of course."

"You see, I told you he was special," interjected Vitellius.
"Praetorians are a breed apart, Sejanus. And this one, if
selected, would be even more so."

Deucalion had been surprised by his superior's compli-
ment, but he knew better than to let his excitement show.

"His arrogance is tempered with logic," continued the
Governor. "And I find his candid observations most refreshing.
Whatever he calls himself, he's a soldier born and bred. It's in
his blood."

"I'll think about it, Vitellius," conceded Sejanus as he
turned to leave.

Knowing that Sejanus was famed for hyperbole laced with
a dash of satire, Deucalion had been determined to make a

final impression. "Cincinnatus was *not* my father's name," he said boldly.

Sejanus stopped and turned slowly.

Several centurions had been milling around, trying not to appear curious, yet obviously interested in the conversation. Deucalion eyed them covertly, knowing they were all well acquainted with his biting wit . . . and his arrogance. Now that he was verbally dueling with the infamous Sejanus, he realized they wanted to see how he would fare. "He's done it now," he heard one named Malkus mutter, continuing, "Sejanus can be cruel when he gets angry."

The smile on Vitellius' face disappeared.

"Cincinnatus was retired and living on his farm when war broke out between Rome and a brutal, tough mountain tribe from central Italy," Deucalion continued. "A Roman army, untrained and under incompetent leadership, was trapped by the fierce Aequi; it was feared they would be slaughtered.

"The former consul from Rome, then sixty, took up his armor and resumed office at the request of the people. Gathering a small force of local herdsmen and farmers, he defeated the Aequi, completely demoralizing them after sixteen days of intense conflict. For his efforts he was rewarded a Triumph by the people." He paused, hoping he hadn't pushed too hard.

"Go on, finish it . . . tell us the rest," prodded Vitellius.

"Like the good Roman he was, Cincinnatus once again resigned his consulship, there being no further need for his services. Not wanting to burden the people with additional expense, he returned to his retirement and his farm beyond the Tiber."

The three men stood in the hot sun for several minutes, caught like insects in the spiderweb of silence. Finally Sejanus smiled. "And just who was this Cincinnatus?"

"My great-grandfather, sir."

"I see . . . " replied the consul as though he really did see this time. Abruptly he slapped the Governor on the back. "I think you're absolutely right, Vitellius. We most certainly have the makings of an exceptional soldier in our midst. See to it that he is appointed to the Guard immediately."

In the darkness of the stable a horse snorted loudly, jerking Deucalion into the present. "Take it easy, boy," he whispered, "you'll give me away." The animal quieted, and Deucalion returned to his thoughts.

That was how he'd come to be in Palestine. Vitellius, ever mindful of political opportunities, had sent him here to help the beleaguered Procurator of Judea curb the rise of civil disobedience. His specific orders had been to train an elite unit to eliminate the rebel leaders, and those orders had suited Pontius Pilate just fine. The Procurator wanted the Judean problem lifted from his back. And he would do whatever it took to eradicate the politically disastrous mark with which he'd been branded as a result of his failures in Palestine. In spite of the fact that Pilate harbored a passionate hatred of the Jews, he detested his estrangement from Rome even more; and even though he despised Antipas, he believed he knew the Tetrarch's political weaknesses well enough to manipulate him.

"Antipas' devotion to his Faith is a contrived affiliation," Pilate had told Deucalion just the other night. "His lust for power is another matter altogether, however."

"I don't understand."

"It's quite simple, really. Herod can't help himself. Most men simply *covet* power. Antipas is *addicted*. And I intend to use that weakness against him."

"How?"

"Given the opportunity, Antipas will sacrifice everything, including his Faith, to sit at the helm of the Hebrew ship of state. I intend to see he has that opportunity."

"But why must *we* become involved?"

"Because, my friend, once Antipas controls the Sanhedrin, I will have the Jews right where I want them. You see, whoever controls the addict's source of supply, controls the addict. And there is no power in Palestine, indeed in the known world, without Roman occupation."

At the time Pilate's words made sense. Now Deucalion wasn't so sure. He'd experienced another kind of power tonight — the power of faith. And it had shaken him to the very depths of his being.

Out of the darkness a man's voice called to him, startling him. "Deucalion?"

"Who goes there?" he asked, suddenly wishing he'd brought a weapon.

Pilate stepped into the light provided by a lone lantern and faced his Commander of the Garrison. "What in the name of the gods are you doing here dressed like that?" he asked, obviously angry.

Deucalion's mind raced. He knew he mustn't act shocked at seeing the Procurator disguised in a hooded robe and in the stable with him. Pilate never did anything without purpose and planning. If the Procurator knew he was here in the stable, he also knew he'd been at the meeting. "I was doing a bit of spying, Pontius," he replied, uncomfortable because he was lying.

Pilate appraised him with hooded eyes. "I see," he said and walked over to one of the horses and began stroking the animal's neck. "You seemed very friendly with that dark-haired woman. Is she one of *them*?"

"Have you been spying on *me*?"

"Not exactly, Commander. But I'd be lying if I didn't say I've had some serious doubts about your loyalty since our last conversation."

"So you followed me here. Why?"

"So we could talk — away from eyes and ears who might be far less sympathetic to your plight."

"Oh?"

"Come now, Deucalion. I know you better than you think. In fact, I know you well enough to say I'm positive that the woman I saw you talking to tonight was the same woman you rescued from Saul. Am I right?"

"Perhaps."

Pilate sighed and stopped stroking the horse. There were several bales of hay piled against one corner of the stable, and he walked over and sat down on top of them. "I know about Doras' failure in the Sanhedrin — and that his daughter, Esther, was the woman you supposedly took to the garrison for questioning. Only neither of you ever arrived."

"You don't understand —"

"Let me finish, Deucalion, then tell me I don't understand," barked Pilate. "I can't believe you're prepared to throw away a promising career in the Guard because of a woman. A Jewess, no less. If you must have her, then take her. But by all the gods, be discreet. I have enough problems without having to deal with rumors that my Commander of the Garrison has fallen for a Jewess."

"Esther is not just another woman."

Pilate arched his brow. "Oh?"

"Why did you marry Claudia, Pontius? Was it just because of who her father was?"

"Of course. Why else?"

"For love."

Pilate snorted. "Love? Certainly you don't expect me to believe that you have come to love this woman?"

Deucalion pondered the Procurator's question. Until this moment he hadn't named his feeling for Esther. But yes, he *did* love her. "What's so wrong with that?"

Pilate waved his hand impatiently. "There is no power in

love. Love only saps the strength of a man — and distracts him from what is important."

"And what *is* important, Pontius?"

"Political power, of course."

"You're beginning to sound like Antipas."

"May the gods take you, Deucalion," Pilate spat. "First you claim the Nazarene rose from the dead, and now you tell me you've fallen in love with a Jewess who believes the same preposterous story."

Deucalion flinched. "So that's what this is truly all about . . . the Nazarene. I had hoped that perhaps you at least believed me when I told you what transpired at the tomb."

"Listen to me, Deucalion. It doesn't matter what *I* believe. The case is closed. The Tribunal determined that the Galilean's body was stolen by thieves — very likely His own disciples — in order to promote rebellion among the populace."

"You weren't there, Pontius. I was."

"And so was Malkus."

"What does he have to do with this?"

"He thinks the whole thing is a hoax."

"A hoax?"

"You find that preposterous?"

Deucalion laughed harshly, and Pilate felt as if he'd been slapped in the face. "Do you remember when you asked me what happened to my hand, the morning after I'd dined with Doras, and I told you that I had been attacked by some men?"

Pilate nodded.

"You also asked me if they were Jews."

"And you told me they weren't."

"That's correct."

"So?"

"They were centurions, Pontius. That is, I'm sure at least three of the four were."

Pilate jumped to his feet. "That's impossible."

"So was what I witnessed on the third morning of guard duty at the tomb of the Nazarene. But both happened."

Pilate groaned. "I curse the day Sejanus appointed me to rule over this stretch of desert. And I curse the day I allowed the Jews to manipulate me into crucifying the Nazarene. But by all the gods, I swear I shall have my revenge." He stared at Deucalion. Light from a lantern flickered in the darkness, turning his eyes to glittering ice. "Don't make me curse the day *you* came into my life too."

Deucalion knew he was being asked to make a choice. What was it Peter had said? *"We can all partake of the divine nature and escape the corruption that is in the world because of lust."*

Pilate coveted power, just as his archenemy Antipas did. But Deucalion realized *he* couldn't choose that path, because now he saw clearly that at its end lay only destruction. Nevertheless, he decided to make one last effort to get through to the man who had treated him as a son.

"Revenge isn't the answer, Pontius," he said compassionately.

"No? What then?"

"Forgiveness."

Pilate stared at him as if he'd uttered a curse. "You *have* become infected with their rot, haven't you?"

"No, Pontius, I have not become *infected*. For the first time in my life I feel *clean*. Totally clean."

Pilate adjusted his robe, then stepped toward the narrow street outside the stable. He turned and said, "I'm going to pretend we never had this conversation. I expect to see you at the garrison first thing tomorrow morning. We have much to do." With that, he disappeared into the night.

Deucalion stared into the darkness, reviewing the conversation. An astounding insight shook him to the core of his soul. Pilate had said it didn't matter what *he* believed about what happened at the tomb. Did the Procurator know the truth but wouldn't, or perhaps couldn't, admit it? Because if he did, he would be accountable. And if he was accountable, he would have to answer to an authority that was much higher, and much more powerful, than Caesar.

Deucalion knew he wouldn't be at the garrison in the morning. That part of his life was over. Something in Peter's words had pierced his emotional armor, and instead of injuring him, it was as if a burden he'd been carrying on his back for as long as he could remember was suddenly lifted. He wasn't sure what he was going to do, but he did know that as soon as he saw Esther he was going to tell her of his decision to accept her God as his own.

XVIII

The two women and the Praetorian arrived at Abigail's house just before midnight, unaware that Malkus had followed them from the city. They went inside, where Abigail lit a solitary lantern, then said, "It's been a long day, and I'm very tired. I'll see you two in the morning." She handed the lantern to Esther, who placed it on the table and sat down. Deucalion joined her.

Abigail had barely disappeared from sight when the door opened and Joseph entered the house.

Deucalion looked up and said, "I don't believe it —"

Joseph smiled. "We meet again, Commander," he said as he closed and latched the door behind him.

"What do you mean 'meet again'?" asked Esther. "You were barely conscious the night Deucalion helped us escape from Saul."

"That's true, Esther, but the commander and I had met prior to that night — the morning after the crucifixion."

"At the Nazarene's tomb . . . " mumbled Deucalion.

"Yet you didn't recognize Joseph the night you rescued us?"

"I was more interested in you than Joseph," confessed Deucalion.

"That's quite understandable," quipped Joseph.

"But, Joseph, you don't seem surprised to see *him* here," prodded Esther, staring at her friend.

Joseph shrugged. "I saw the commander at the meeting tonight — with you. I assumed he must be one of us now."

"Please, call me Deucalion — I'm no longer Commander of Pilate's Praetorian Guard —"

"What?" exclaimed Esther.

"And after tomorrow morning I'll be a rogue soldier — a hunted man."

"But why?" Esther inquired.

"Because I've chosen to defy the Procurator's orders . . . and because I know too much."

The room grew suddenly silent. Joseph walked over to the table and sat down on a small stool across from Esther and Deucalion.

Esther's mind was racing. *What is going to happen to us now?* Suddenly an idea came to her. "All three of us are outcasts," she said, breaking the silence. "Consequently we, like many others, are without family or friends save those who believe as we do."

Esther paused, surprised at herself. She couldn't remember ever being as bold and confident as she was now. Joseph and Deucalion were listening attentively, and she saw curiosity and encouragement in their eyes. Relieved, she continued, "As long as Caiaphas and the Council, including my father, continue to ignore the truth — that Jesus was who He claimed to be — the nation of Israel will continue to suffer. And if Rome continues to view us as insurgent rebels, with no respect for authority — secular or religious— there will be no end to the slaughter of innocent men, women and children."

"What are you suggesting?" asked Deucalion.

"Somehow we must make both the Sanhedrin and Rome see that this insane hatred of one another cannot continue. We have to find a way to open the eyes of both Caiaphas and Pilate before it's too late."

In the ensuing silence, an odd kind of stillness settled over

Deucalion, Esther and Joseph. A soft haze permeated the dining area. Deucalion had the same feeling he'd had the night he was ambushed — like he'd had too much wine, only he had had none to drink. He looked at Esther, who was suddenly subdued. Her eyes shimmered with a sparkling luminescence; they looked like two agates lying in a stream of rushing water, reflecting the brilliant sunlight. Then he stared at Joseph, the man he'd once thought was a thief come to rob the grave of a dead man. He realized now just how foolish that thought had been.

Joseph was pensive. Esther's prophetic words struck a chord deep within him. As she'd talked, part of his mind had been on his conversations with Uriel — first at the edge of the Great Salt Sea, then later on the road from Bethany. Now understanding flooded his mind. "Before you continue," he said softly, "there's something you should know, Esther. I'm one of the disciples now."

"That's wonderful!"

"Yes, it is, although I'm a little surprised at how fast things have been happening. I've even been given a new name — Barnabas."

"'Son of prophecy,'" translated Deucalion.

"You know Aramaic?" asked Joseph.

"A little."

"He also speaks *a little* Hebrew," interjected Esther mischievously.

Deucalion frowned at her, but said nothing.

The glimmer of an idea began to grow in Joseph as he digested the information. "Can you *read* Hebrew?" he asked abruptly.

"Not as well as I speak it, but well enough to understand what's written."

Joseph made a decision. But before he told Deucalion and Esther what he was thinking, there was one very important matter to be taken care of. "I think I understand now why Peter shared his story about Lazarus," he said. "We have all had an intense personal experience with the Lord Jesus, the *Christos*. And each of us has had our lives resurrected, even as Lazarus was raised from the dead. Even though we haven't experienced physical death, as he did, we are truly dead to the lives we once lived —"

"You're mistaken," interrupted Deucalion, suddenly agitated. "*I* haven't experienced such a moment as you describe."

Joseph — Barnabas — glanced at Deucalion with understanding and compassion. "When we met — at the tomb — were you not there to insure that Jesus' body would remain undisturbed? And three days later, didn't you experience something you didn't understand?"

"But how —"

"*How* I know isn't important. What is important is that you share that experience with us."

"Now?"

Barnabas nodded.

Deucalion recounted what had happened at the tomb during the morning of the third day of his guard duty. When he finished, Esther said, "To think you were there when he rose from the dead! How wonderful!" She stared at him, wondering why he seemed so sullen. He should be excited — *the Lord had spoken directly to him.*

"There's something more you haven't told us, isn't there?" said Barnabas, reading Deucalion like an open book.

Deucalion stood and walked over to the window, staring out into the blackness of the night. After several minutes he whispered, "It was *my* spear that pierced the Nazarene's side."

"What did you say?" asked Esther, her stomach suddenly tied in knots.

Deucalion turned. He looked defeated, broken. "I was the one who made certain Jesus was dead," he said in a hollow voice.

"Yet the Lord spoke to you and comforted you when He rose from the dead three days later," said Barnabas. "He *forgave* you."

"I don't deserve to be forgiven."

"None of us *deserves* what the Lord freely gives by grace. If we received what we deserved, we'd all be in *Gehenna*."

Deucalion remembered that Pilate had said something about *Gehenna* a few weeks ago. "What is *Gehenna*?" he asked.

"Physically, it's the Valley of Hinnom."

"The narrow ravine southwest of the city?" exclaimed Deucalion, remembering bits and pieces of his dream.

Barnabas nodded. "It separates Mount Zion from the Hill of Evil Counsel and the Plain of Rephaim. Unfortunately, we Jews suffered under a number of our own idolatrous kings before coming under Caesar. From the time of Solomon, infants were sacrificed to the fire-god Molech, until Josiah rendered the ravine's depths unclean by spreading human bones over it. Afterwards it came to be known by its spiritual name; it is a place of eternal torment."

"I feel like I'm there now."

"You can put an end to that feeling forever," Esther said softly, wanting desperately to take his pain from him.

"But I *killed* him," groaned Deucalion, feeling like his soul was being torn asunder.

"No, brother, that's a lie," Barnabas said forcefully. "He *chose* to *give* His life at the appointed time so we might never die."

"Never die?"

Esther smiled. "To be absent from the body is to be present with the Lord — in Paradise."

Deucalion's eyes flickered between Esther and Barnabas. They didn't hate him? There was hope for him yet then. "What must I do?" he asked humbly.

"Admit your sin, and ask Jesus into your life," answered Barnabas.

"And confess with your mouth that you believe Jesus was the Son of God and that He died on the cross that you might live," finished Esther.

Esther and Barnabas closed their eyes and began to pray out loud. At first Deucalion understood what they were saying; but after a few moments the words rushing out of their mouths sounded odd, incomprehensible. He had the strangest feeling that they were speaking a special language. In fact, it occurred to him that they might be speaking the very language of God.

Overwhelmed by the idea, and overcome with emotion, he bowed his knee, as he'd seen soldiers do when surrendering on the battlefield, closed his eyes, and called upon the Lord to forgive him.

The haze thickened, and the room filled imperceptibly with the scent of frankincense.

For the first time in his life Deucalion felt as if he were truly loved. He began to weep. And instead of fighting the emotion, he gave himself over to it, without reservation, feeling as if he'd been washed clean of every foul thing he'd ever experienced. He kept muttering, "Thank You, Lord. I praise Your holy name . . . "

Barnabas was the first to open his eyes. He watched Esther and Deucalion praying together for several minutes. Just before they both opened their eyes, Esther knelt down beside Deucalion and grasped his hand in hers. Then they stood up together, arm in arm.

"Uriel was right — I've found my answer," Barnabas said, eyeing them appreciatively.

"What answer?" asked Esther.

"Now that neither of you can return to Jerusalem, what will the two of you do?"

"My face is well-known in Judea and Syria," replied Deucalion, realizing he hadn't really given the problem much thought. "Pilate will send word to the garrisons throughout Palestine to watch for me. It will be difficult to hide from the probing eyes of Rome. Alive, I'm a dangerous liability — not only to the Procurator, but to the Empire as well. Truth revealed is more frightening to the elite of Rome than an army of men knocking at their doors."

"And more difficult for the Sanhedrin to deal with than a backslidden Jew," added Esther.

"Don't be so quick to mock the elders, Esther," scolded Barnabas. "We serve the same God — it's just that they don't believe He has already fulfilled His promise to send the *masiyach*."

"Moses believed and confronted Pharaoh. Lot believed and was saved from the destruction of Sodom and Gomorrah. Joshua believed, and the walls of Jericho fell. Why won't my father and the others believe?"

"Because they are men whose vision of God is molded from their fear of living lives without worth or purpose," suggested Deucalion. "Your priests serve God to the degree it pleases their sense of ritual. For them, tradition has replaced faith. Men like Caiaphas and Doras have become hardened to the truth. Their unwillingness to change masks their unbelief."

"I don't understand."

"Without tradition and ritual they slowly starve, like a man without food. At first the body survives by getting nourishment from the excess it has stored; once those reserves are depleted, the body begins to feed upon itself. The less important organs are sacrificed first, in an attempt to protect the more vital ones. If no new nourishment is forthcoming, the flesh dies. It is no less with the spirit."

Barnabas and Esther were stunned by Deucalion's assessment. Neither had known the Praetorian for very long, but both knew that he was now a very different man than when they had first met him.

"The Jews aren't alone in their narrow-mindedness," he continued, excited by the sudden realizations flooding his mind. "The night I first saw you, Esther — at your father's house — I was ambushed as I returned to the garrison by four men dressed as centurions. I never got a good look at any of them, and even though each spoke to me, at the time I didn't recognize any of their voices. One voice did seem familiar, however, and I learned later who it was. But I wasn't sure until this moment that I had recognized yet another voice."

"Why would centurions attack *you*?" asked Barnabas?

"I've asked myself that same question a hundred times."

"Well?" prodded Esther.

"It was Annas who led the other three."

"Annas!" exclaimed Barnabas. "Are you certain?"

"Absolutely."

"And the other voice you recognized?"

"My second-in-command, Malkus."

"This is incredible! A former High Priest and a Roman Praetorian working together. But why?"

"Since the crucifixion certain members of the Sanhedrin have been conspiring with high-ranking members of the Legion to keep the truth about the resurrection of Jesus from the populace. They're afraid of what might happen if they admit that Jesus was who He claimed to be. They're afraid they will lose their power."

"But we cannot just sit by and watch them slaughter innocent people in order to protect their authority," said Esther, angry at the thought of such self-serving brutality.

"I may have a solution," said Barnabas as he picked up the bundle of leather parchments entrusted to him by Uriel and set them on the table.

XIX

"And I followed the three of them for over an hour," said Malkus, delivering his report to Pilate. The sun had only been up for half an hour — unlike the Procurator, who had never really slept — and it was already over 90 degrees.

"Well?" prodded Pilate, sweating profusely.

"They stopped and went inside a house just off the road to Bethany, about eight furlongs from the city. A short time later they were joined by another man."

"And you're absolutely certain it was Deucalion with the two women?"

Malkus nodded.

"By the gods . . . " muttered Pilate, suddenly distraught. "Why does he tempt me so?"

"Your orders, Procurator?"

Pilate snapped from his reverie. "I'm promoting you to Commander of the Garrison, and I'm ordering that Deucalion be killed on sight. You are to find him and deal with him immediately. He has betrayed not only me, but Rome as well."

"What about the Syrian Governor?"

"Vitellius has notified me he has 'washed his hands' of this rogue Praetorian." Pilate grimaced, remembering he'd spoken the same words when the Nazarene was brought before him. "The Governor also made it unmistakably clear that he will similarly wash his hands of *me* if I fail." He glared at his new commander. "Need I say more?"

"No," replied Malkus grimly. "I will not fail you."

"Good," Pilate said, forcing a note of confidence into his voice that he didn't feel in his heart. Malkus was no Deucalion. The Procurator had the distressing feeling that Malkus harbored a "lone wolf" mentality — an attitude that could prove dangerous. Even though this was Judea, and even though Sejanus had been dead and buried two years, the Senate had a very long arm.

Rome still suffered under the judicial turbulence of the days of "treason trials." A scroll would arrive from Capri, where Tiberius lived in self-imposed exile, with charges of complicity in the Sejanian conspiracy, usually on the basis of slim evidence. If the Senate found the man guilty, he was executed — or allowed to commit suicide. There were many among the most prominent of Rome's pyramidal hierarchy who lived in daily dread of being cited for *maiestas* — treason against State and Emperor.

It wasn't just that Pilate's record in Palestine left much to be desired in the eyes of his superiors. No, what he worried about most was that Sejanus himself had appointed him Procurator of Judea.

Pilate eyed Malkus appraisingly. He needed to know what motivated this man. "Tell me what you think," he commanded.

Malkus spoke hesitantly at first, until he realized the Procurator was no longer frowning. Then he grew bold. "Many of us in the Legion, particularly those of us who were with Deucalion on guard duty at the tomb of the Nazarene, have felt for some time that his behavior was suspect."

Pilate grimaced. In spite of his order to kill Deucalion, he still felt anguish. Ironically, he wasn't sure whether he was more angry at Deucalion for failing him or at himself for cultivating such a deep friendship.

"As you are well aware, Procurator," continued Malkus,

"Deucalion was the only one of us who refused to accept the Tribunal's finding that the Nazarene's body had been stolen. It's clear that the theft was orchestrated by the Nazarene's followers in order to arouse the populace into rebellion — by claiming that their 'king' had risen from the dead. Deucalion was adamant that he would not participate in any attempt to discredit that idea." Malkus paused, then added, "I believe Deucalion was *convinced* the Jew had indeed risen from the dead."

Pilate's eyes went vacant as color drained from his face. But he said nothing. Malkus wasn't sure if he was more uncomfortable with the silence or with the vacuous stare on Pilate's face. Deciding it was the former that worried him most, he said, "Ironically, it was a Jew who provided us with a solution —"

"A Jew?" interrupted Pilate in a hollow voice. His head jerked spasmodically, as if it were a ball hanging on the end of a piece of twine being swatted by a playful cat.

"But . . . but I thought you knew. It's not possible that you didn't," stammered Malkus, wondering how he was going to get himself out of the very deep hole he seemed to have unwittingly stumbled into.

"Tell me *everything*," demanded the Procurator.

Suddenly nauseous, Malkus complied. "About a month after the Tribunal handed down its findings — early in June, I think — a heavy-set man approached me in the market. It was crowded, and I didn't notice him until he was standing right beside me. Actually, I *smelled* him before I saw him."

"What?"

"He was heavily scented, almost to the point of making me gag — like he'd just stepped out of the baths."

"Go on."

"He called me by name, and that surprised me more than his furtive approach, because I had no idea who he was. When

I asked how he knew me, he told me it didn't matter. What was important, he said, was that there were certain matters which remained unresolved in the case of Jesus of Nazareth. I told him the case was closed. That's when he told me he knew about Deucalion's refusal to cooperate with the Tribunal. He also knew about Deucalion's declining to accept the money the rest of us had taken."

Pilate's mind raced. "He knew Deucalion's name?"

"Yes."

"Did he tell you *how* he knew so much?"

"No. I pressed him, but he refused to answer."

The frown on Pilate's face deepened.

"When I threatened to take him to the garrison and question him further with the help of some centurions, he just laughed. That's when he told me he had a solution — one, he said, that even the Syrian Governor would be most pleased with. One that had been approved by the highest authority. I thought he was referring to you."

"How do you know he was a Jew?"

"Because I followed him to the Temple and watched him disappear inside."

"What does all this have to do with our problem?"

"A week later I received instructions to select two of my best men and meet a fourth centurion near Antipas' residence, just before sunset."

"Who gave that order?"

Malkus looked shocked. "I thought *you* did."

"What?"

"But the scroll —"

"Was it signed?"

"No, but it had your seal on it."

"By all the gods, this smells of Annas," snapped Pilate. "What happened when you met this anonymous centurion?"

By now Malkus' legs were trembling. He was suddenly

fearful that Pilate would strip him of his newly acquired authority — or decree a worse fate for him. Unfortunately, the new commander had no choice — he would have to tell the Procurator about the ambush.

Pilate was livid when he heard what had happened. "You fool!" he bellowed. "Deucalion was acting on my orders. He went to that house to gather important information on Caiaphas and the Sanhedrin. The Jew who lived there gave Deucalion valuable information on the High Priest's plans to disrupt our administration of Judea," he shouted, immediately realizing by the look on Malkus' face that he'd said too much.

Angry with himself for losing his control and entrusting his secret to a man he barely knew, he walked over to the marble table and poured himself a goblet of wine, hoping it would dull his throbbing headache. He took several gulps, then walked over to the balcony and stood, looking out beyond the Royal Bridge, straining to see the distant mountains through the blue-grey haze.

Invariably his gaze was drawn to the Temple. "It has to be Annas," he muttered. "No one else would have the audacity to meddle in my affairs so brazenly. And he's the only one who could possibly have known about Doras *and* have the ear of Vitellius."

Pilate turned and faced Malkus. His eyes were twins — cold points of steel. "You will never discuss this matter again — with anyone — on pain of death. Is that clear?"

Malkus nodded obediently and averted his eyes, hoping they hadn't given him away. There was something here he could use later.

"I want you to find Deucalion," continued the Procurator. "You know his habits — how he thinks. And when you do, make sure his death is swift and, above all, quiet. I want no evidence, no curious spectators. Is that clear?"

"Yes, Procurator. Perfectly clear."

"Whatever else he may be, Deucalion is first and foremost a Praetorian. And as such he deserves to die with dignity." The harshness suddenly left Pilate's voice, and he grew thoughtful. "Be careful, Malkus. Deucalion is a formidable enemy, especially when he believes in something." He paused and sighed, then whispered, "And I know he passionately believes in what he saw and heard that morning at the Nazarene's tomb."

"Is that all?"

"Not quite. I want you to go back to the house Deucalion left just before the ambush and arrest the man who lives there. His name is Doras."

"What about the girl who has become Deucalion's companion?"

Pilate glared at him and replied in a voice as void of emotion as when he'd been speaking about the moon, "When you find them, kill her as well."

The summer was barely half over, and already it had indelibly etched itself into Deucalion's memory.

In the space of four short months his life had changed forever. There were moments when he imagined that if he were to meet himself in the streets of Jerusalem, he would not recognize himself. *The old me is no more, and the new life within me grows steadily stronger*, he thought as he stood up from the table, then walked over to the window.

He stared at Abigail's garden, thinking. He'd been up all the previous night reading the parchments, occasionally stopping to stare at the waning moon. Now it was early afternoon, and the sun reigned unchallenged in the heavens.

Abigail had gone shopping in the city, and Esther had gone to see her father. "I can't just leave without telling him how I feel," she'd said just before dawn. He'd agreed and told her to be careful, then added, "Be sure you're back before twilight. We have to leave here tonight. Pilate has many spies. If he doesn't already know about this house, he soon will."

The door opened behind him, and Barnabas' voice pulled Deucalion from his reverie. "I'm leaving for Joppa, but before I go, you must tell me your plans."

Deucalion turned and replied, "You're right, of course, about the parchments. They *are* incredible. But I don't understand why you've given them to me."

"Who knows whether you are come to the kingdom for such a time as this?"

"What?"

Barnabas smiled and sat down at the table. "It's a quote from the Book of Esther. She lived during the time of King Ahasuerus."

"I've studied about him. The Greeks call him Xerxes. He was a Persian monarch whose kingdom extended from Media to Ethiopia."

Barnabas nodded. "Ahasuerus was married to Queen Vashti, an extraordinarily beautiful woman. However, Vashti failed to honor her husband and rebelled against him. Consequently, Ahasuerus ordered his advisors to seek out a virgin to be his new queen. A Benjamite by the name of Mordecai had been carried away from Jerusalem by Nebuchadnezzar, King of Babylon, and was later taken to Shushan, the capital of Persia. Mordecai, in turn, had raised Esther, because her father and mother were dead. When the King's decree was published, Esther was among the virgins brought before Ahasuerus."

"What does all this have to do with me?"

"Patience, my friend. Esther so impressed the King that he made her his wife and queen. Not long after, Haman, one of the King's trusted advisors and a man who had nothing but scorn for Jews, conceived a plan to destroy all the Jews in

Ahaseurus' kingdom. Mordecai informed Esther of Haman's plan, but she was reluctant to go to the King because she was fearful. Mordecai pointed out to her that if Haman's plot was successful, not only might her people be destroyed, but she also, because she was Jewish. He also prophesied to her that if she failed to speak out, God would perhaps provide another to deliver the nation of Israel — but she and her father's house would be destroyed."

"And her decision?"

"She prayed and fasted, and God gave her a solution. The Jews were saved from extermination, and Haman and his ten sons were hung. A yearly feast was instituted to commemorate our deliverance under Queen Esther."

"The Feast of Purim," muttered Deucalion, overwhelmed by the magnitude of God's sudden revelation to him.

"You know it?"

Deucalion shook his head. "No, but Esther told me about it the night I rescued you two from Saul."

"It seems a great deal happened that night."

"More than you know, Barnabas."

Barnabas stood and walked to the door. "It is time for my departure to Joppa."

"I still haven't answered your question."

"Maybe not in words, Deucalion. But I see the answer in your eyes . . . and I believe God knows your heart. That is all I need."

Deucalion stuck out his hand. "Good-bye, Barnabas. The Lord be with you."

Barnabas turned and grasped Deucalion's hand. "One last thing before I go," he said. "I lived for a time in a cave, at the edge of the Great Salt Sea. You and Esther can hide there until you decide what to do. No one will bother you. The only people who frequent the area are the Essenes, and they keep to themselves, shunning all contact with the world."

"How far is it?"

"About twenty miles. I'll tell you how to find it."

"We'll need food and water."

"Water is no problem; there's a small, hidden spring. Food you'll have to acquire along the way. I take it you have some money?"

Deucalion smiled and reached inside his tunic. "How fitting that the Tribunal shall finance this adventure," he said, lifting the small bag of money from his belt.

"Hello, Father," Esther said as she walked onto the veranda.

Doras had been gazing intently at the city below, and he turned at the sound of his daughter's voice. "What are you doing here?" He was surprised at how well she looked — not like one who had been cut off.

"I came to say good-bye. Deucalion and I are leaving the city."

"You've been with *him* the last two weeks?"

"No, Father. I've been living with another outcast."

"I see. You look healthy."

"We've managed . . . and the Lord is faithful."

Doras flinched. "Where will you go?"

"It's best you don't know." Esther stared at her father, surprised that he wasn't angry. She'd expected him to yell at her at the very least. But he seemed distant, as though his thoughts were far away. Her heart went out to him. "I'm sorry I failed you," she said, searching for the right words to express what she was feeling.

Her father sighed heavily. "It is not you who has failed me, my little *hadassah*. It is I who have failed. I have failed the Sanhedrin . . . you . . . and most of all, God."

"I don't understand."

"Sit," he said and motioned for her to take one of the cushions, then sat down across from her.

Suddenly she realized how quiet it was. "Where are the servants? They should be preparing dinner."

"Gone."

"Where?"

Doras shrugged. "It's not important now. What is important, however, is something I should have told you a long time ago."

"Father —"

Doras raised his hand and said, "Please, let me finish. I've wanted to share this with you since your twelfth birthday, but because of my selfishness I never found the time. It's about your real father — and how you came to be my daughter."

"You never lied to me, did you, about my being adopted?"

"No, Esther, I never lied to you — I just didn't tell you the whole story. And for that I am truly sorry."

"Oh, Father, I wish we'd had this conversation sooner. So much has happened in the past few months. I've grown up in ways I never thought possible."

"And we've grown . . . *apart*."

"It doesn't have to be that way anymore. Deucalion and I don't have to leave. We can —"

Doras shook his head and said, "It's too late, Esther."

"What do you mean, 'too late'?"

"As always, you ask too many difficult questions. Let me tell you what I haven't had the courage to tell you about your father."

"Alright, Father, but then you must explain to me why you're acting so strangely."

"I've told you many times how Rachel became sick in the sixth month of her pregnancy and lost our child. And that we traveled to Caesarea Philippi where we met your father — a bedouin." Doras continued talking as the memory resurrected

itself inside his head, as though it had happened only yesterday.

*He and Rachel were walking down one of the side streets of
the city situated near the base of Mount Hermon. It was late
afternoon, just before twilight, and they were on their way back
to their lodgings when he noticed the tall, broad-shouldered man
with dark, almost black skin staring at them.*

*Oddly, Doras wasn't afraid, even though he carried a large
amount of money hidden inside his robe. The stranger reminded
him of a very old olive tree. One that had borne much fruit in its
time and was near the end of its productive life.*

*The man approached them boldly, his hands stretched forth
in greeting, as if he'd just encountered a pair of long-lost friends.
When he was only a few feet away, Doras noticed a long scar that
ran from the man's left ear, along his jawline, and ended at the
top of his Adam's apple. It was jagged and wide, and obviously
very old, because there was virtually no discoloration between it
and the rest of his wind-burned face.*

*"I've watched you closely these past three days," the stranger
said, addressing Doras in broken Hebrew. His voice was clear
and crisp, almost melodious. "And it seems that your wife is most
unhappy. I come from the desert, and I am also acquainted with
the kind of grief your wife harbors inside her belly."*

*"What do you know of our grief?" replied Doras, speaking
in Aramaic.*

*"Thank you," said the stranger, positioning himself between
Doras and Rachel and taking their arms in his. "It is much easier if we converse in Aramaic. I know so very little Hebrew."*

*They continued walking arm in arm, and Doras was too
astounded to be afraid. He glanced at Rachel and saw that she
was equally mesmerized by the man.*

"My wife died a few days ago," continued the stranger as if

he were sharing sad news with old friends. "But, God be praised, in her death she left me life — a daughter."

"Why have you come to us in this way? And why are you telling us all this?" Doras asked, starting to feel foolish.

The stranger stopped walking. "Because I've seen your wife staring at the children in the streets," he replied, then sighed heavily. "Because you, like my wife, are Jewish. And because God told me to give you my daughter."

"You're mad!" said Doras, grabbing Rachel by the arm. They started to leave, but the stranger stopped them with his words.

"God has also told me that the ones I seek prayed for a child and conceived, but lost the baby in the sixth month. He instructed me to bring my infant daughter here to Caesarea and seek out a man and woman of your description."

Rachel gasped as if she'd been struck. Doras was about to rebuke the man sternly when his wife asked, "How do you know it was God who spoke?"

The stranger stared at them for several moments. That's when they both realized how unusual the man's eyes were. The iris and the pupil were the same color, both dark brown, almost ebony, with specks of gold, shimmering with an odd kind of light that seemed to reach out and envelop them. Both had the sense that they were standing next to a brightly burning fire, fueled by coals of the purest power they had ever experienced.

"There is no other voice like the voice of God," the man replied in a voice that was soothing, like a cool balm applied to a throbbing, burning wound. "I'd been praying to Him for guidance, asking Him what to do with the girl-child after my wife died, when suddenly my tent was filled with smoke — but there was no fire.

"Then a warm, soft wind shook the canvas, and I thought at first that it was the beginnings of a sirocco. Yet when I looked out the flap, the sand was still — not a grain had been displaced.

"Also, there was a strange kind of light. A light that was soft and penetrating at the same time. And I heard singing! Out of

*the light a man's voice spoke: 'I am the Beginning and the End.
I have always been and I shall always be. You have been faithful
with little and so you shall be given much. Go and find what you
seek in Caesarea.'*

"Never, in all the years of my life, nor in all the years of my
father's life, and his father's, and his before him, has God ever
spoken to a bedouin in such fashion. That is how I know it was
the voice of God."

Doras started to say something, but Rachel cut him short.
"We will take the child. Where is she?"

Doras paused and stared at his daughter.

Esther was tingling all over. She felt like she'd been
immersed in a pool of warm, scented oil. And she thought she
smelled frankincense. "I . . . I don't know what to say. It's all
so incredible. But what does it mean?"

"When your father, wild-eyed, uncircumcised bedouin that
he was, appeared to us in the streets of Caesarea and told us
that story, Rachel and I knew God had indeed spoken — He
had answered our prayers."

"How did you know?"

Doras stood up and stared at the city once again, as if he
were seeing it for the last time. "You see, it was the month of
Adar, and the particular day we met your father was the
fifteenth. The Feast of Purim. The Fast of *Esther*. Three months
after Rachel lost the baby."

"Why is that so special?"

"Because it had been nine months, to the day, since Rachel
had heard from God during the previous Pentecost."

The sudden silence was deafening. Esther began to weep.

Suddenly there was a knock at the front door. Both Esther
and Doras were startled by the insistent banging.

"Who can that be, at this hour?" mumbled Doras, heading
for the door.

It was Abigail, and she was terrified. "We have to go!" she pleaded as soon as Doras let her in and brought her to Esther.

"What is wrong, Abigail?" Esther asked, wiping the tears from her cheeks.

"Pilate has a new Commander of the Garrison, and he's on his way here now!"

"Malkus . . . " muttered Doras.

"But why would —"

"Esther, you must leave immediately," interrupted her father. "Do as your friend says."

"I—I don't understand . . . "

"There's no time to explain. Just go."

Esther stared at her father and was frightened by what she saw in his eyes. She hugged him and whispered in his ear, "I love you, Father . . . "I will *always* love you."

Doras pushed her away and said, "Go now, before Malkus arrives and finds you here."

"Hurry, Esther," Abigail said, grabbing her by the arm. "You promised Deucalion you'd be back before twilight."

"Good-bye, Father," Esther said over her shoulder as she and Abigail scrambled out the door.

"Good-bye, my precious *hadassah*," muttered Doras.

XX

The Hebrew way of life during the calendar year is, for the most part, a life filled with an odd mixture of feasting and fasting. August is no exception. It is the month for harvesting grapes, figs, walnuts and olives in Palestine. The Jews wisely call it *'ab*, meaning "fruitful."

At the new moon there had been a fast for the death of Aaron, the older brother of Moses and the first High Priest of Israel. And in a few days another fast would be initiated, one that recalled God's declaration against murmurers entering Canaan. Because of their sin, neither Moses nor Aaron was allowed to enter the Promised Land. Indeed, of all the people over twenty, only Joshua and Caleb were allowed into Palestine.

Esther looked wistfully outward from the mouth of the cave, hidden in the rocks on the eastern shore of the Great Salt Sea, and thought about the way of life she'd left behind. It made her sad, and she felt like crying, but didn't. It was too hot, too dry for tears.

The air had remained still for days. The heat was intense. When there was wind, it achieved character by virtue of having blown in from the east, acquiring scent from the *Arabah*, the Sea of the Plain.

Esther shook her head, clearing it of melancholy thoughts, replacing them with thoughts of Deucalion. In her mind's eye she could see the two of them as they had stood side by side at the highest point on the cliff, looking over the vast panorama of desert below. She'd asked him what *Arabah* meant, and he patiently explained the subtleties of translating words that had many meanings for many people.

"Actually the term is somewhat misapplied," he'd continued in a strong, deep-throated voice. "The literal translation is 'desert.' In its purest and most proper sense the expression is most often used to indicate the whole valley lying between Mount Hermon and the Red Sea. The bedouin refer to the area as *El Ghor*, because there is so much fertility."

"How do you know so much about this place?"

"I read much and ask many questions."

"I see."

"I'm not finished."

"Oh?"

"Look."

"Where?"

"Over there," he said, pointing. "See the line of white cliffs crossing the valley?"

She nodded excitedly. "They're beautiful!"

"Well, because we Romans are so smart, we split the valley in two and recognize *both* names. The point of division between *El Ghor* and *El Arabah* is those cliffs. Beyond them are flat marshlands that run all the way to the south end of the Great Salt Sea. From there south to Akabah is the *Arabah*, and north, to the Lake of Galilee, lies the *Ghor*."

"How clever. But I bet there's something not even a smart Roman such as yourself knows."

"Try me."

"Doras once told me this area is like the wilderness our ancestors wandered in for forty years."

"That's a long time."

"It's also an extremely significant period of time."

"Why?"

"See, I told you you're not as smart as you think."

"I confess. Now tell me why forty is such an important number."

"Because Jews believe it's the number of probation, trial, and chastisement. Moses was forty when he was forced to flee Egypt, and eighty when God spoke to him from the burning bush and commanded him to return to Egypt to rescue his people. And Caleb was forty when he was sent out from Kadesh-Barnea by the great patriarch to explore Canaan."

"Canaan?"

"The Promised Land."

"And where might that be?"

"We're standing in the middle of it."

Esther sighed with the memory. That conversation was typical of their time together. They'd spent their days alternating between getting to know one another and studying the parchments. At night they prayed together around the fire, asking God for wisdom and guidance — and for strength to accomplish whatever He told them to do.

All of a sudden Esther jumped to her feet and ran outside. The day was almost over, and vibrant colors were beginning to separate the dark-blue ceiling of the sky into a rare mosaic of pale pastels and strikingly resonant hues. She'd felt the beginnings of a breeze on her face and didn't want to miss a moment of it. Outside the cave, the wind was blowing in short bursts, cleansing the air of its staleness. "Thank You, Lord," she shouted to the heavens, relishing the welcome relief from the heat.

Before she turned and went back inside, she glanced down the cliff, through the shimmering ocean of heat that lapped at the limestone cliffs below the cave, to the beach below. Deucalion was somewhere down there. Even though she couldn't see him, she knew he was walking along the beach — a mixture of crackling gravel mixed with deeply stained marl and chalk — as the two of them had done, hand in hand, many times the past few days.

Abruptly the prophetic words of Ezekiel flooded her mind:

> . . . a river of water, bubbling forth from the Temple, sweeping eastward, down to the Sea, increasing in force and power as it flowed, healing the bitter waters upon contact, restoring life to the dead.

She remembered Simon ben Gamaliel talking about that vision once, at one of her father's many parties. "Ezekiel's vision teaches us there is nothing too sunken . . . too useless . . . too doomed, but by the grace of God it may be redeemed, lifted, and made rich with life."

Later when she saw that Simon was alone, she'd asked him what he'd meant. Surprised by her interest, he'd smiled and replied, "Ezekiel was speaking of our nation, Esther. However, his vision was not only a vision for Israel, but a metaphor for the life of one who dedicates himself to the service of God. We who serve in the priesthood must have the persistence of Habakkuk."

"I'm not sure I understand."

"'Write the vision, and make it plain upon tables, that he may run who reads it,'" he continued, quoting the prophet's words. "'For the vision is yet for an appointed time, but at the end it shall speak, and not lie: though it tarry, wait for it; because it shall surely come, it will not tarry.'"

At the time she'd wondered if those words applied to a *woman* who desired to serve God. Later that same night she received her answer.

After her father's guests had gone, she was cleaning the house, singing to herself quietly, praising God. Suddenly the room filled with a soft, barely discernible haze. And she had smelled frankincense.

Then a quiet, firm voice from within reminded her of the significance of her name and of the fact that it was Esther, with the help of Mordecai, who had hearkened to the voice of God and in so doing had saved the nation of Israel from certain destruction.

Not long after that, she'd heard Jesus speaking to a large crowd of people. She'd been overcome with emotion when she realized that the voice which had spoken to her that night and the voice of Jesus were one and the same. That was how she'd come to her salvation.

As the sun slipped below the horizon, she walked to the back of the cave, where she began preparing the evening meal. She glanced at the parchments and prayed that people would listen — and believe.

Deucalion returned just after darkness robbed the twilight of its beauty, but before the stars awakened from their daytime slumber. Venus, queen of the dusk, had disappeared with June from the nighttime ensemble and no longer bridged the gap between last light and starshine.

"I have our answer," he said as he stepped from the deep shadows outside the cave into the dancing light coming from the small fire inside. "It finally came to me today as I walked along the beach." He paused and took a sip of water from the bucket Barnabas had left behind, then continued, "We must take the scrolls to Capri. I'm convinced that's the only way Tiberius can be made to see that the people of the Way are not his enemies."

"He won't believe us," Esther said softly, "even if we're able to get to him before the Legion gets to us."

"Why do you say that?"

"Think of what it's taken for *us* to believe. We've spent hours in prayer over the last few days, and still we both have difficulty dealing with the enormity of the truth."

Deucalion replaced the ladle in the bucket and sat down.

"Still, we must try. We can't ignore the burden the Lord has placed in our hearts."

Esther looked into Deucalion's eyes as the firelight danced across his face. The strength of his gentleness and the depth of his caring filled her more with his essence than any physical act ever would. She was glad they'd agreed to remain celibate in their time together and let God provide the time and place of their union in marriage.

She walked over and sat down beside him, and he pulled her close and wrapped his arms around her, making her feel safe and secure. "Whatever happens in the days to come," she said, looking into his eyes, "I want you to know that I love you more than you can imagine . . . more than mere words can express."

Deucalion grasped her chin in his hand and kissed her, slowly and unhesitatingly. She felt passion surge, but knew she mustn't give herself over to it completely. It wasn't time yet.

Sensing that Esther was holding back, Deucalion pulled away and said, "We leave for Capri tomorrow, my love. And once we've seen Caesar, I want us to marry."

Esther hugged him fiercely and said, "Nothing would make me happier."

Pontius Pilate wrestled with the night.

The demons that plagued his dreams seemed to feed off his torment and misery. And each night they grew in stature and number.

He was lost in the dark abyss of Hades. Charon had deposited him, along with his fellow lepers, on the dark side of the River Styx. At any moment he expected to encounter Orcus — the Greeks called him Pluto — and he was sweating blood.

He cringed with fear, certain the god of the underworld would see the rotting lesions on his body and feed him to his three-headed dog, Cerberus.

He gagged as a horrible stench filled his nostrils. It was worse than the smell that rose from the Valley of Hinnom. He cried out with fear, although his voice was weak and tremulous.

Sweat covered the Procurator's quaking body. He was lying askew on his bed, and an ocean of fear escaped through the pores of his mottled skin, soaking his silken bedclothes. He cried out again, this time screaming, and the raspy sound yanked him from his nightmare.

He opened his eyes, disoriented. The darkness covered his soiled clothing and hid his uncontrollable trembling. "What have I done?" he moaned to the empty room, then reached over to the table beside his bed and grabbed the flagon of wine he'd placed there before retiring. It was empty.

With a great deal of effort, he pulled himself into a sitting position, as if he were truly a man who had leprosy, or one who was so advanced in age he could not move easily without help. When he realized this, he felt like weeping, but his despair was beyond tears.

Instead, he sat in the darkness, trembling, and thought about the decision he had made.

After Pilate's conversation with Malkus, Annas had come forth and revealed his intentions. "You've wavered long enough, Procurator," he'd said, his voice harsh and uncompromising. "Vitellius has demanded that you remedy the unstable situation here in Judea . . . immediately. Yet you delay carrying out your orders. Need I remind you that you neglected a dangerous and potentially catastrophic situation once before."

Pilate had flinched and glared at his adversary. Annas was right, of course, but he hated the Jew all the more for his rightness. "You're exaggerating, Annas," he said calmly, keeping the gnawing frustration he felt in his belly out of his voice.

Annas laughed derisively. "Hardly, Pontius."

"Rome isn't what she was in my father's day," countered the Procurator. "Augustus would never have tolerated such insolence from a man like you."

"Speaking of emperors," Annas had said, "I understand that Tiberius languishes in Capri. It is rumored that his skin has broken out in large red blotches and that his whole body is covered with pus-filled eruptions which exude the most unpleasant of smells and cause him a great deal of pain."

"Your words have you on cliff's edge, priest."

"I meant no disrespect, Pontius. It's just that I have also heard that Tiberius has planned well for his death —"

"What are you insinuating?" interrupted Pilate.

"I'm surprised you don't know."

"Know what?"

"Why, that Tiberius has chosen Gaius Caesar to be his successor." Annas' smile was almost a sneer. "I believe his fellow legionnaires refer to him as 'little boots.'"

"Caligula!" spat Pilate, shocked by the Jew's revelation. "I don't believe it!" He turned and walked over to his desk, then sat down heavily. His head sagged forward as if it were too heavy for him to hold up. "*My* spies tell me Tiberius hates his adopted son. In fact, if rumors are to be believed, the Emperor reportedly told a group of Senate representatives that Caligula was 'a viper being nursed in Rome's bosom.' Why would Tiberius chose such a successor? He is a child, a boy whose morals and habits are contemptible."

"The *child*, as you refer to him, has a claim that is as good as any previous ruler's. He is, after all, the great-grandson of Augustus, through Julia. And since the death of his son Drusus, Tiberius has been unable to produce progeny of any gender. On the other hand, who are we to question a man who allows himself to be worshiped as a god?" finished Annas tauntingly.

Pilate glared at the titular head of the Sanhedrin and changed the subject. "You are in no position to gloat, Annas," he said sternly. "I understand Antipas and Doras are determined to remove *your* son-in-law from the position he has held for fifteen years. I'm also informed they are close to succeeding."

Annas laughed loudly, then poured himself a goblet of wine, intentionally infuriating Pilate with his breach of manners. "You poor, beguiled man," he said, enjoying the moment. "Do you not know? Doras is dead."

"What?"

"He hung himself this afternoon. It seems he couldn't stand the pain of losing his daughter." Annas stared at the Procurator and added, "I'm told he chose the very tree Judas Iscariot used."

Pilate's face was blank. "Who?"

"The man who betrayed Jesus to us for thirty pieces of silver."

Pilate was suddenly beyond words.

"So you see," continued Annas, "it's highly unlikely Herod will try to continue his efforts to unseat my son-in-law." He walked over to the balcony and stared down at the Temple, wondering what Pilate thought about whenever he looked at the Royal Bridge. "As for you, Pontius . . . your problem remains alive, walking the streets of the city."

Pilate looked at Annas, all but defeated, and said with his last bit of defiance, "Not exactly."

"Oh?"

"We've located Deucalion . . . and the girl. I've sent Malkus and a cohort of men to take care of both of them."

"How did you find them?" Annas asked, amazed that the Procurator had the situation under control.

"We discovered she was hiding with an outcast — a woman named Abigail."

"An outcast?"

"A leper," Pilate said, fighting to control the nausea germinating like a poison weed in his belly.

"I see. And what has become of this *leper*?" asked Annas, not knowing the significance her leprosy held for the beleaguered Procurator.

"She told us what we needed to know. Unfortunately, she didn't survive the interrogation."

"A pity," sighed Annas. "Although I imagine her death is as fortuitous for Rome as Doras' death was for us."

Pilate remained silent.

"Where are Deucalion and Esther?"

"Esther?"

"Doras' daughter. I'm surprised you didn't know."

Pilate waved his hand casually and shrugged. "Names are of no consequence to me at this point. I care only about the swift resolution of our problem."

"As you say, it is *our* problem. Where are they?"

"Somewhere along the shore of the Great Salt Sea, in a cave."

"What do you mean, 'somewhere'?"

Pilate grunted. "Perhaps you should pray to your God and ask Him. And while you're at it, ask Him to make sure your sleep isn't as troubled as mine has been these past weeks. Perhaps, if He is merciful He won't probe your conscience. I doubt your image could stand the strain."

The Procurator's thoughts returned to the present. The night remained still. The *Arabah* had swallowed all the wind. Pilate got out of bed and walked to the balcony. He absentmindedly rubbed his hand across the marble balustrade ringing the suspended veranda, and it came away wet with dew. "That's strange," he muttered, "it feels like oil."

He wiped the sticky wetness on his bedclothes and thought about his nightmare.

The reason he'd screamed himself awake was not because of what he'd seen in *Hades*. It was because of what had happened *after* that.

Immediately after he'd smelled the horrible stench, the scene had changed abruptly.

From the center of darkness in the pit beneath him, a blinding white light had raced toward him and enveloped him. He'd tried to close his eyes, but couldn't. Standing in front of him was the Galilean. Jesus was dressed in white, and He was glowing brightly, as if He were on fire. He had spoken thirteen words: "You are forgiven, for in your ignorance, you know not what you did." Then the brightness increased and became a consuming fire.

All of a sudden the leper, Abigail, was standing in front of him . . . beside Jesus. And she was also glowing. Then came the thief who'd been crucified with Jesus. Finally Deucalion and a strange dark-haired woman appeared beside the Galilean.

That was when he awoke in terror. The light had become so intense, he thought the sun had fallen on him. His body had felt as if it were on fire.

He shuddered, knowing that had he not screamed himself awake, the faces would have continued to appear — faces of all the men, women, and children he'd been responsible for killing. "Yes, *Gehenna* is worse than I ever imagined," he mumbled, grateful he couldn't see the Royal Bridge at night.

Perhaps it's not too late, he thought hopefully, running his hand through the cool wetness on the marble railing. Abruptly he turned and stumbled towards the door. "Antonius . . . " he cried out hoarsely. "Wake up! I must get a message to Malkus. Wake up! Do you hear me?"

XXI

Five miles east of the Great Salt Sea and the cave, Malkus awoke, drained and irritable. He sat up groggily and watched the sun rise, big and round, over the camp he and his men had hurriedly made late last night. Dawn was only minutes old, and the day was already hot. The absence of any wind didn't help the cloying weather, or his mood.

The soldiers who were already awake were doing their best to cleanse themselves. There had been yet another heavy dew during the night, and yesterday's dust now clung with irritating tenacity to their damp clothing.

"What a contradiction in terms this land is," muttered Malkus, wondering if the people took their cue from the weather.

He marveled at Palestine's idiosyncrasies. The inhabitants were irascible and stubborn, with little tolerance for the uncircumcised; yet they would renounce their own flesh and blood in order to keep themselves pure.

His reflections were interrupted by the arrival of Tacitus, his second-in-command, who announced, "The men await your orders, sir." Malkus stood and secured his sword — once Deucalion's — in the scabbard tied to his waist, then looked east, toward the sunrise, squinting his eyes against the harsh glare. When he spoke, his voice was thick with exhaustion, and the dark circles beneath his eyes made his face look bruised, as if he'd been in battle during the night.

"I'll be glad when we've completed our duty, Tacitus," he

said, his mind elsewhere. "I grow weary of Palestine. Rome beckons to me in my dreams. She calls to me insistently, like a Siren. But I'm bound to this parched and inhospitable country by the bonds of another man's destiny." He shivered despite the heat, then whispered, "We're all doomed, Tacitus — all of us who stood against the Nazarene."

"Commander?"

Malkus blinked, then stared at Tacitus as if he were only just recognizing his presence. The chill left him as abruptly as it had come upon him. "What . . . ?"

"The men are waiting. Your orders, sir?"

Malkus brushed the dirt off his sandals and straightened his crumpled, damp robe. "Come, Tacitus," he replied in a somber voice, "we march to the Great Salt Sea." The deep purple-blue of dawn was already fading into the pastel-blue of morning as the two men began walking through the camp.

Pontius Pilate paced the marble floor of Herod the Great's Palace. The haggard look on his face was accentuated by the long, deep lines that looked like crow's feet spreading outward from the corners of his sullen brown eyes.

He'd roused Antonius from sleep and had hastily prepared new orders, rescinding his command to kill Deucalion and the girl. Instead, Malkus was to arrest them and bring them to him for questioning.

The runner had left before just before dawn. The Procurator knew that Malkus, though camped only a short distance from his destination, would not begin the search for the cave until the sun was risen.

The courier must reach Malkus in time, he thought. *He must!*

Herod Antipas lay passed out on the floor of his residence. The prostitute with whom he'd feverishly shared his bed had unknowingly, and rather unceremoniously, pushed him off his bed in her sleep. The Tetrarch had been too drunk to care.

He'd finished off the last of the spring wine four months early, attempting to drown his latest failure in an ocean of fermented grapes. Doras was dead, having supposedly committed suicide. Two years of planning and preparation had died with him.

First his demented father had failed him. Then Augustus had denied him the full measure of his rightful inheritance, and his brother had married the woman he desired. His plans to control the Sanhedrin had developed nicely until Pilate sent that accursed Jew from Bethlehem to him. Now Doras was dead, and all hope with him. Herod would have to content himself with his building projects.

"Perhaps mortar and stone will prevail against time, where flesh and blood have failed," he had muttered just before he passed out.

Caiaphas had risen early and walked downstairs to the court-yard. He stood in front of the solitary acacia and smiled. Annas had informed him late last night of the death of Doras, and of the fate of Pilate's Praetorian. "It seems as though the fire Simon spoke about with such trepidation has burned itself out," he told the tree, stroking the dark *shit'tim* wood with his right hand. "I have nothing more to worry about. The old men who sit on the Council have short memories — especially where their own fail-ures are concerned. They will support me now." He laughed heartily, then hugged the tree as if it were a long-lost friend.

Annas stood in the shadows of his upstairs room and observed his son-in-law's strange behavior for the second time in less than a month. "He's lost his mind," he said under his breath. *It was wise for me to arrange for Jonathan to become High Priest. Perhaps it would be even wiser for me to escalate his rise to power.*

XXII

Deucalion walked along the beach and watched the large, round, bright yellow ball of fire rise majestically over the shimmering green expanse of saltwater stretching before him. As the sun began to reclaim its authority over the earth, he prayed, thanking God for the day. He was glad to be alive and eager to get started on the journey to Capri. *Tiberius will see us, and we will make a difference,* he thought as he headed back towards the cave and Esther.

Suddenly the ground beneath his feet rippled. There was no warning, no sound, just the abrupt, startling tremor, as if the earth had heaved a heavy sigh.

Concerned about Esther's safety, Deucalion began to run along the shore, heading towards the cliffs. That was when he heard the faint shout. He stopped running. In the distance he thought he saw a group of men, but he couldn't be sure because there was a haze between him and whoever had shouted.

Nevertheless, he knew in his heart they were centurions. Pilate had found them!

He uttered a quick prayer, hoping they were shouting because of the tremor and not because he'd been seen. *Plan, don't panic!* he scolded himself. He knew if he could get to the cliffs without being seen, he had a better than average chance of eluding his pursuers. The cave was well hidden, and the legionnaires would be fighting the heat as they searched for him. He started running again, this time in a crouch, hoping he was right.

Malkus reined in his horse and fought to stay on his mount as the earth trembled beneath the bay stallion's hoofs. The horse whinnied and snorted. Several of his men cried out in surprise. He and the reddish-brown horse were both sweating heavily, and from a distance the animal's coat appeared to be the color of dried blood.

Tacitus ran up beside horse and rider and grabbed the stallion by the bit. "One of the men saw someone running down the beach," he said.

"Where?"

"There, ahead of us on the beach, at the base of the cliffs."

Malkus stared at the edge of the great inland sea, only half listening. The glistening green water was rippling spasmodically. Unlike a normal wave pattern, the water moved in concentric circles, as though a huge rock had dropped from the sky, sending giant ripples outward from the center of impact. Before the tremor, the sea had been flat and quiet, the surface of the water a mirror upon which the sun danced.

"Commander . . . "

Malkus blinked. "Was it Deucalion?"

"I'm not sure, sir. But there's no one living near here."

"Except the Essenes. Have you forgotten about them?"

"The community of religious fanatics is behind us, Commander, and it's located some distance from the shore."

"Send a man to follow, quickly," barked Malkus, his pulse accelerating as it always did before he went into battle. "And make certain the man you choose remains unseen."

"Hail Caesar," responded Tacitus as he released the horse. He turned and started in the direction of the men.

"And, Tacitus . . . "

"Yes, Commander?" Tacitus turned to face Malkus' hooded stare.

"If it is indeed Deucalion, remember, we are under strict orders not to reveal who we've been chasing until the last possible moment."

"I understand, Commander. I'll tell the tracker we don't want to lose our quarry in the rocks, and nothing more."

Tacitus moved off to select his man, and Malkus turned his gaze to the cliffs. "I know you are out there, Deucalion — I can feel your presence," he muttered. The horse whinnied again, and Malkus stroked its neck, calming him. "Easy, boy," he whispered as he reached for the oilskin water bag hanging on his saddle, anxious to wash a bitter, burning taste from his throat.

Deucalion was sweating heavily as he climbed up the steep cliff. Even though it was still early, the sun beat down upon the earth relentlessly, and the intense heat reflected off the white, limestone rocks.

He crouched as low as possible as he darted among the crags and crevices of the rock face, using the larger boulders to shield him from any prying eyes that might be watching from below. He glanced over his shoulders from time to time, making sure no one was following him. But his checking was perfunctory — he didn't believe he'd been seen.

He was wrong. One hundred feet below, a lone centurion tracked his prey with the cunning and silence of a wolf.

Deucalion reached the cave, exhausted. The climb itself was not particularly difficult, but he'd virtually run up the side of the cliff. In his haste he'd scraped his legs in several places, and he was bleeding from a number of small but painful cuts on his hands and feet.

Esther, startled by Deucalion's abrupt appearance, looked

up as he stumbled into the cave out of breath. "What happened? You're bleeding," she cried.

"Water!" was all he could manage to say.

Esther filled the ladle and waited expectantly as Deucalion
gulped it down and asked for another. He drank half of the
second ladle, then poured the rest over his head. He told her,
"There was someone else on the beach . . . perhaps a large
number of men."

Esther's eyes grew wide with fear. "Centurions?"

"I'm not sure. They were too far away. And there was a
strange haze hovering above the shore."

"Did they see you?"

"I don't think so."

"But you're not certain?"

"No."

Esther looked anxiously towards the entrance of the cave.
"Did you feel the tremor?" she asked.

Deucalion nodded.

"What are we going to do?"

Deucalion shrugged. "Wait . . . and watch. If it looks safe,
we'll leave tonight. If they are centurions, it should be dark
enough for us to sneak past them." He stared at her and added
softly, "In the meantime, I think we'd better pray."

XXIII

The sun had reached its zenith. The day was hot and still.

Malkus and his men were sweating profusely under the weight of their armor. Only Malkus' horse seemed unaffected by the heat. The animal stood in the loose gravel, his head erect, his muscular body glistening in the harsh, unrelenting afternoon sun.

The tracker Tacitus had chosen had returned and confirmed Malkus' suspicion: the lone figure sighted on the beach just before the tremor was Deucalion; he'd disappeared into a cave on the backside of the cliff.

Just then, a messenger from Pilate arrived. The man was out of breath because he'd run the entire distance from Jerusalem. When he regained his composure Tacitus took him to Malkus, who was standing by his horse. The messenger bowed, then said, "The Procurator sends word that you are not to harm the Praetorian. You are to place him under arrest and return him to Jerusalem."

Malkus pondered the messenger's words briefly, drew his sword, and pierced the messenger through the heart, killing him instantly. As the man's body slumped to the ground, Malkus said, "I will not be denied what is rightfully mine." He stared at his second-in-command with expressionless eyes and added, "Get rid of this body, Tacitus, and tell the men to leave behind everything but their weapons. We've a long climb ahead of us."

Ten men climbed the cliffs, grumbling all the while about the heat, the dust, and the salt stinging their eyes. Now, as they stood facing the well-concealed cave, Malkus realized that had they not seen Deucalion on the beach, they might never have found the refuge.

"Deucalion Cincinnatus Quinctus! It is Malkus," he shouted. "We know you're in there. There's nowhere for you to go. Come out immediately — and bring the woman with you."

There was no reply from inside the cave, but several of Malkus' men began murmuring among themselves. They'd known they were tracking an enemy of Rome — but a Praetorian? One of their own? Their former commander? "May the gods protect us," one of them mumbled.

Malkus called again, "Do you hear me, Deucalion? Pilate has stripped you of your rank. I am now Commander of the Garrison. The Procurator has ordered me to arrest you and the woman and to bring you back to Jerusalem." *The lie comes so easily*, thought Malkus. "Do you hear me, Deucalion? You have nothing to fear. Pilate is a just man. He will deal with you fairly."

"Like he dealt with Jesus, no doubt," came a voice from within the darkness of the cave. "You forget, Malkus — I was at the crucifixion . . . I watched *you* nail the Nazarene's body to the cross . . . And I plunged *my* spear into His side."

Malkus looked at his men, suddenly uneasy, as Deucalion's voice paused, then continued, "I was at the tomb. I know what I saw and heard. Yet you and the others have denied the truth. I listened to the Tribunal's lies and later witnessed the slaughter of innocent men and women at the hands of that madman, Saul. All of this was sanctioned by the 'just man' you speak about."

Deucalion had yet to appear, and the sound of his voice echoing off the limestone rock sounded strange and guttural.

The murmuring was spreading among Malkus' men. As each heard Deucalion's voice, they grew pensive and restless. All of them knew that their former commander was no coward, and those who knew him well knew he loved Rome. There wasn't a man among them who wasn't grateful for the temporary peace he'd brought to Jerusalem by setting up provisional grievance committees, giving the Jews an opportunity to release their anger and frustration verbally rather than by attacking and killing centurions. What madness of Pilate's was this? they wondered.

Inside the cave, Deucalion's military mind assessed the situation. He knew that for him there could be no escape; he would die here, at the edge of the Great Salt Sea. But perhaps he could bargain for Esther's life.

"Malkus, I want to talk with you alone. Come to the front of the cave."

"We've nothing to discuss, Deucalion."

"You're wrong, Malkus. I have something Pilate wants . . . something he desperately needs in order to free himself from the domination of Vitellius and regain the favor of Caesar."

Malkus listened to the voice of his former commander, wondering if Deucalion was lying. Sweat ran down his face, back, and legs in rivulets. He looked at the sun, then at his men. "Curse this heat," he muttered, then added under his breath, "and curse you too, Deucalion." He knew he had to make a decision . . . fast. The scorching sun had robbed him of time.

"All right, Deucalion . . . I'm coming up."

Esther grabbed Deucalion. "What are you doing?" she cried. "They're going to kill us both." Her eyes and voice pleaded with him. "If Pilate gets his hands on the parchments, he'll destroy them."

Deucalion stared at her, his eyes clouded with emotion. "I know, my love," he said, reassuring her with a gentle touch of his strong hands. "But maybe I can prevent them from killing you. If Malkus will guarantee your safety, we can hide the scrolls, and you can come back later and retrieve them. Then when you have the opportunity, you can give them to someone who will understand . . . someone who believes as we do . . . someone who will use them for their intended purpose."

"No! I love you, Deucalion. My life is nothing without you."

"We have no other choice, my love. The information contained in those scrolls is more important than one life. You must live to see that they are read by others. You must tell others the truth."

"Jesus tried, and they crucified Him. And He was the Son of God. Why should they believe me?"

Deucalion grasped her shoulders, saying, "They will believe *because* Jesus came and *because* He was crucified. Barnabas told us that even he didn't believe . . . at first. It will take time, but the word will spread. Whether or not people believe is between them and God. But they must be *told*. At least then they have the opportunity to choose." Deucalion paused, searching for the right words to convince her. "Just before we left Abigail's, Barnabas said something to me that I'd forgotten about until now. I wasn't sure what he was trying to tell me at the time, but now I think I understand."

"Tell me."

"He said that faith is the fabric of God's web . . . that it is the substance of things we hope for, the evidence of things we cannot see. Faith is the fabric, and the shed blood of His Son, Jesus, is the scarlet thread. God is the Master Weaver. He weaves the fabric of our faith, through the power of the blood, together with His Faith, in the loom of His heart, binding all of us who believe into one massive quilt — the Master's Quilt."

Esther clung to him, overwhelmed. His passionate words brought to memory the words of the great Hebrew prophet Hosea: *"My people perish for lack of knowledge."*

"You're right, my love," she said, on the verge of weeping. "We must have faith in Him. Once the seed is planted, if the soil is fertile, the tree will grow and bear fruit." Esther reached down and took hold of the manuscripts, then leaned over to kiss Deucalion.

"I'm waiting, Deucalion," Malkus called from the cave entrance, interrupting their fleeting embrace.

Their kiss forestalled, Deucalion motioned for Esther to wait at the rear of the cave, out of sight.

When Deucalion stepped from the shadows into the light, Malkus stifled a gasp. His former commander seemed to radiate light. There was a calmness and certainty about him that was beyond anything Malkus had ever seen in a man — especially in one who must know he was about to die.

No, that wasn't quite true. He had seen another who behaved the same way, just before *He* died. The Nazarene had radiated that same light. Malkus had looked into Jesus' eyes just before he'd driven the nails into His hands and feet, and what he'd seen there had frightened him, just as the glow he saw in Deucalion's eyes frightened him now.

Suddenly confused, Malkus pulled his eyes from Deucalion's searching gaze. Where else had he seen such light? Of course! At the tomb. The morning the body of the Jew disappeared. The morning all the madness started.

Malkus began to tremble, then clenched his teeth and ordered his mind to take control of his quivering flesh. He would not fall apart in front of Deucalion. "Your time in hiding has been harsh on you, Commander," he said, angry with himself for adopting the tone and title of respect he'd told himself he wouldn't use.

"Less harsh than your conscience has been on you,

Malkus," replied Deucalion sympathetically. He glanced at the sword hanging from Malkus' waist, knowing that Pilate must have entrusted both the sword and his favor upon Malkus. "There was never any love lost between us, Malkus," he continued, "but I've never wished ill for you. Neither do I wish ill of Rome. You, as much as anyone, should know that I have always had the Empire's best interest in my heart."

"Until now."

"You're wrong, Malkus. I still love Rome — perhaps now more than ever. It is the madness that rots within her I seek to eliminate." Deucalion sighed. "There was a time when the Empire was respected throughout the known world. Now we are feared . . . and reviled. The world no longer trusts our judgment. Rome and her people have become enfeebled with their lusts. The citizenry have become blinded to truth. Because they have been fed lies for so long, they can no longer distinguish between what is real and what is illusion."

Malkus frowned, uncertain how to respond. Deucalion wasn't saying anything that he himself hadn't thought more than once. But he had his orders. "About the documents, Deucalion . . . "

"I've hidden them in the city," lied Deucalion, feeling guilty about his deceit. "They are the results of my investigation of the Sanhedrin. A man named Doras — one of the members of the Jerusalem Council — has been conspiring with Antipas to overthrow Caiaphas and —"

"Doras is dead," interrupted Malkus.

The news stunned Deucalion. Unseen powers had obviously been at work in his absence. He hoped Esther hadn't overheard their conversation. "Malkus, I am the one Pilate wants," he said hurriedly. "I know he believes I betrayed him; but believe me, all I did I've done for the good of Pilate and Rome."

"So you say!"

"Think, Malkus! We are not butchers. Think about why *you're* in the Legion, why you're willing to die for the Empire in some strange and foreign land. You believe in what you're doing."

"I believe only that Rome must impose order where there is chaos. Nothing more, nothing less."

Deucalion tried another tack. "Let Esther go and I'll return with you to Jerusalem. She's not a threat to Pilate . . . or to Rome."

Malkus was exhausted. Suddenly he was having trouble thinking clearly. Deucalion's words were having their intended effect. "Perhaps you're right, Commander," he said tiredly. "Unfortunately, it is Annas, not Pilate, who demands the woman's death."

Deucalion's eyes widened at the truth.

Malkus cursed himself silently for his mistake. Now Deucalion would know that he'd lied about taking them back to Jerusalem. He stared at the imposing figure standing before him and winced. There was no fear, no anger in his former commander's eyes. Most unnerving of all, there wasn't even resignation. There was only light. A disconcerting, *brilliant* light.

Malkus snapped, "You've nothing to bargain with, Deucalion." He drew his sword, realizing for the first time that Deucalion wasn't armed. "The decision is not mine. It's over, Deucalion."

"Yes, you're right, Malkus. It *is* finished," he said, remembering the words Jesus had spoken on the cross: *"Forgive them, Father, for they know not what they do."* He added, "I must die with my failure — but you and Pilate must live with yours. I forgive you, Malkus, and I pray to God that He is merciful when you stand before Him in judgment."

Deucalion's penetrating words stung Malkus as if he'd been struck repeatedly with a scourge. His legs went weak, and he began to tremble. Cursing his weakness, he started to raise his sword, but the earth heaved violently, throwing both him and Deucalion to the ground.

Suddenly the rocks surrounding the cave entrance rolled frantically every which way, scattering chunks of limestone, dust and debris in all directions. The earth heaved again, this time even more violently, and an ominous roar thundered through the ravine. The entire cliff seemed to sway.

Dust and pieces of rock hung suspended in the air, choking and smothering both men. Deucalion covered his head with his hands and arms, as if to somehow ward off the flying rocks. Then he heard Esther scream. Her voice immediately blended with the cacophonous sound of the earth being torn apart at the seams. He tried to stand, tried to go to her, but couldn't. The earth was shaking too violently.

Chaos reigned.

Malkus fought his way to his knees at the edge of the cave entrance. Suddenly a huge boulder was ripped loosed from the ceiling. It clipped him on the shoulder and knocked him from the ledge. He disappeared into the ravine below with a muffled scream of agony.

Deucalion scrambled towards the rear of the cave just as several chunks of limestone, ripped from the ceiling, came crashing to the floor inches from his legs and feet. "Esther, are you all right?" he yelled.

There was no reply.

Again the earth shook violently. More rocks came crashing to the floor. The light in the cave began to dim rapidly as the entrance filled with rocks and dirt.

Outside the cave, Tacitus attempted to organize his men. The earth screamed and groaned, as if it were dying. "Gods, protect us!" he cried out, shaking with fear.

He looked across the ravine, wondering what had happened to Malkus, just as a huge, round slab of glistening white rock detached itself from the side of the cliff above the cave. In the blink of an eye it slid down the slope, filling the small oval of darkness that was the cave entrance. There was a horrible crunching sound as the mountainous section of limestone crashed to the bottom of the ravine.

Within a matter of minutes the violent quaking stopped.

An eerie silence, punctuated by shrill cries of pain, settled on the ravine. As the dust and debris began to settle, Tacitus scrambled towards where the cave had been.

He searched the rubble for Malkus as he went, calling his commander's name in a hoarse voice. Minutes later he saw his superior below. Malkus was unconscious, and his leg was twisted in a sickening direction. Tacitus looked around for help. A few of the men had been fortunate; like himself, they weren't injured.

He called them by name, ordering them to help him.

XIV

The darkness inside the cave was as solid as the rock that now sealed its entrance.

Deucalion called out to Esther again, his voice raspy and choked with emotion. There was still no reply.

The violent shaking had stopped, and he tried to stand. A sharp stab of pain raced up the length of his left leg. When he reached back and felt his calf, his hand came away wet and sticky. He knew it was blood, and he could feel the jagged edge of a broken bone protruding through his skin.

He crawled towards the back of the cave, gritting his teeth against the pain, but stopped when his hand scraped something hot. There were still some live coals from the fire. Also, he felt a slight draft of air. *At least we won't suffocate*, he thought.

He fumbled in the darkness, burning himself repeatedly, until he'd gathered up a small pile of embers. Next he groped for and found a piece of wood, half-buried under debris that had been the ceiling of the small refuge turned tomb.

It took some doing, but he finally managed to get a small fire started. The flickering light cast eerie shadows on the cave walls. He squinted, trying to see better. Fear clutched his heart. *Where was she?*

Suddenly his eyes stopped roaming the piles of rubble. He saw her lying at the very back of the cave, covered with fragments of rock, and she wasn't moving. Frantic, he crawled over to her. Blood trickled from her ear. She was badly injured, but she was alive! He stroked her face, wiping away dust and grime, then pulled himself into a sitting position and cradled her head in his lap. The effort left him weak. He dozed off.

In his arms, Esther moaned. Her eyes fluttered open. She blinked, trying to orient herself. Her mouth was dry, and her tongue felt swollen. The lower half of her body felt numb. Frightened, she spoke Deucalion's name in a voice that sounded like wind caressing a field of dry, dead wheat.

When he didn't respond, she called to him again, more loudly, more desperately.

Deucalion's eyes opened instantly. "Esther?"

"What . . . what happened?"

"Earthquake," he rasped. "You were struck on the head by part of the ceiling." A sharp pain coursed through his body, and he grimaced.

"You're hurt!" she said.

"My leg's broken."

She tried to sit up, but couldn't. "I can't move *anything*, Deucalion!" she cried, more frightened than she could ever remember being.

"Shhh, it's alright, my love. Everything is alright."

Esther whispered, "I love you."

"And I love you — more than I could ever begin to tell you," he replied, then adjusted her head so she would be more comfortable.

"We're going to die in this cave, aren't we?"

Deucalion nodded.

"I thought it would be more painful," she continued, "but it doesn't hurt at all. I just feel so tired . . . "

"Rest, my love. Close your eyes and sleep. And when you awake, we'll be together."

"Forever?"

"Yes, my little *hadassah*, forever. I promise."

Esther smiled. "*Hadassah* . . . That's what my father used to call me." Her eyelids fluttered closed.

Helplessly, Deucalion watched her life slip away. He held his hand above her half-parted lips, as if to catch the breath of life and force it back inside her. He thought of Peter's captivating words, "Jesus wept," and he wanted to cry, but he hurt too much to cry.

He remembered other words of God Peter had said near the end of his speech that fateful night he had made the decision to accept Esther's God as his own. "The life of the flesh is in the blood: and I have given it to you upon the altar to make an atonement for your souls: for it is the blood that makes atonement for the soul . . . except you eat the flesh of the Son of man, and drink His blood, you have no life in you. Whoever eats His flesh and drinks His blood has eternal life; and He will raise him at the last day."

Afterwards, when he'd questioned Esther about it, she told him the apostle had quoted the first portion from a book called Leviticus — one of five constituting the Jewish Pentateuch and written by the great Hebrew patriarch Moses — but that she wasn't sure about the second part. Both of them had asked Barnabas about it, and he'd told them that the night before Jesus was crucified the Master had eaten a final meal with his twelve closest disciples and explained that he was speaking about the blood of *the* Lamb of God, the blood of the New Covenant, which was to be shed for the remission of the sins of many.

Now, hours passed like minutes. Weak from loss of blood, Deucalion slipped in and out of consciousness. While he was conscious, he was extremely thirsty. When he was unconscious, he dreamed a strange, disconcerting dream.

The land was flat, the air hot and dry.
The two men working the field were forced to squint in order

to block out the harsh glare reflecting off the dusty, rock-strewn landscape.

No rain had ever fallen upon the field they now tilled.

They had worked the fields every day for months now, from dawn until midday, when the heat became so intolerable that they were forced to rest until late afternoon. Only then could they return to the tilling and planting.

The younger of the two men — although both were youthful in appearance — sang quietly to himself as he worked, oblivious to the inhospitable environment. Small rivulets of sweat trickled down the crevices of his back as he stabbed the desiccated skin of the planet with his crude wooden hoe. His perspiration evaporated quickly upon contact with the air, leaving his body coated with a crystalline veneer of salt.

Although the two men were brothers, upon close scrutiny one might believe they had sprung from the loins of different fathers. Where his younger brother was tall, lean and fine-boned with narrow shoulders, the older was short and squat. His broad body sat atop stubby, thick legs, and his whole frame was covered with a thick carpet of jet, coarse, curly hair.

It was apparent from the way the older one lashed out at the earth in feverish abandon that he was very angry. Every few minutes he looked up from where he labored, sweat pouring off his face, and shouted something unintelligible at the sky, carrying on a conversation with some unseen tormentor.

Finally, having given himself over to the voice inside his head, he threw down his tool and headed in the direction of the small hut he and his brother had constructed as shelter against the sweltering intensity of the day.

Abel looked up and wondered why Cain had left his work unfinished.

The relentless, uncompromising onslaught of the sun campaigned throughout the morning. After a time Abel finally headed for shelter, leaving the earth to battle the implacable heat in its own way.

He searched the small hut for Cain, but it was empty. Fatigued, he took several sips of water from the clay pot sitting near the entrance of the shelter, then sat down on the ground in the shadow of the hut.

He fell into a fitful sleep, and when he awoke, the sun was gradually slipping over the edge of creation. The dull orange-red glow of day's last light reflected off the opaque blue-purple canvas of the sky. The moon, hazy and lavender-white, hung low in the east, suspended like a giant pearl.

He attempted to sit up, but found he could not. His hands and feet were securely bound, stretching him upon the still-warm earth like a four-point star fallen from Heaven. He was firmly anchored to the ground by four small but strong wooden stakes.

A dull, throbbing ache pulsed painfully at the back of his eyes, making it difficult for him to focus. His mouth tasted like he had eaten sour fruit. He felt like vomiting.

Dazed and confused, he called out his brother's name, his voice barely above a whisper. Minutes passed without response.

Again he called out — more loudly this time. Again nothing.

Suddenly, a shadow fell across him, etched upon the twilight, silent and unmoving. Raising his head a few inches off the ground, he cried out, "What is happening, Cain? What is it you want? I am bound as one would bind an animal in preparation for sacrifice."

When his brother finally replied, a look of madness glazed his eyes. "You are most observant, brother . . . and it is to your credit that you remain so calm in the face of your fate." Cain looked down at the helpless figure before him. The intensity of his anger pierced the veil of composure on Abel's face. "Truly the sacrifice I offer up this night shall be worthy of the one who shall receive it," he added.

"You must not do this," pleaded Abel. Fear welled up inside

him, threatening to overflow his normally tranquil state of mind. Oddly he was not afraid for himself, but for his brother. "You are deceived," he placated, regaining control. "Your lack of faith has opened the door, allowing the evil one to gain a further stronghold. He uses you to seal his covenant with death. Do not give place to him. Resist him . . . he is a lie."

For a moment it seemed as though the soft words of the younger would be able to turn the older from his chosen course of action. Yet before Abel could speak further, Cain withdrew his sacrificial knife, raised it high, and plunged it deep into the chest of his offering.

Blood flowed down Abel's stilled chest, mixing with the dusty, brown earth, blending into the blackness of night.

Again there was silence.

The sun disappeared over the rim of the world.

Darkness reigned.

Deucalion awoke with a start. The fire had burned down to embers, and the dull, orange-red coals glowed softly in the quiet stillness, casting an eerie light. He blinked repeatedly, trying to wash away the stinging salt of a cold sweat, and shivered uncontrollably.

"What —" he muttered, then remembered where he was and all that had happened. He shifted position, trying to make himself more comfortable, then stared at Esther's crumpled form. Her once-warm, honey-colored skin had taken on an ash-grey tint. He glanced down at his leg and realized he was still bleeding. The burgundy-red, liquid life blended with the yellow-brown dust, producing a copper-colored mud. "Not a dream . . . " he mumbled deliriously and grimaced in pain as he stroked Esther's hair.

Abruptly he thought about the parchments. Where were they? He scanned the immediate area, but couldn't see them. He groaned, realizing how foolish his concern was. It didn't really matter if he found them or not. *Not only am I going to lose the only woman I ever loved*, he thought morosely, *but I've failed God as well.*

All at once the cave was filled with a brilliant white light — a shimmering luminescence that was both soothing and penetrating.

Deucalion gasped.

Before him stood a man dressed in white. "I am Uriel," said the silver-haired stranger, "and I've come to tell you that you and Esther will not die in this cave."

"What?" Deucalion moaned and thought, *I'm hallucinating.*

Uriel nodded and smiled, then said, "No, you're not imagining — I am *real*."

Oddly, Deucalion felt light as a feather. And he thought he heard singing. Suddenly recognition dawned. "You were at the tomb!" he cried.

Uriel nodded again.

The light . . . the sound . . . the *singing*. It all came back to him. It had *all* been real!

"The parchments," he pleaded, full of remorse. "You must take the parchments! How will the believers know the truth if they don't read the scrolls?"

Uriel shook his head, thinking of the wild-eyed Saul. "The Lord has many servants," he replied cryptically. "Chosen ones you cannot imagine . . . and purposes no man can fathom." Then he disappeared as suddenly as he'd come.

Darkness reigned outside the cave. The moon was barely a sliver of light in the starry sky.

Tacitus and three men had managed to carry their semiconscious commander to the temporary camp they'd set up along the shore of the Great Salt Sea.

Malkus winced in agonizing pain, but still managed to give orders. "What happened to Deucalion?" he wheezed, coughing up bright-red blood.

"Buried in the cave," answered Tacitus.

"How . . . many . . . lost?"

"Five, sir."

"How long was I unconscious?"

"Several hours."

"My leg —"

"It's broken in three places."

"It's hard to breathe. I feel like I've been kicked in the chest by a horse — no, by several horses."

"I think you've also broken several ribs."

Malkus grimaced. "I'm sure it's nothing life-threatening."

"No, provided you don't lose too much blood," Tacitus warned.

Malkus stared at his second-in-command for several minutes, then said, "I am *not* responsible for Deucalion's death. Do you understand? His blood is on the hands of his God." A spasm of pain racked him, but he didn't cry out. "We shall return to Jerusalem at once," he added. "I must report to Pilate."

"But, Commander —"

"At once, I said!"

"As you wish, Commander. Hail Caesar."

XXV

Deucalion Cincinnatus Quinctus tasted fear. The flavor was cold, like iron, and it lay on his tongue with the sharpness of a battle sword.

Around him stretched a stark and shadowy landscape. He gripped a spear in his sweaty right hand, tight enough to soak the wooden handle. Cautiously he walked towards a mound littered with skulls. The mound, adjacent to the deep, narrow glen called Hinnom by the Jews, held three wooden crosses.

In the distance a wild dog howled. He turned in the direction of the unnerving sound and saw the city of Rome — or was it Babylon? Sweat burned in his eye, and when he blinked the scene dissolved.

Around him the shadows shifted, seemingly alive with things that made his skin crawl. Even though it was almost summer and he was in the middle of the desert, he suddenly felt chilled to the bone. He walked on, shivering uncontrollably. Finally he stopped before the center cross and looked up.

Above him a man hung with His head slumped forward, so that His chin touched His chest. He wasn't breathing. There were three bloodied holes in His body; one each in the palms of his hands and one through both feet, where the two-pound nails that secured Him to the crossbars had punctured His olive-colored skin. He reminded Deucalion of a flayed animal pelt, stretched taut to dry.

Deucalion began to weep, full of remorse, knowing that he,

and indeed all mankind, was responsible for the man's crucifixion. He cried out with all his heart, "Father, forgive me . . . "

Suddenly there was a sound as a rushing, mighty wind and a blinding white light consumed Deucalion. In the midst of the light stood the Nazarene, dressed in white linen, His hair white as snow. When He spoke, His voice was soft yet resonant, penetrating but not intrusive. And His words were full of power. "Know this, Deucalion Quinctus — I am the resurrection and the life: he that believes in Me, though he were dead, yet shall he live."

Then, as abruptly as he'd appeared, Jesus was gone.

Startled, Deucalion cried out and was immediately awake. He blinked repeatedly, adjusting to the harsh light that still burned in his eyes, then realized it was the *sun* that was causing his discomfort. He stared at the crystal-blue heavens until his eyes flooded with tears.

He was *outside* the cave!

He sat up and stared down at his leg, amazed at what he saw and felt, or rather what he *didn't* see or feel. There was no pain . . . no blood . . . no evidence at all of the horrible wound he'd sustained in the earthquake.

Beside him he heard a groan.

"Esther!"

"Deucalion?" came the muffled reply. "Wha — what happened?" she asked groggily.

Deucalion shook his head. "I'm not sure." He stared at her in amazement as she sat up. "How do you . . . feel?"

"Strange . . . like laughing and crying at the same time. What about you? I thought I heard you cry out a moment ago."

Deucalion grew pensive. "I was dreaming about that day at the cross. It was a dream I've had many times the past few months, yet this time something was different."

"I don't understand."

He told her about the original dream, then explained, "This time the Nazarene appeared before me in a blaze of light. And He *spoke* to me! Then He just *disappeared*. That's when I cried out and . . . woke up . . . outside the cave . . . here beside you."

Still dazed, Esther shook her head. "So it was all just a dream — the cave, the soldiers, the earthquake and —" She shuddered, unable to finish the thought.

Deucalion continued to stare at her, a strange gleam in his eyes. Finally he reached out, touched the back of her head, and gently probed her hair with his fingers. Satisfied, he stood up and walked several feet to a narrow hole in the side of the cliff, where he knelt down and examined the ground around the opening.

He found dried blood on the rocks.

"Not a dream —"

"What?"

Deucalion stood slowly and walked over to where she was still sitting. "No, my darling," he replied, then laughed loudly. "It wasn't a dream." Feeling more alive than he could ever remember, he reached down and helped her to her feet.

"Then how — ?"

Deucalion smiled and took her in his arms. He could feel her heart pounding against his chest, and that caused his own heart to beat more quickly. In an instant he saw realization come to life in her beautifully alive jade-green eyes.

"A miracle," he announced loudly just before she too smiled and kissed him with abandon.

EPILOGUE

My name is Vashti, and I was born thirty-three years ago on the island of Crete, where my father, a Roman, married my mother, a Jewess. I was named after the first wife of King Ahaseurus because my father said I was extraordinarily beautiful and because I, like my mother, Esther, have eyes the color of the purest jade.

It has been seven years since Mother and I came to Alexandria. Seven years since the Romans destroyed our Temple at Jerusalem. Seven long years since Father died. I never understood why he thought he had to return, why he thought he could make a difference, or why my brother Cincinnatus went with him. Now, after what Mother told me last night, I think at last I understand. And for the first time since Father left us my heart is at peace.

Mother died this morning, after a brief illness. Although I'm deeply grieved, the words she spoke to me before she went to be with the Lord give me hope. As we Jews are fond of saying, "I now have an anchor for my soul."

I'm not sure why I'm writing this — perhaps because I do not want to forget one jot or tittle of it as I grow old. No, that's not entirely true. My real desire is that my husband, Flavius, will consent to my bequeathing this letter to our newborn son, Justus, when he is of age, as a legacy of his *true* heritage. I pray that God will soften my husband's heart and reveal to him the truth about *His* Son. It's not that Flavius is an unkind man, far from it. But he is a scholar, descended of the Hasmoneans and born to a lineage of priests, *and* a Pharisee. I am his second wife, and we have been married but seven short years. Even though I know he loves me, I fear he loves the law more. It was that deep abiding faith I saw in him that first drew me to him, and, ironically it is the newly rediscovered faith within me that may yet draw us apart. I pray not.

I know that I am taking a great risk speaking of things which some deem heretical. Nevertheless, I feel compelled to write down what Mother shared with me in the early-morning hours, just before the column of dawn. If nothing else, this simple act of obedience to the Voice, God's Voice, my constant companion since I was a child, makes me feel *restored* somehow.

I cannot, however, confirm the veracity of what I'm about to pen, for I was not even conceived when the events took place. But I have heard others, besides Mother and Father, talk of the Nazarene, and I have seen the indescribable light in both my parents' eyes whenever they have spoken His name.

So, my son, if you are reading this, and if I am not alive to explain further, all I ask of you is what your grandmother, Esther, asked of me — that even if you don't believe, pass it on to your son or daughter and let them decide for themselves whether or not they believe.

I must write quickly, before Flavius returns from his work at the Great Library, and before my resolve falters. The historical account I urge you to consider is this:

The heat from the scorching morning sun pulled the city from its slumberous lethargy, sucking the cool forgetfulness of night from the belly of Jerusalem.

The sky was cloudless . . . a dispassionate spectator. Its

countenance was the color of a sapphire. The last vestige of the full moon hung low in the eastern sky; the nightly brilliance had rapidly given way to a spectral translucence.

There had been no breeze for three days. To say that the morning was stifling would have been a gross understatement.

It was the time of the spring equinox. The barley that had been planted in October and November was being harvested in the Plain of Jericho and in the Jordan Valley. Jews throughout Palestine had been diligently preparing during the past month for the Feast of the Paschal Lamb. Bridges and roads had been repaired for the use of pilgrims, the red heifer was burned as a sin offering, and holes were bored into the ears of those who wished to remain in bondage to their masters. Any dead body discovered in the field was buried where found. To insure that pilgrims coming to the feast did not contract any uncleanness by unwittingly touching such graves, the priests ordered that "all sepulchres should be whitened."

The first sacred month — the seventh civil month of the Hebrew calendar — was replete with festivals: the fast for Nadab and Abihu; the fast for Miriam and for the death of Joshua; and the festival of unleavened bread. But this particular April was to be very different than any other. The coming of the "latter" or spring rains would arrive sooner than expected and with such force that when combined with the melting snows of Lebanon they would cause the Jordan channel to fill beyond bursting, inundating the entire lower plain.

However, that climatic irregularity was of little significance when compared with the events that would transpire simultaneously with the advent of this, the tenth celebration of Passover since the Exodus.

The noise originating within the walls of Jerusalem was as stifling as the stillness of the air. From one particular section a cacophony of voices rose above the hum of the huge city, like filth overflowing a bursting sewer.

A portable Tribunal had been erected on the *Gabbatha*, a tesselated pavement in front of the palace. A throng of angry citizens pummeled Pontius Pilate, the morose Governor of Judea, with abusive rhetoric. Pilate had failed in his bid to give his "problem" to Herod Antipas.

The Nazarene some called *Christos* stood before Pilate silent and irreproachable. In an uncharacteristically poignant moment of compassion, Pilate made a frantic attempt to sever himself from the blood-guiltiness that entwined his heart. The cancerous ache in his belly seemed like sticky, leavened dough in what he imagined was a rotting cavity in his soul. He had magnanimously offered, according to custom, to free the Jewish prophet who had been hailed as Messiah just three short days ago. His conciliatory gesture had been ridiculed by the maddened crowd. Caught up in the fevered mindlessness of a rabid dog, they chose to forgive the murderer Barabbas instead.

The Procurator's cheeks were hollow depressions in a sagging façade of hopefulness. The paucity of color in his skin heightened the aura of death that haloed his disconsolate demeanor. The large, dark semicircular stains underneath his sunken eyes were visible from a distance. He stared resignedly at the battered man standing stoically before him.

Jesus had yet to speak.

Pilate, sitting uncomfortably in his magistrate's chair, wiped sweat from his brow and marveled at the endurance of the man. He then cast a furtive glance at the uncompromising morning sun. "It is barely the third hour," he muttered miserably, "and already the day is scorched — and I along with it."

The minutes passed like hours.

Finally Pilate, Governor of Judea, realized he had no choice but to crucify Jesus. He stood up wearily and turned his back on the madness. As he began to wash his hands listlessly in the porcelain basin that sat on the inlaid, marble table he'd imported from Babylon during happier days, his jaw began to twitch uncontrollably.

The human mass of fury, hovering angrily around the lone figure, surged forward, as if on cue.

Jesus, although acutely aware of the multitude's presence, remained stolid. Gethsemane was now but a memory. The crisis was past. The cross was a necessity. Reconciliation between God and man was less than seven hours away, as man reckoned time.

The crowd screamed in unison, myriad angry voices crying out for blood: "The law says He must die" . . . "Death to the blasphemer" . . . "Let Him be crucified" . . . "His blood be on us and on our children . . ."

The clamorous sounds escaping from their snarling lips sounded very much like the hungered growling that came from the packs of wild dogs roaming Jerusalem unchecked.

The man from Galilee was barely able to stand. His skin was like pulp, the bones beneath His disfigured flesh laid bare by the brutal scourging. The bits and pieces of metal and glass tied to the end of the Roman whip had viciously scoured His sun-darkened, olive-colored skin.

Thirty-nine times.

One shy of death.

Clumps of His hair had been torn from His head during the beatings, and the sweat-stained strands that remained were knotted together by dried blood. Yet, for all His pain, there was a serenity in His eyes that cried out for recognition.

The rabid crowd never saw the silent, sagacious plea in Jesus' serene eyes. Their mouths shouted caustically for vindication. Their hearts were hardened to truth.

Large red drops of liquid life trickled from the man who had fed the hungry, healed the sick, made the blind to see, and raised the dead. His undefiled blood mixed with the stale, dry earth, foreshadowing the outcome of His unselfish sacrifice.

The rising hum of anger enveloping the seething mass of people sounded like a hive of highly agitated bees. The air was filled with the scent of death. No one would speak in favor of the Son of God.

Pilate's soldiers took Jesus into the common hall. There, they stripped Him naked and put a scarlet robe upon His torn and bleeding back, a reed in His right hand, and a crown of thorns upon His head.

They laughed viciously, mocking Him, saying, "Hail King of the Jews."

One of them slapped His face.

Another spit on Him.

Time slowed . . .

The crowd lining the *Via Dolorosa* was a gauntlet of screaming spectators. Jesus stoically carried the iron weight of His own cross towards the outskirts of the city, staggering under the painful burden of the rough hewn wood until Simon of Cyrene was compelled by an impatient centurion to intercede.

The procession arrived at Golgotha . . . the place of the skull . . . the mound of death outside the Holy City.

To the south was a deep, narrow glen. There, in times past, the Jews had offered up their children in sacrifice to Molech, the fire-god. Now it served as a receptacle for all sorts of putrefying matter from the city. Small fires smoldered constantly in the ravine's belly, and the heat from the fires, combined with the heat from the blazing sun, released foul-smelling gases that defiled the otherwise fresh air around Jerusalem.

A slight breeze began to blow, carrying with it the nauseous smells from the Valley of Hinnom: *Gehenna . . . Hades . . . Sheol.*

Hell.

The day seemed to buckle under the weight of the burden

of the atrocity about to occur, its shudder felt in the wails of those who knew innocence.

Jesus groaned three times as each of the two-pound iron spikes securing Him to the cross pierced His body. Miraculously missing bone, they settled with muffled *thuds!* into their wooden cradles.

Several women began to wail loudly.

In the distance, just outside the city gate, a lone Praetorian watched the savage proceedings. Bewildered, he wondered why tears kept welling up in his eyes like fat drops of rain, overflowing them and running down the parched dryness of his sunburned face. He stared unblinking at the cloudless, brilliantly blue sky, ignoring the ache in his belly.

How long will it be?

Shortly after the sun reached its zenith, the sky above Jerusalem and Golgotha suddenly turned black and ominous. It remained that way for three hours. At about the ninth hour of the day, Jesus cried out from where He hung with a loud voice saying, "*Eli, Eli, lama sabachthani!*"

Without warning, a howling wind arose.

The four soldiers guarding the cross looked at one another fearfully.

From the cross, Jesus spoke for the last time. "*It is finished.*"

The dry, dusty earth began to quake violently, throwing two of the soldiers to the ground. Rain fell from the blackened, cloudless sky. Propelled by the howling wind, it pummeled the earth for several minutes, then stopped as abruptly as it had started.

Suddenly there was a total absence of sound.

All eternity stood still for a heartbeat.

The unnatural silence was unnerving.

One of the Roman centurions stared at the cross and said in a hushed voice, "Truly this man was the Son of God."

Another, the Praetorian, pierced the Nazarene's side with the hardened point of his spear. He watched with glazed, weary blue-grey eyes as blood and water gushed from the wound, splattering his tunic. Earth and blood blended together into a copper-colored mud, staining his sandals.

Later, inside the city, Joseph Caiaphas gasped and clutched at his chest in pain when he heard the news that the veil of the Temple had been rent in half. That night he cried out in agony from the midst of a nightmare, saying, *"Ecce homo . . . "*

Behold the man.